Mother of Faith

Mother of Faith

Thom Lemmons

Multnomah Publishers® *Sisters, Oregon*

MOTHER OF FAITH
published by Multnomah Publishers, Inc.
© 2001 by Thom Lemmons

International Standard Book Number: 9781590528341

Cover illustration by Dan Brown/Artworks, Inc.

Multnomah is a trademark of Multnomah Publishers, Inc.,
and is registered in the U.S. Patent and Trademark Office.

The colophon is a trademark of Multnomah Publishers, Inc.

For information:
Multnomah Publishers, Inc. • P.O. Box 1720 • Sisters, OR 97759

Library of Congress Cataloging-in-Publication Data

Lemmons, Thom.
    Mother of faith: Amanis, friend of the last apostle / Thom Lemmons.
        p. cm. — (Daughters of faith; Book 3)
    ISBN 9781590528341
    1. Church history—Primitive and early church, ca. 30-600-Fiction.
    2. Ephesus (Extinct city)—Fiction. 3. Women slaves—Fiction. I. Title
        PS3562.E474 M68 2000
        613'.64—dc21

                                                00-012756

01 02 03 04 05 06 07 08 09 — 10 9 8 7 6 5 4 3 2 1 0

Acknowledgments

I read somewhere that a novel might best be defined as a prose work of indeterminate length which contains one or more problems. I heartily agree. However, this novel would contain many more problems than it does if not for the considerable aid rendered by the following resources:

The Perseus Project at Tufts University (www.perseus.tufts.edu), an online resource for the study of ancient Greece; Gregory Crane, Editor-in-Chief. An endless trove of information and inspiration.

Everett Ferguson, *Backgrounds of Early Christianity*, 2d ed., Wm. B. Eerdmans Publishing Co., 1993. Dr. Ferguson's mastery of the milieu of the church's early centuries is well known. Any historical faux pas discovered in my work can only be blamed on my poor interpretation of his excellent work.

_____, *Early Christians Speak: Faith and Life in the First Three Centuries*, rev. ed., ACU Press, 1981. Dr. Ferguson's translations of early Christian hymns and prayers were especially influential.

Argos (http://argos.evansville.edu), a limited-area search engine for ancient and medieval online documents and resources; Anthony F. Beavers, managing editor, University of Evansville, Evansville, Indiana. One interested in the vast body of antiquities scholarship could scarcely do better than this as a starting place.

This book has only one author but it has many midwives: My family, whose support and encouragement is a great blessing; Sherry Rankin, who helped me thrash out the overall plot design and loaned me books from her personal library to aid the effort; and, as always, Rod Morris, whose patient skill and quiet attention to editorial detail are the literary equivalent of the best prenatal care. He has guided each book in this series through a successful gestation and delivery, and my respect for him continues to grow.

PART ONE

Fugitive

One

*A*manis grunted as she eased herself down onto the stool. "Let go of me, now; let go," she said, waving away the hands of the three younger women hovering around her. "I'm all right, I tell you. I can put myself onto a stool."

She pulled her robe closer. She had never gotten used to these inland winters. On days like today, when the wind whistled down out of the Taurus highlands, it seemed there weren't enough blankets in all of Antioch to get her as warm as she wanted to be.

"Go get it for me, one of you. Please?"

"I will, Grandmother. Where is it?" It was Berenice who answered.

Amanis pointed at the battered oak chest, banded with rusted iron straps. The chest sat on the floor beside her pallet—close, so that Amanis could reach out and touch it during the night. It helped, knowing everything was nearby.

"You put it in there?"

"Of course. Where else would I keep it?"

Berenice walked across the small room and lifted the lid of

the chest. The young ones were always asking her to take out all her old stuff, to tell again the stories of the odd objects she had collected through the years. They just liked the stories, and Amanis couldn't blame them for that. She liked the telling. But there was a little sadness attached to each of the things.

Berenice had reached into the chest; Amanis heard the clicking of the wooden balls. She saw the bone handle of the knife for an instant as the girl moved it aside while looking for the letter. She heard the brittle rustle of the parchment she had gotten from Patroclus all those years ago. "Have a care, Berenice. I don't want my things damaged."

"Yes, Grandmother."

Amanis briefly wished she hadn't put the letter at the very bottom. But of all the mementos, this letter was her most precious.

Finally, Berenice withdrew a small leather pouch and brought it back toward the rest of them, huddled around the brazier near the doorway. Berenice pulled from the pouch a piece of parchment. She settled herself on the floor near the brazier, unfolded the parchment, and began to read aloud.

Amanis smiled and closed her eyes, nodding. How many times had she listened to this letter—a hundred, perhaps?—since that first time, when she had proudly handed to the president of the assembly the small packet containing these words? And yet, every so often, she had to hear them again. Many had come to her asking to see the letter, to make a copy. People with strange clothing and accents, smelling of faraway places. That was fine. But she wouldn't let the letter out of her sight. It slept each night in the chest with the other things. Memory was the most precious treasure a person could own. She hoped these girls had learned that.

Berenice had a good voice. Amanis was glad she had insisted

on the girl's learning to read. The words of the letter uncoiled slowly, sweetly in her mind. She was so glad Berenice was here. Amanis wanted to do some more remembering.

The wailing of the infant came down the wind to Amanis as she climbed the steep, rocky trail that wound across the shoulder of the barren hillside. She stopped walking and turned her head this way and that, trying to pinpoint the source of the sound. She forced herself to breathe slowly, trying to tame the fearful thoughts scrambling about in her head. She stood in the deep orange light of the late afternoon and listened. There! That out-cropping, just upslope from where she stood. She glanced down the path toward the town. No sign of pursuit. Maybe she hadn't been missed yet. She picked her way as quickly as she could across the flinty slope toward the outcropping.

At the base of the three large stones she found it: a baby girl, barely two hours old. They hadn't even had the decency to put the child on the leeward side out of the wind. Amanis gathered the baby into her arms. She wrapped the little girl in the blanket she had filched from the mistress's bedchamber. She held the baby close as she moved to the other side of the boulder, crouching low to get away from the wind.

The stones of the outcropping made a kind of wall, about shoulder height. Amanis squatted with her back against the rocks and fumbled beneath her robe for the skin of goat's milk. She soaked the corner of a clean rag and dangled it near the little girl's mouth. The baby sucked at the rag until the milk was gone. Amanis soaked the rag once more, and the greedy little mouth pulled at it again and again. The child quieted. Finally she slept.

With the infant curled in her arms and breathing in soft,

quick puffs, Amanis thought about what she had to do next. Ephesus was a large place, but her master would soon be searching for her, if he wasn't already. A dark-skinned woman with a light-skinned baby would be noticed—even if the baby weren't still caked with the residue of its birth. If they found her, she'd be lucky if she were merely whipped. And the baby—

Her head snapped up. A noise—two rocks clicking together somewhere down the slope. Then, footsteps crunching up the path. Only one set of feet from the sound of it. Her master would surely have sent more than one searcher. The footsteps came nearer, and she heard a man mumbling to himself.

"Came this way, I'm sure of it. Must have dumped the brat somewhere nearby. Ought to be hearing it scream by now, though. Dead already?"

She heard him shuffling back and forth across the slope, cursing the wind under his breath.

The baby gave a sudden jerk and let out a fitful whine.

There was a quick silence, broken only by the wind among the broomweed and juniper. Then fast footsteps coming toward her.

Amanis swiftly bundled the child and placed it at the base of the rock. She stood in front of the baby, her feet wide, knees bent, her hands held at the ready, clawlike. The man was rounding the edge of the outcropping. He was five paces away when he saw her. He straightened and took a startled step backward.

"Who are you?" he asked.

"Go away," Amanis hissed. "I warn you."

His eyes flickered over her, then toward the bundle on the ground behind her. "I came for the child. It's no concern of yours. Get out of the way."

"Go away," Amanis said.

His hand strayed toward his belt. Quick as a cat, Amanis

grabbed a palm-sized stone from the ground and hurled it with an underarm motion at the man's face. It caught him on the cheekbone, just below his left eye. He gave a yelp and put both hands to his injured cheek, staggering back a pace or two. Amanis found two more stones. She cocked one back in her right hand and held the other in her left.

"Have a care, wench! Scaevolus won't be pleased when I tell him what's happened here."

Amanis remembered all too well the day she was hauled like a market animal into the courtyard of Marcus Licinius Scaevolus. She made as if to launch the rock in her right hand. The man flinched and raised an elbow to protect his head.

"If you take this baby to Scaevolus, you'll have to kill me first," she told him. "And that won't be easy."

He glared at her a moment, then shook his fist and spat toward her. "You'll be sorry, woman! Whoever you may be, Scaevolus will find you and have you flayed alive. I swear it."

He backed away, cursing and shaking his fist at her. When he was maybe twenty paces distant, he turned and hurried down the path toward Marble Street. Amanis flung a stone; it struck the path just behind him. He gave a scared little hop and broke into a stumbling trot.

Amanis watched him go for a moment, then went to the screaming baby. She rocked and shushed her and gave the little one the rag to suck. Finally the infant quieted again. She settled the baby in the crook of her arm and arranged the blanket to keep the child's head out of the cooling air. She stood and stared down the hillside at the city. The sun was sliding toward the sea beyond the harbor. Lights twinkled here and there among the clusters of houses. Amanis turned and angled up the slope of Mount Pion toward the north.

She worked her way over Mount Pion as dark deepened, and by nightfall had come out onto the plain where the temple of Diana gleamed in the moonlight. She skirted the southern edge of the temple complex and soon came to the road that ran past the athletic grounds north of the city. She waited in the darkness until a group of travelers approached the Koressos Gate, then slipped through at the back of the crowd.

Amanis sidled along alleys and backstreets, angling toward the harbor. She found the building with the six-pointed star painted above the doorway. She went to the door and knocked, then waited, glancing nervously up and down the street. The docks were maybe two streets over. Amanis could hear the shouts of the seamen and dockworkers trying to get the last of the cargo secured before the night got any later. She knocked again, as loud as she dared.

Footsteps. Amanis ducked into the shadows around the corner of the synagogue and prayed to every god and goddess she knew that the baby would keep still. Two men were approaching—longshoremen from the sound of their conversation. One wanted to know if the other had any money. The other cursed and assured his companion he was as poor as a rock badger. The first wondered why they were bothering to walk to the tavern, then, if neither of them had the price of a cup of wine.

Amanis tried to make herself part of the wall as they drew even with her.

"Well, I ain't got much on me right now," the other man replied, "but I guess the Two Brothers'll always have a sheep or two to be sheared this time of evening."

The other man gave a low chuckle as they passed Amanis's hiding place and made their way up the street.

Amanis stepped back to the doorway and knocked a third

time. The baby began to fret. She followed the wall of the synagogue to the rear of the building and found a low house separated by only a few paces from the back door into the synagogue. Lamplight flickered in the windows.

The baby grew more restive. Amanis went to the door of the dwelling and rapped loudly. She heard the sound of a stool scooting across the floor, then sandals scuffing on bare dirt. The latch slid back, and the door opened the width of two fingers.

"What do you want?" A woman's voice.

"I found this child on the hillside above the town. No one was around."

The door opened another finger's width. "What does that have to do with me?" Amanis could see a sliver of the woman's face. Her eye was dark in the lamp's shadow.

"Please. I have heard that you—that your people take in orphans. Sometimes."

"A Roman or Greek brat, no doubt. Why should I care?"

"Who is it, Hannah?" A man's voice came from the small room. Amanis heard the sound of another chair scooting, then the thump of a cane or crutch and a shuffling sound approaching the door.

"Never mind, Papa. It's just some Ethiopian woman with a foundling. I told her to go away."

"Sir, I beg you! This child was abandoned; she has nowhere to go." Amanis tried to push the door open with her shoulder, but the woman held it against her.

"Get away, you! Take the brat somewhere else!"

"Please, you must listen—"

"Get away, I said!"

"Hannah! Moses himself was a foundling—have you forgotten?"

"Papa, this isn't—"

"'Do not deprive the alien or fatherless of justice.' So says the Law."

"Papa, we're the aliens in this cursed place."

"All the more reason. Open the door, Hannah."

Amanis heard the woman exhale loudly in disgust. The door fell open. An old man stood there, balancing on one leg and a crutch. He had a gray beard that straggled down over his chest and the most wrinkled face Amanis had ever seen. He wore a round little cap on the back of his head.

"Let me see the child," he said.

Amanis angled the baby's face toward him.

"I can't tell anything in the dark," said the old man. "Step into the lamplight."

Amanis cautiously stepped across the threshold. The woman sat at a small table in the middle of the room. She was taller and heavier than her father, and she sat with her arms crossed in front of her. Her face looked as hard as a pebble in a shoe. She wouldn't look at Amanis or the baby.

"Oh, my—this little one hasn't even been cleaned from her birthing," the old man said. He leaned in over Amanis's elbow, looking into the tiny girl's face.

"No. As soon as the midwife cut and bound the cord, the master sent someone in to take her away."

Alis was the one he had sent, Amanis remembered—the mousy, Gaulish-looking girl whose favorite pastime was household gossip. "The master says to expose it," she had told them, then picked up the squawling, bloody bundle and walked out—without even a backward glance.

She had stared at the mistress, lying limp beneath the midwife's busy hands. Would she not protest? She had grunted and screamed and strained this child toward the light of day; now would she allow it to be tossed on the rocks of Mount Pion without even a word of protest?

Amanis had watched for her chance to grab the blanket and hide it under her robe. Then when the midwife had finished her work and fussed them all out of the room, Amanis grabbed a water skin and marched toward the main gate.

The chamberlain had been standing in the courtyard, and he looked at her curiously as she made for the street. Amanis held up the skin. "The mistress wants water from the fountain by the theater," she had said.

"But—the cistern here is full," he had protested. No matter—by then she was through the gate. At that point she had been beyond caring whether he believed her or not.

The sound of the baby's cry cut like a knife through Amanis's thoughts. The baby opened her eyes: They were the blue-black of the newborn and shone like wet pebbles. The old Jewish man put out a finger and touched the baby's cheek.

"So tiny. So helpless," he murmured. "Kicking about in her own blood..." He glanced at Amanis. "One of our women has just lost a child. It may be that this baby will find a home with her."

"It's goy," said the daughter coldly.

"It's also a living soul." His tone was firm. "Go, Hannah. To the house of Thomas the tanner. Bring Heracleia back here."

The woman smote the table. "Why? It's a fool's errand, Papa. And it's already nighttime."

"*Hannah.*" The single sharply-spoken word bode no further protest.

She flung herself from the table, stomped to a corner, and grabbed the robe that was draped over a water urn. With an exasperated sigh she left, slamming the door behind her.

"Hannah has her moods," the old man murmured after a few moments had passed. "But she will do as I say."

"You will take the child then?"

"Yes. As the God of Abraham is my witness, I will see that this child receives care." He stumped over to a chair and lowered himself into the seat. He propped his crutch beside him, then looked at Amanis and held out his arms.

Amanis looked at him, then down into the tiny face. She felt a sudden surge of regret as she gazed into the dark eyes. Why the sudden urgency to save this infant? Babies were abandoned almost daily. A daughter too many to feed…a misshapen body…a child too easily identified as the fruit of loins other than its mother's husband… or a grown daughter comely enough to help pay down a debt. Yes, there were many reasons for abandonment. The accidents of birth and parentage were no assurance of anything.

Amanis bent slowly and put the girl in the man's arms. She took the skin of goat's milk from around her neck and set it on the table. "You'll want that. She'll be hungry soon, I'd guess."

He looked at her. "What will you do? Do you have a place?"

"Maybe. It's time I was finding out." She pulled her robe tighter about her shoulders and turned for the door.

"Wait. What you have done here will follow you," the old man said. "For good or ill, I don't know. But it doesn't stop here."

Her hand was on the door handle. As she pulled it open she said, "I think I knew that already."

Two

he gates had been locked long before Amanis arrived
in front of them. She had to pound repeatedly to
awaken old Urbanis. The only reason the master
allowed the fat, aged Cilician to continue as a night watchman
was because Urbanis had tutored him in his boyhood. Finally
she heard the bolt creaking across the hasp.

"Who is it?" demanded the sleepy voice of the gate warden.

"Urbanis, let me in. It's Amanis."

The gate groaned open a span, then part of another. Amanis
shouldered her way inside.

"Where have you been, Amanis? The master has sent people
everywhere—"

"Never mind. I'm back now."

"But he will demand to know—"

"And I will tell him. But not you."

The chamberlain spotted her before she was halfway across
the atrium. She turned at his call, facing him with what she
hoped was a casual expression.

"Amanis. The master wants you brought to him as soon as you are found."

"Found? I wasn't lost, Demetrius. I just returned from—"

"Come with me, Amanis," the tall Thracian said. She followed him past the well in the center of the atrium, toward the master's suite.

Patroclus was sitting in one of his backless Roman chairs when Demetrius ushered her into the andron. She knelt before him, her eyes fixed on the floor, as he put aside the parchment scroll he had been reading.

"Amanis. So they found you. Where was she, Demetrius?"

"Actually, Master, she was crossing the courtyard."

"She was here the whole time?"

"No, Master. She had just come through the gate when I saw her."

"I see. Thank you, Demetrius. You may leave us."

Amanis heard the door close softly behind her. For a few moments Patroclus didn't speak.

"Well, Amanis. Apparently no one sent you on an errand that should have taken most of the afternoon and this much of the evening. At least no one will admit doing so. Why were you gone for such a long time without permission?"

"The mistress says the water from the fountain by the theater tastes sweeter than the water from our well. She was thirsty, and I thought she would like water from the fountain. That is why I left the house."

"And did you bring back water for your mistress?"

"No, Master. I was…detained."

"Detained? I'd say you were. Who detained you, Amanis?" His voice was still calm, curious.

"There were ruffians, Master. In the agora. They harassed

me—even took my water skin."

"Did they? I must have some stern words with the urban prefect. But I fail to understand why, even with such difficulties, you were away until after the gates were locked for the night. Surely, after such an upsetting experience, you should have come back here immediately."

"Yes, Master, I…that is what I should have done. I see that now. But I wasn't thinking clearly." She hoped her tone was convincing.

Patroclus sat silent for a long time. Then he got up and paced across the andron, toward the windows. She risked a glance at him. He was leaning against the sill, peering down the hillside. The villa was nestled on the upper slopes of Mount Koressos and owned a fine view of the town below, sprawled between Koressos and Pion to the north. If her master looked to the left, he would be able to see the setting moon's glimmer on the waters of the harbor.

"This has been a disappointing day, Amanis. A girl-child I didn't need. Distressing news from the currency markets. And, to cap it off, a slave out of place." He sighed and scratched his beard. Then he turned to look at her. She quickly let her eyes fall.

"You are a good servant, Amanis. I've heard the mistress say so. You are efficient, quiet, and you don't tire easily. And, for my part, you are pleasing to look at." He took a few steps toward her. "I like beautiful things—like to have them around me. Stand, Amanis."

She rose, keeping her face averted.

"I want my things where I can find them, Amanis. Always. Do you understand?"

"Yes, Master."

"Good. I'm going to have Demetrius give you three brisk ones. Just to remind you to take more care the next time you run into ruffians in the agora."

She could feel him studying her.

"You may go now. And send in Demetrius."

Amanis rose, holding the chamber pot, and winced. Her back was still tender. She shifted her shoulders about, trying to find a position where her garments didn't chafe.

She stepped outside the front gate and dumped the night slops into the street. The sunlight sparkled on the harbor far below, and the handful of ships riding at anchor appeared as smudges against the gleam. Amanis's eyes roved the harbor district as she thought of the tiny girl she had taken to the old Jew. Had the woman accepted the child? Would her grief make her grateful for the chance to feel tiny gums nuzzling her breasts once more? Grief could do that—or it could make a person hard and unforgiving. Amanis had seen it happen both ways.

She had just stepped back inside when she heard the mistress's chief body servant calling her name. Clio beckoned impatiently to her. Amanis crossed the courtyard toward the older woman.

"Amanis, the mistress wants fresh dates. I don't have time to fetch them and watch those lazy girls in the scullery at the same time. Here." She held out a small bag of coins. "Make sure they're fresh."

Amanis shifted the pot into one arm and took the money. But Clio held onto the bag. Amanis looked at her.

"And make sure you come back straightaway. No wandering about the city until after dark."

Amanis lowered her eyes and nodded. Clio strode past her, shouting at a girl lounging outside the scullery.

Amanis went into the women's suite. The mistress was reclining on a pile of cushions in the atrium. Alis sat near her, waving a fan of palm fronds. A brass ewer and cup sat on the floor beside Alis. As Amanis passed, she could see a single swallow of watered-down wine in the bottom of the cup.

Eurydeme's eyes opened as Amanis passed. "Amanis. Did Clio find you?"

"Yes, Mistress."

"Alis, my cup."

The girl put down the fan and held the cup toward her mistress. Eurydeme took a tiny sip, then handed the cup back to the girl.

"Did she give you the money?"

"Yes, Mistress."

"Good." She sighed and closed her eyes as she lay back on the cushions. "Some fresh dates would be so nice. First thing I've really felt like eating since…"

Amanis waited another moment, but the mistress said nothing else. She went quickly into the bedchamber and set the pot in the corner by the mistress's linen-draped bed. She went to the spice cabinet and scooped a handful of lavender pods from one of the urns. She squeezed them until the delicate scent floated through her fingers, then tossed them into the pot.

Eurydeme had been lethargic since the birth, and Amanis thought it was due to more than the rigors of childbearing. There was a sadness in the mistress's face, a silent mourning in the long spaces between her words. But Eurydeme would never say anything, of course. It wasn't her place to have an opinion about the wishes of her husband and lord. In such matters she was as bound as any of her slaves and as powerless.

Amanis remembered hearing the stories of her people in their African homeland. It was said that many mighty queens had once ruled in Nubia, female warriors who fought as fiercely as any man. To this day, Nubian parents taught their daughters to fight, as well as their sons. That was perhaps the only useful thing Amanis had learned from her father.

She remembered the shining look on her mother's face as she told of Shakhta, who wore the skin of a panther she had killed herself; of Merope, who, it was said, could outrun horses; and above all, of one-eyed Amanirenas, who defied the armies of Rome during the days of Caesar Augustus. Amanis's name, her mother never ceased to remind her, was taken from this great queen.

The day of her mother's death, the light began to fade in Amanis's life. Oh, how she longed for her mother's face, for the calm strength of her voice! If her mother had lived, so many things would have been better. If she had lived, maybe Amanis's father could have held out against the despair that finally bested him.

She could hear Clio scolding inside the scullery as she crossed the main courtyard on the way to the gate. The street was crowded even though it wasn't a market day. Maybe a merchant ship had docked this morning. When the spice ships from Africa or Arabia came into the harbor—even on festival days—all the wealthy households in Ephesus made sure their managers were on hand, carrying plenty of silver. Or maybe one of the grain ships had come from Alexandria. The local barley and wheat harvests had been poor the past year or two. If cheap grain was to be had, there would be plenty of traffic to and from the harbor until the ship's holds were cleaned out.

Amanis turned onto Marble Street. She walked between the colonnades and arcaded shops, looking at the wares hung and stacked and piled along both sides of the street. She went through the archway, framed by huge Ionian pillars, and entered the agora.

A group of wealthy-looking men stood between the sundial and the water clock in the center of the main courtyard. Patroclus was probably among them; he spent most of his days here or on the steps of the civic temple, conducting business or listening to news and rumors from Rome and her provinces. In all the time she had been in the household, Amanis had been unable to guess exactly what sort of ventures her master engaged in. He was evidently good at it; he received many important-looking guests and was treated with deference.

There was vacant floor space in some of the porticoes on the perimeter of the marketplace. On market days vendors would be crammed in cheek to jowl, jostling one another for frontage on the agora. But even today there were a variety of vendors to choose from: potters, oil sellers, carpet weavers, leather workers, and wood carvers. As always, several silversmiths were hawking miniatures of the multi-breasted image of Diana, whose magnificent temple drew so many sightseers to Ephesus. There was even a small troupe of acrobats and jugglers working the crowd.

As Amanis watched, one of the performers tried to gain the attention of some of the men on the fringes of the group near the sundial. His limbs were wrapped in multicolored strips of cloth and a bustle of saffron-and-purple-colored rags hung on his backside. His arms were a bright blur as he kept aloft five or six brightly-colored wooden balls. He beckoned jokingly to the men near the sundial, feinting as though he were about to toss them one of his balls. But the well-dressed citizens of Ephesus scowled at the juggler and turned their backs on him.

Amanis located a fruit peddler near the northwest corner of the agora. He was as thin as a lath and crouched like an overgrown mantis among baskets of figs, olives, dried apricots, walnuts, raisins, and dates. Amanis asked him the price of his dates, and when he answered she saw that he had no teeth.

She handed him a coin, and he reached behind him and picked up a small wooden bowl, polished by much handling. He scooped a bowlful of dates from a basket. Amanis held out a corner of her robe and he poured the dates in. She knotted her garment and made a quick retreat.

Crossing the agora, she looked around until she spotted the juggler, then walked over to him. He stood before a group of children, juggling objects as they tossed them to him. He had one of his colored balls, a small sandal, a toy flute, and a round rock about the size of a quince. As he juggled the objects the children threw, he made up rhymes with their names. Amanis watched him for a few moments, then reached into her bag and flicked a sestertius at his feet.

"Thank you, kind lady," he said as he caught a rag doll flung at him by one of the little girls. He winked at Amanis. She smiled and walked toward the archway. Then she heard the shouting.

A mob was coming down Marble Street from the harbor district. Shoved in front of it were two unfortunates, pinioned by their arms. As Amanis watched, the crowd turned and began to pour into the amphitheater. Drawn by the commotion, people were coming from the agora and even from the Harbor Baths. Soon she heard a chant coming from hundreds of throats, echoing through the amphitheater: "Great is Diana of the Ephesians!" Strange. Today was not a ceremonial day for the goddess, was it? And why were they shoving those two men at the front of the crowd?

When Amanis saw one of the city magistrates accompanied by his bodyguards and marching sternly toward the theater, she walked quickly the other way.

A thong on her sandal had come untied. She stooped in the roadway to refasten it. As she rose, she turned to take in the view of the city and the harbor. A sudden flash of movement drew her eye to the side of the road, maybe twenty paces down the slope from where she stood. A figure ducked around a house near the street. Amanis drew a startled breath.

She forced herself to gaze nonchalantly over the harbor for a moment, then to turn slowly and proceed up the street. When she had gone a little way, she strolled into an alley between two houses. Amanis strode to the rear of the houses and doubled back along the gap between their walls and the slope of the hillside. She flattened herself against one of the houses and craned her neck around the corner to watch the street.

An instant later, a man hurried past. It was the agent of Scaevolus.

When he had passed, she went around the corner toward the street and half-ran back down the hill until she reached the first crossing. She turned into this street and followed its switchbacked path until she was well above the street where she had seen the man. When she was certain she had left him behind, she hurried on up the steep avenue.

Amanis kept to the sides of the road, always watching for the next space between two houses or the niche in a wall where she could conceal herself if the slaver came into view. But she didn't see him, and at last she ducked through the main gate of the villa.

Eurydeme was still lying on the bed of cushions in the atrium. She appeared to be asleep. Alis was gone. Amanis untied her garment and emptied the glistening fruit into a glass bowl on the table beside Eurydeme's couch. She rose and turned to leave.

"Amanis. You brought the dates?"

"Yes, Mistress."

"You had money left over?" Eurydeme kept her eyes shut as she talked, but she limply held out a hand in Amanis's direction. Amanis pulled the money bag from her belt and laid it in the woman's palm.

"Thank you, Amanis. You may return to your duties now."

She walked through the doorway into the main atrium. She paused, looking back at her mistress's listless form. *Your daughter lives,* Amanis thought. *You don't know it and probably don't care, but she lives all the same.*

It was nearing midday, and a group of Patroclus's clients were trooping out of the men's suite toward the gate. Amanis hurried toward the scullery, away from them. She didn't know if her father had presented himself today or not, but she made herself scarce when any of her master's freedmen were about.

Clio was waiting for her in the scullery. "You're back, finally. What kept you?"

Amanis gave her what she hoped was a sincerely puzzled look.

"Even at my age, I could have gone to the agora twice while you ran the errand once."

"I went and got the mistress's dates and came back, just as she told me to."

Clio scowled at her, then shrugged. "Oh, well. Fill four small bowls with oil and take them to those lazy girls at the ovens." She turned and went outside. Amanis took a deep breath and left to fetch the oil.

Three

The lion crouched upslope from the small, muddy river. Amanis could see its eyes, its panting mouth with the pink tongue lolling out. And then the small knot of gazelles began picking its way down the opposite slope. The lion's mouth closed, and it all but disappeared behind the clump of tall dried grass where it lay.

The gazelles approached carefully. One would inch its way a few steps toward the water while the others glanced warily about, nostrils flaring as they tested the wind. Then the leader would stand watch as the others encroached. They looked as if they were stalking the water.

The lion crouched undetected in the grass. Amanis could see the powerful muscles in its hindquarters tensing for the spring. One of the gazelles minced to the water's edge—about to lower its head to drink.

Amanis ran down the slope, yelling and waving her arms. The gazelles leaped into the air and raced away from the stream's edge. She watched them for an instant, then turned to see where the lion waited.

The beast rose from its hiding place, his eyes never leaving Amanis. She could sense it measuring her as it came slowly, slowly down the slope. She realized she held no spear, not even a knife.

Amanis backed up the slope and suddenly realized her feet were not on dried grass and flinty soil, but on flagstone. There were stone buildings and colonnades on both sides of her. Masts of ships sprouted from behind the low buildings at the end of the street; seagulls cried overhead.

She was on Arcadian Way, near its harbor end. She glanced quickly over her shoulder and saw the theater, its tiers and tiers of stone seats carved into the hillside that rose from the street.

And still the lion came, padding toward her, its eyes fixed on her with steady intention. Its mouth hung open now. She could see the tongue pulsing with each breath. Its teeth stood out like pointed pearls against the dark gums.

If she turned to flee, the beast would be on her in an instant. Why were there no other people on this, the busiest street in Ephesus? She opened her mouth to cry for help, and the sound that came out was the cry of a newborn baby.

Amanis's eyes snapped open in the darkness. Without moving, she looked around: The shelves of the storage room behind the scullery surrounded her, filled with jars and vases and urns and baskets. Shadowy clusters of onions and garlic and leeks and dried herbs hung from the rafters above her head.

There was a small, grilled window high in the west wall above the shelves. Outside the window was the street that led downhill toward the town. A tilted rectangle of pale blue moonlight lay along the opposite wall, striped by the bars of the grille.

Amanis heard footsteps and a tuneless whistle pass the window. Some restless soul wandering the night, much as her spirit wandered in strange places within her.

She laid aside the blankets, went over to the shelves, and climbed until she could put her face to the window.

She closed her eyes and breathed in the night. It had a cool scent of lavender and jasmine and the sea. What would it be like out in the dark air, guided only by starlight and moonlight? Where would she go if somehow she found herself loosed upon the night? Which star would she choose as her guide? Or would she simply follow the moon's slow progress, hunting by its light as did the great, wild cats of her homeland, hunting for the place where she might finally come to rest and peace?

Amanis found herself wondering about the figure she had seen coming from the agora. Was it really the slaver's agent, or had her anxiety caused a similar person to resemble her adversary? She wasn't sure. In the quiet of the moonlight it didn't seem to matter.

She heard feet scuffing on the floor of the scullery, coming toward her. Quickly she climbed down the shelves and lay on her pallet, pulling the blankets over her just as Clio stooped through the doorway.

"Amanis! Get up! I need your help."

Amanis shifted the blankets off and rolled over, shading her eyes against the lamp Clio held. "What's the matter?"

"The mistress is burning with fever. I need you to help me make a poultice."

Amanis pulled down a cluster each of onions, garlic, and dried mustard. The two women went into the scullery. Amanis lit a lamp from Clio's flame and began dicing an onion and a large clove of garlic into small pieces while Clio ground the mustard between a mortar and pestle.

Tears stung Amanis's eyes; she could hardly see to finish chopping the onion. Clio rummaged in a corner and found a square of loosely woven cloth. She scraped the onion, garlic, and mustard into the center of the cloth, then tied it into a bundle.

"Somewhere we have some mint," she muttered as she turned to go back to the women's suite. "Make an infusion and bring it to me in a ewer, along with a drinking cup."

When Amanis arrived in Eurydeme's bedchamber with the steaming ewer, Clio was holding the poultice to Eurydeme's chest and daubing her forehead and neck with a damp cloth. The odor of onion and garlic filled the room. Eurydeme moaned and moved restlessly on the bed. Her cheeks were flushed, but the flesh around her mouth and eyes was pallid.

Clio held out her hands for the mint infusion. She poured some into the drinking cup and held it to her mistress's lips with one hand, cradling her head with the other. Eurydeme took a weak sip or two, then turned her head away.

"Go soak this in water," Clio said, holding out the cloth to Amanis and gesturing toward the water urn in the corner. "When you've done that, go back to the storerooms and find me some vinegar."

By dawn, Eurydeme was no better. Still in his sleeping robe, Patroclus came in and stood for a moment over his wife's bed, looking into her glazed eyes. He turned on his heel and left, calling loudly for Demetrius.

Not long after, a humped man in dark robes came in, carrying a leather bag over his shoulder. He set the bag beside the bed and peered at Eurydeme. He ran the back of his hand along her cheek and grunted softly. He lifted the poultice, holding it between a finger and thumb. He nodded and placed it back on Eurydeme's chest.

"How long since she was in childbed?" he asked Clio.

"Five days."

He bent to pick up the cloth soaking in the bowl near the head of the bed and sniffed it. He cocked an eyebrow at Clio. "Vinegar and water?"

She nodded.

He peered at Eurydeme, chewing on his lip, then he picked up his satchel and rummaged inside for a moment or two. He let the bag drop to the floor, shaking his head.

"You're doing everything that can be done. If the fever doesn't break in another day or two she'll most likely die."

Clio gasped.

Amanis felt her eyes go wide, staring from the physician to Clio.

"Who's got my drachma?" he asked, extending a hand.

Clio gestured toward the main atrium. "Demetrius, the chamberlain. The—the man who fetched you here."

The physician took a last long look at Eurydeme. He shook his head and went out.

Clio held her face in her hands. Amanis heard the sobs start, low and quiet.

"Should I go get the master?" she asked.

The older woman shook her head. "No...Demetrius," she finally managed.

The fever didn't break; the mistress got worse and worse. Patroclus was in and out of her room all day, alternately pacing and kneeling beside the bed, holding his wife's hand.

Amanis spent the day running between the mistress's chamber and the scullery, bringing Clio clean cloths, more water, more vinegar, a fresh poultice.

Toward evening, Eurydeme lapsed into delirium.

"My baby," she panted, staring wildly around the room. "Where is my baby?"

"Now, wife," Patroclus said, brushing the hair back from her face. "Theon and Eugenia are hardly babies."

"My baby…I must find her. I'm going to look for her."

Amanis risked a glance at the master. If Patroclus felt any remorse, he didn't allow it to register on his face.

Eurydeme died not long after midnight. Patroclus was holding her hand when her last breath shuddered in, then out. Her head fell to one side. Clio began a low keening as the master, his expression stricken, placed in his wife's mouth a coin for Charon. He stood very slowly and left the room, moving like one afraid he might collapse with each step.

Amanis, Alis, Clio, and the other women set about washing and wrapping their mistress's body. They sent Urbanis to the agora to buy fresh flowers, and Alis fashioned a garland which they placed on Eurydeme's head. They smoothed olive oil along her limbs and dressed her in her best purple chiton and robe. Sometime just after midday, when everything was ready, they sent Demetrius to notify the master. The men lifted the bier, and the musicians Demetrius had engaged led the way through the gate of the villa and into the street that wound down through the town. Patroclus, ash smeared on his cheeks and clad in a hemp shirt and kilt, walked in front of the bier and his son and daughter followed just behind. The wailing of the aulos and the pounding and ringing of the tabor and finger cymbals competed with the clamor of the paid mourners, and a crowd quickly formed to watch the procession.

Clio had served Eurydeme since the mistress's childhood, so Patroclus allowed Clio to accompany them to the crematorium behind the temple of Juno, then to the family's mausoleum on the eastern face of Mount Pion. Amanis and the other women watched from the gate as they went, until a curve in the street took them from sight.

Amanis turned toward the scullery and her sleeping place. She had hardly shut her eyes since the night before last, and she just wanted to crawl onto her pallet and sleep for as long as she could.

When she woke, the dim light coming through the window told her it was getting on toward evening. She got up, stretched, and wandered out toward the well to wash her face.

Urbanis was standing at the gate speaking to someone in the street. He made as if to shut the gate, but evidently the one he had been speaking to tried to prevent him. Urbanis threatened the caller with Patroclus's reputation and influence, struggled a moment or two more, then succeeded in closing and barring the gate. He walked back toward the center of the courtyard, dusting his hands on his tunic and muttering to himself.

"Urbanis, who was that?" Amanis asked, drying her face with a sleeve.

"Some slave trader's fetching boy. Wanted to know if we had any Africans here. I told him it was none of his business." He shook his head and clucked his tongue, strolling off toward the formal garden at the west end of the atrium.

Amanis felt her insides going cold. Why should a run-in with a Nubian slave woman make such a difference to Scaevolus that he sent his man to search the streets for her? In a place the size of Ephesus there was usually no shortage of unwanted babies. What was special about this one that he was eager to find the person who had taken her?

Patroclus's routine altered dramatically after the funeral. Normally he would go to the agora an hour or two after sunrise. When the heat mounted, he would come back to the villa for a bit of food and a nap. In the midafternoon he might go to the commercial temple or perhaps back to the agora. But for days after the funeral, Patroclus was absent from the villa from sunrise to sunset. No one, not even Demetrius, knew where he was keeping himself. And then he took to closeting himself in the men's suite, not going out at all. Men began calling at the villa. Some Amanis remembered as business associates of the master, and these usually left with scowls on their faces. But a few of them were strangers who wore the cap and amulet of the magicians' guild. When they arrived at the gate, they were ushered hastily to the men's suite. Sometimes Amanis would take wine and bread to the doorway of the suite where Demetrius waited. Sometimes she could smell incense. Once she heard what sounded like the clicking of bones and a high-pitched chant.

If the chamberlain knew anything about the goings on in the andron, he wouldn't say. Even Clio and Urbanis, both of whom had been in the household as long as he, could extract nothing from him.

Amanis mistrusted the magicians. The guild was influential in Ephesus; its members were a common sight, hurrying along the streets with scrolls tucked under their arms, their dark robes furling behind them. A delegation of the guild attended every important civic assembly, participated in every festival. But everyone had heard rumors of dark deeds in the temple of Hecate. None but their initiates ever witnessed their ceremonies, and they were sworn to secrecy on pain of death. They were well-spoken, the magicians; their behavior was unfailingly proper, as far as Amanis could see. But somehow that just made it worse.

On the second market day after the funeral, just before lamp-lighting, Demetrius assembled all the household slaves in the main atrium. The master had asked him to tell them about some of the unusual happenings lately. The master had suffered a number of misfortunes, he said, the most calamitous, of course, being the death of his wife. In his grief the master had consulted the augurs to determine which of the gods he had offended, for surely such suffering was due to some failing or unwitting insult. But the auguries had revealed nothing, Demetrius said.

So the master had called in the seers of the guild. By their arts they had seen that the troubles plaguing the household were due to some upset in the cosmic order. Patroclus or someone in his house had altered the essential forces. Fortuna was angry at some alteration of her usual prerogatives

The magicians had not yet determined the source of the troubles, but they would continue their divinations. In the meantime, Demetrius said, the master urged each of them to reflect on his or her actions. Until the source of the imbalance was found, the woes would continue. Who knew which of them might be next to suffer the consequences?

The servants dispersed, murmuring among themselves. Amanis kept her head down and said nothing. As soon as she could, she went to her room.

What should she do? Go to Patroclus and confess what she had done, take whatever punishment he and his advisors might concoct? She could imagine nothing other than her own demise that might appease *numen* angry enough to cause the death of the mistress. And Amanis was merely a slave, after all—hardly a fair exchange for the wife of a respected citizen.

And then she thought of the baby's cry as she first heard it: thin and unprotected, shuddering in the wind among the rocks of Mount Pion. She thought of the tiny face crusted with blood, of lips sucking greedily at the milk-soaked rag. How could it be wrong to rescue something so defenseless, something that could grow into a human being who could feel fear, anger, grief—or love? How could Fortuna begrudge the tiny girl a chance for life? Was the goddess, like Scaevolus, so jealous of what she considered hers that she would hunt down any who cheated her?

Amanis paced the tiny room like a leopard in a cage. What should she do? The only money she had was what little she had accumulated in her peculium, and she couldn't very well ask Patroclus for that. Besides, even a free woman couldn't survive for long without resources or a place of shelter. And where would she hide? Ephesus wouldn't long conceal a *fugitiva* from the household of one as well known as Patroclus. She would be caught; the *F* would be branded on her forehead; and the master would probably have her crucified.

A day passed, then another. The servants moved about the villa like people trying to avoid notice. Conversations were held in whispers, accompanied by wary glances. Patroclus remained shut within the men's suite, and aside from the magicians, Demetrius was the only one who went inside. Even the businessmen had ceased coming. Amanis overheard Demetrius complaining to Urbanis that the master's depleted financial resources would not long tolerate the sums he was handing over to these wizards. Urbanis clucked his tongue and said something about the curse hanging over them all.

That evening, as Amanis was settling herself for the night,

Clio called from her doorway.

"Make sure you're up before dawn. Demetrius says the magicians are going to cast lots on everyone in the household."

"Why?"

"Because no one's come forward to confess an offense. The master has decided the only way to get to the bottom of it is to have them examine everyone in the house." She stared hard at Amanis for a moment. "So be up early. When the last star in the tail of the Great Bear has faded, they'll cast the letters, then start taking us into the andron, one by one."

With a final look at her, Clio turned and went out.

Four

*A*manis sat unmoving for a long time. One by one, Clio said. The magicians were sure to find out what she'd done. The thought of sitting alone in front of them, of having their eyes on her, studying her, watching every move she made as they performed whatever spell they used to test a person's guilt or innocence—it made Amanis feel as if cold fingers were running up and down her spine. Fortuna was sure to whisper her guilt to them.

She forced herself to be still until all sounds from the villa had ceased. Alis slept in the next storeroom where provisions were kept that Amanis would need: dried fruit, parched grain, and maybe some nuts, she decided. She'd have to find water along the way.

Along the way to where? She shoved the question back down in her mind. Maybe the moon and stars would tell her. She got up and searched quietly along the shelves in the darkness, her fingers gliding over the glazed surfaces of the pots. This room was mostly devoted to spices and herbs, but somewhere there was a container of walnuts and another of filberts. She found them and carried them to her pallet. In another corner she located the gauzy cloths used to strain oil and sift meal. She grabbed a handful and dropped them beside the pots with the nuts. Amanis scooped several double-handfuls of nuts onto two of the cloths and tied them into bundles.

She stepped silently to the doorway of the next room and stood still until she heard the slow, steady breathing of Alis coming from the corner. This room was windowless, so Amanis had to tread slowly and carefully to miss the urns and baskets stacked here and there on the floor. Amanis wished Alis weren't so slovenly in the way she kept her sleeping quarters. The tall grain urns stood in the corner nearest where the Gaulish girl slept. Scrabbling around in the darkness, Amanis found an empty basket. The lid of the first urn scraped as Amanis lifted it. She froze, not daring to turn her head. But Alis's soft snoring continued on unbroken. Amanis set the lid on the floor and scooped grain into the basket. She tiptoed back across the floor and into her cubicle, setting the basket beside the other bundles. She returned to Alis's room, found the pot of dried figs, and carried it into her room.

Amanis made bundles of the grain and the figs, then piled all the parcels together in the middle of her blanket. She tied the corners of the blanket, then found a bit of rope and fashioned a strap.

She pulled on her robe and sandals, slung her bundle over her shoulder, and crept silently through the scullery and into the main atrium. The moon hung in the sky above the villa like a half-full skin of wine. From across the courtyard she could hear Urbanis snoring on his pallet beside the gate. She padded to the entryway of the master's quarters, took a deep breath, and went inside.

Hanging above the doorway into Patroclus's bedchamber was the sikhimi of a Nubian warrior. Her father had crafted it as a gift to Patroclus upon receiving his freedom. Its long bone handle protruded from the leather-wrapped sheath, bleached almost white; her father had painted totems on it in blue, red, and black. Carved into the haft was a likeness of Apedemak, the Nubian lion god; he stood with a bow in one hand and a blade in the other.

It was a much younger Patroclus who had gratefully accepted the sikhimi on that day long ago, Amanis remembered. He had smiled at his freedman and the shy little girl at his side. He had declared himself well pleased with the gift and sent the freedman and his daughter back to his metal shop with promises of future assistance.

The sikhimi was too high to reach unless she found something to stand on. She peered around in the darkened anteroom. At the far end was a large stone urn, and beside it a small footstool. Amanis retrieved the stool and placed it on the floor in front of the doorway. She removed the sikhimi from the peg, stepped off the stool, and turned around to find a magician standing in the courtyard door.

He stared at her, his face still in the moonlight. "Have we found our curse, even before the lots, I wonder?" he said in a low voice.

The sikhimi flashed from the sheath and its point pressed into the flesh below the man's beard. "One word," Amanis whispered fiercely, "and it will be your last."

The magician's eyes widened. He stepped back into the main atrium, his gaze never leaving Amanis's face. She took hold of the amulet dangling from his neck and backed him slowly toward the gate where Urbanis snored. When they neared the gate, Amanis realized with dismay that Urbanis was leaning against it, his head lolling to one side and his mouth hanging open.

"Turn around," she whispered. "If you touch him or try to

wake him, you'll die right here. Do you understand?"

The magician nodded. He turned until he was facing the gate.

"Now, slide back the bolt—silently!"

The magician's hand went to the bolt and moved it cautiously until it almost reached the release point. Amanis gave the magician a sudden shove to one side and threw the bolt the rest of the way. The gate, propelled by Urbanis's weight, swung open, dumping the old man onto the ground.

"What...? Help!" he sputtered as Amanis leaped over him and dashed into the street. Behind her she heard the magician's shouts, joined soon by Urbanis's.

There were houses on both sides of the road, but Amanis soon came to a place where the slope fell away on the left side. Houses were built there, but farther down the hillside, fronted by a different street. She saw a house with stairs descending an outside wall. Amanis jumped onto the roof and pounded down the stairs to the street, then continued her downhill race.

Already she could hear the sounds of pursuit behind her. She risked a glance over her shoulder and saw a line of torches making its way down the sloping street in front of the villa.

She came to a narrow crossing street—little more than an alley—and veered into it. It opened onto another, larger street. She was nearing the bottom of Mount Koressos and the road flattened out ahead of her. Farther up the hillside she could hear dogs barking.

She darted through the streets of the sleeping town, wishing her sandals didn't slap so loudly against the pavement, unable to stop long enough to remove them. Following the contour of the land, she let it lead her toward the harbor district. She flew along Marble Street, its pillars and colonnades like silent sentinels. The agora stood eerily silent and empty in the light of the moon.

Her legs were beginning to ache. Between the agora and the theater she came to a fountain with an alcove built into it; a small niche covered the basin where the water gathered. She staggered between the Ionian columns into the shadows of the alcove and leaned forward, her hands on her knees and her back against the stone wall. Her breaths came out as sobs as she tried to catch her wind.

"Welcome. I'm afraid you've missed the supper hour, but there's plenty of water, and we can still offer one of our fine beds."

Amanis's hand went to the handle of the sikhimi. The blade slid from the sheath, and she pointed it at the dark corner from which the voice had come.

"Now, now. No need to threaten. If you want the place to yourself, I'm happy to oblige. I have no money, so robbing me would only be a waste of your time."

She heard the rustle of clothing. One foot slid into a patch of moonlight, followed by another. The legs were short, stubby, and bent inward at the knees. The stranger's height barely met her waist.

The dwarf bowed. "Tarquinius, at your service."

"What are you doing here?"

He cocked his head at her. "I might ask you the same thing. I was here first, after all. But since you're the one holding the knife, I'll tell you that—"

They both froze. The sound of feet and voices racketed along Marble Street from the direction Amanis had come. Tarquinius slid back into his dark corner, and Amanis flattened herself against the opposite wall. Soon she could see the flicker of torches reflected on the polished surfaces of the alcove's supporting pillars. A band of six men jogged past them, headed toward the harbor district. "If we don't spot her, we'll wake the centurion," said a voice that sounded like Demetrius's. "They'll search every ship in the harbor." The men trotted on by, and the torches winked out of sight as they turned a corner just beyond the fountain.

Amanis cursed under her breath.

"Friends of yours?" asked the dwarf.

Amanis looked at him a moment, then sheathed the sikhimi. She kneeled beside the bowl of the fountain, cupping cool water in her hands and bringing it to her mouth. When she had quenched her thirst, she straightened and asked, "Why didn't you call out to them?"

"Let's just say I likely have more in common with you than with them." He stepped into the patch of moonlight. "Where will you go?"

"Why do you care?"

"I don't, especially." He looked at the sheathed blade in her belt. "Maybe I just want to make sure we don't share another hiding place."

Amanis shrugged the pack from her shoulder. She leaned back against the wall, then slid down to the ground and hugged her knees to her chest. "I'm sorry. I'm just afraid. If they catch me..."

Tarquinius was silent for a while, watching her. He gave a loud sniff and stepped to the edge of the alcove and peered up and down Marble Street. He turned back to her with a decisive motion. "Come on. I know a place."

Amanis looked at him, uncomprehending.

"Well, do you want to go while it's dark, or would you rather wait until the sun is up?"

She stood, pulling the pack into place on her shoulder. "Why?" she asked.

"Like I said, I've got reasons for hiding, too. At least until the others are ready to leave Ephesus."

"Who are the others?"

"Never mind. Just come on. And stay close to the edge of the road. Better a colonnade to duck behind than nothing." He set off toward the harbor with a quick, waddling gait.

"They just went that way," she said. "Should we really follow behind them?"

Tarquinius neither answered nor slowed his pace. Amanis shook her head, then followed.

They made their way cautiously along Marble Street. At every crossing Tarquinius halted, listening. Then he peered up and down the crossing street until he was satisfied the way was clear. When they had passed the theater, the dwarf ducked suddenly into an alley between two buildings. The space was so narrow that Amanis had to turn sideways to negotiate it. She heard rats scurrying away into the darkness. Tarquinius didn't seem to notice; he hurried down the alley until they reached the end of one of the buildings, then set off down another byway no wider than the last. At the end of the passage he stopped, gesturing for Amanis to do the same.

"This is where we cross Arcadian Way," he whispered over his shoulder. "If your friends were going to the harbor commander, they'll be down at the other end, in the barracks beside the customhouse. But I don't want to chance being seen."

He craned his neck around the corner of the building. Looking both ways, he ducked back into the alley. They heard the sound of sandaled feet trotting on stone pavement. A band of torchbearing men appeared not a stone's throw distance where Marble Street bisected Arcadian Way. They talked together in low voices for a moment, then Amanis heard someone hail them from the direction of the harbor.

"Ho! Demetrius! Any sign of her?"

"No. We just informed the centurion on duty in the harbor barracks. Which way did you come?"

"Down the hillside to Curetes Street, then along Marble Street to here. We looked everywhere—around the agora, in all the corners. Even in the fountain alcove. No sign of her."

Tarquinius turned to look at her. "There must be twelve of them out there!" he whispered. "What'd you do, slit the governor's throat with that fingernail cleaner of yours?"

The men in the street conferred a while longer; then Demetrius posted two of them to stay in the harbor area. "I'm going to talk with the centurion a little more. The rest of you, go back to the villa. Fortunatus, you'd better give the master a report."

Fortunatus said something that didn't sound happy. The men began drifting away as Demetrius left quickly for the barracks.

Tarquinius waited until the street was empty. He turned to Amanis. "We're going to turn right here, go a few paces, then turn back along another alley on the other side. It'll take us around the barracks and the customhouse. I'll go first; if they see me I can draw them away and you can get across. Wait for me a few paces down the alley, and I'll catch up with you. If you don't hear anything by the time you've taken twenty breaths, it'll mean I'm on the other side, waiting for you." He turned to go.

Amanis put a hand on his shoulder. "Why are you doing this for me?"

He grinned at her in the darkness. "I don't know. When I figure it out, I'll tell you."

He stepped into the street and skittered to the right, out of her view. She suddenly realized she was forgetting to count her breaths. She tried to breathe as slowly as possible. The closer she came to twenty, the harder it became. She finally made herself peer slowly around the corner. The street was empty. She stepped into Arcadian Way and turned right, toward the theater. She walked briskly, but forced herself not to run. The opening of the alley was maybe six paces away. With every step, she expected to hear someone shout her name from behind, followed by the sound of running feet.

But nothing happened. She reached the alley and ducked into the shadows between the buildings.

Tarquinius was there, and behind him stood a tall, burly figure.

Her hand went to the knife.

"Hold on! You don't need that," Tarquinius said. "This is Othar. He's a friend."

Amanis leaned against a wall, trying to slow her panting. "How many times in one night will you frighten the life out of me?"

"It wasn't me; it was Othar. Can I help it if his timing's not so great?" He turned and swatted at the huge man with the back of his hand. "Were you worried about me, Othar? Admit it; you missed me and came to see if I was all right."

"Shut up, wart," Othar said in a thick, unfamiliar accent. "I missed you like a case of the ague."

"Same here. By the way, Othar, this is—" He stopped, blinking at Amanis. "I just realized I don't know your name."

She looked from one of them to the other. "Amanis," she said finally.

"We were just about to retire to the private chamber, good Othar. Would you care to join us?" Tarquinius swaggered off down the alley. Othar shook his head and gave a low grunt as he followed. Amanis stared after them for a moment, then hurried along behind.

Tarquinius led them through a maze of back streets and alleys, some hardly worthy of even that name. They crawled under overhanging ledges, they crept up side stairs and along the edges of roofs, they scrambled in one window of an unguarded building and out a window on the other side. After a while, Amanis became less worried about getting caught and more worried about getting lost. It seemed the dwarf knew every dark corner, every hidden way, every stealthy route in Ephesus.

Finally they climbed a wall of crumbling masonry and arrived at the back of a stone building. The only visible feature in the wall was a square window, set four cubits off the ground. The window was maybe an arm length in width, but iron bars were set from top to bottom across the opening, leaving only enough space between for a large cat to get through.

"Ah, here we are," announced Tarquinius. "Home at last."

"What?" said Amanis. "How are we supposed to—"

"Othar? Would you oblige me?"

Othar walked over to the ground beneath the window and braced himself against the wall with one knee bent forward. Tarquinius used the big man's knee as a step, then Othar boosted him the rest of the way up to the window. Amanis saw Tarquinius doing something to the mortar around one of the bars, and soon he pulled the bar out of its bottom socket. He then repeated the process with another of the bars, then another. The window was now big enough to admit even Othar. Tarquinius disappeared through the opening.

Othar beckoned to Amanis. Gingerly she placed her foot on his knee. She vaulted to the window and climbed into the darkness.

Five

S he felt her feet touch surface not far below the window. She climbed down makeshift steps constructed of old crates, bricks, and broken building stones.

From behind came the sound of grunting and flesh scraping over stone. The entire opening was blocked by Othar's bulk; his legs and lower torso protruded from the window. After some wriggling and more grunting, he slid through onto the steps.

"Welcome to our townhouse," Tarquinius said with a broad gesture. "Please make yourself at home. I can't imagine where the servants have gotten off to, but we'll do the best we can in their absence."

"What is this place?"

"By day, a warehouse." Tarquinius rummaged at the base of the wall near the rickety steps and emerged with a badly soiled bag. He reached inside and scooped out a handful of what looked like moist clay. He climbed the steps to the window. "Othar, if you please."

The giant handed him one of the window bars. The dwarf set the bar back in its top socket, then fit it along the bottom of the opening. He smeared clay on the outside of the sill to hold the bar in place. He did the same with the other two bars.

"I stumbled across this place by luck the last time we were in Ephesus," Tarquinius went on. "By the way, Othar, are we still leaving tomorrow morning?"

Othar nodded.

"Meet at the usual place?"

Another nod.

"Who is this 'we' you keep talking about?" Amanis asked.

"Our band. Our troupe. Surely you didn't think this big oaf and I were the whole act? Jupiter's eyebrows, I'd starve clean to death if I had to depend on this great lout to draw a crowd."

"More likely you'd talk them to death," muttered Othar.

"Anyway, I've got a special knack for remembering good hideouts. An occupational gift, you might call it."

"Scared rat can always find a hole," said Othar.

Tarquinius ignored him. "But enough about me," he said to Amanis. "Why are you on the run?"

Amanis opened her mouth, but had a hard time making the words come out. "I ran away from my master," she said finally in a near whisper.

"Oh. Got any food in that pack, have you?" Tarquinius asked.

"Not much…just a few things I grabbed before I left."

"A few more than either of us have. Suppose you could share a bit?"

"I have a little parched grain, some dried fruit and nuts." Slowly, she began untying the corners of the blanket. "I…I don't know how long this will have to last—"

"Oh, never mind about that. Tomorrow we'll be back with the others, and they'll have provisions before they start out, don't worry. Just a little something to tide us over until morning." Tarquinius had scooted over next to her and was watching as she undid the parcels.

"Why do you think I'd go with you?"

"From what I saw out there, Ephesus is no place for you. We're on our way to Smyrna for the midsummer festival. Pretty good pickings there; you might as well come along. Anyhow, a fugitiva is safer with a few folk who'll help keep an eye out."

"But your friends—"

"They'll do whatever I tell them to do," Tarquinius said flatly. Othar snorted. The dwarf shot him an annoyed glance. "Besides, I need a new assistant. I think you'd attract a much better sort of customer than Othar. No offense, old friend, but don't you think she'd do admirably as a spotter? Now give us a handful of those filberts, how about it?"

His rapid dialogue was making her dizzy. Questions sprouted in her mind with everything he said, but before she could get a word in, he said something that sent her down a new trail, racing to catch up with him as he prattled on about yet another topic. It was simpler, she finally decided, to just let him talk. No wonder Othar kept so quiet. Amanis began to wonder why the giant hadn't long ago squashed Tarquinius like a bug.

Tarquinius gave a huge yawn. "Well, all this late night exercise has made me sleepy. How about you?"

Amanis stood and peered about in the darkness. She began to move away.

"I wouldn't go far if I were you," Tarquinius called. She turned and looked at him.

"I've never seen anybody in here before daylight, but I'd still stay close to this window. I'd hate to have a bale of flax or a stack of crates between me and the way out, in case some industrious merchant decided to drop in for an early morning delivery."

Amanis moved back toward the window. She found a place along the wall near where the dwarf had thrown himself, bundled in his robe. Othar was on the other side of the steps, studying the floor, muttering under his breath.

"Othar, will you stop worrying about the mice? Why would any self-respecting rodent want to chew on your smelly hide?"

Othar glared at the dwarf, then arranged himself on the steps in a crumpled position. He leaned an elbow on one of the stacks of brick and propped his head in his hand. He looked about as miserable as anyone Amanis had ever seen. Every so often he would jerk upright and stare at the floor and the base of the steps.

Amanis pulled the blanket over herself, cradled her head in the crook of an arm and tried to sleep. The floor of the warehouse was packed earth, and it was cool and hard against the back of her hand. Through the window she could see a slice of night sky.

When she closed her eyes, she fancied the sound of footfalls outside the window. She opened her eyes and held her breath in the darkness. Nothing. In the morning she would leave from the north gate with Tarquinius, Othar, and whoever else might be in such a strange troupe. She would trek with them to Smyrna; she didn't know what else to do.

Amanis had a sudden, sharp memory from her childhood. Not long after Patroclus freed him, her father fashioned a decorative gate for the atrium of the country villa of one of Patroclus's associates. While he loaded the finished work onto his cart, Mother packed food in a satchel for him. Amanis followed her out to take the food to Father. She remembered listening to them talk about where he was going and when he might return. She remembered watching their scraggly chickens scratch about in the dust of the courtyard. A desire had risen in Amanis to accompany her father, to travel through the gates of Ephesus and see the wide world beyond the town's walls. She wanted to go, to see, to smell the air and watch the road roll slowly by under the wheels of the donkey cart.

She asked to go, then pleaded. She remembered her mother and father looking softly down at her and smiling. They shook their heads and said no, little one, it's not time for you to venture out into the countryside beyond the gates. Perhaps when you are older, her father said.

But Amanis had remained unconvinced, and still begged to go. Finally her mother and father embraced, and then her mother led her, gently but firmly, back to the house. When they got inside, she kneeled on the floor and took Amanis in her lap. She sang a song of home and warm food and a soft bed. She sang of a mother's arms and the way a little girl fit so perfectly there. She rocked Amanis until her protests and her childish wanderlust dissolved slowly into forgetfulness and drowsiness.

When she had awoken, the first thing she saw was her mother bent over the hearth. And the first thing she smelled was the warm, yeasty smell of fresh bread. Later, as she ate the hot bread with melted butter and honey and drank cool water from her own special cup, she and Mother heard the sound of Father's wheels creak as he drove the cart past the door and around to the forge behind their small house. She ran out the door to watch as her father unhitched the donkey and rubbed him down with an old piece of sackcloth.

He told her about the people he had seen and spoken to while he was there. He told her about the problems he had had installing his work: how he had to chisel at the stone facing where the gate was to be mounted; how he had to fit small wedges of iron in along the top and bottom of the hinge plates so the gate would swing smoothly and evenly. He told her how pleased his customers were, how they promised to speak highly of his work to others. He showed her the money they had paid him: ten shiny bronze sestertia. It was almost as good as going there herself, to hear the happiness in his voice and see the way he smiled when he showed her what he had earned for his labor. He let her hold the coins; they felt heavy in her small hand. Then he let her carry the coins in to Mother.

It wasn't long after that, Amanis remembered, that the wasting sickness took Mother. Father never spoke again to Amanis of his work. She didn't remember him smiling anymore.

Tomorrow she would leave Ephesus at last; she would finally see the countryside beyond the walls. There would be no one to tell a story to draw her mind away from going.

Amanis awakened to the sound of low voices. It was still dark. Tarquinius and Othar were huddled together on the bottom step. Every so often one of them would glance at her. Their faces told her something was amiss. She raised herself to a sitting position. "What's the matter?"

"Othar couldn't sleep, so a while ago he went out to get the lay the land. He says there are people prowling all through the streets, asking anyone who's stirring if he's seen an African woman, a runaway slave." Tarquinius glanced through the window, then back at her. "It's still well before dawn, and already they're out—in numbers." His eyes narrowed as he looked at her. "What else did you take from your master, besides that tickler in the sheath at your belt?"

His authority. His good fortune. His wife, maybe. And a child he'd already discarded. "Nothing," she replied.

They both studied her in silence for a while. "It'll be tricky," Tarquinius said at last, drawing a deep breath. "We'd better get going, while we've still got the dark working for us."

Othar climbed to the window and began digging the clay out from around the bottom of the bars. Amanis gathered her remaining provisions and tied up the bundle for traveling. Tarquinius stood, yawned, and stretched his stubby arms. "I could do with a bit of bread. I don't suppose—?" He looked hopefully at Amanis.

She shook her head as she shouldered the pack.

"Ready?" Othar asked, one leg already across the sill.

When Othar had stuffed himself through the opening, Tarquinius hopped quickly through. Amanis cautiously put her head out and looked up and down. The other two waited for her just on the other side of the decrepit masonry rampart. Tarquinius motioned impatiently to her, and she clambered out feet first, dropping lightly to the ground. They set off down the narrow alley that fronted the low, broken-down wall.

They came to a street. They were near the harbor, so even this early, a few men moved sleepily toward the wharves and the storage sheds along the waterfront.

Amanis was able to make out the six-pointed star on the light stone building across the way. She thought of the baby girl and the old Jewish man who had taken her in. She took a quick look up and down the street, then dashed across toward the place of worship.

"What are you doing?" Tarquinius hissed, close behind her.

Amanis ducked quickly around the corner of the building and went to the small house behind. She rapped at the door.

"Please. Open the door." She knocked again.

She heard the tapping of a cane, followed by the sound of someone fumbling with the bolt. The door opened the barest crack. "Who is it?" came the old man's voice.

"I'm the one who brought the baby to you a few nights ago."

He opened the door wide enough to let her see his eyes.

"Is the child well? Did the family take her in?"

The old man's eyes widened. He was looking at something behind her. Amanis whirled around to find Othar hovering over her left shoulder.

"We need to go," he said, his eyes darting this way and that.

She turned back to the old Jew. "It's all right. He's with me. What about the little girl?"

"Whom could you possibly fear with this one as your companion?" the old man said.

"Please. The girl?"

"She is in the home of Thomas the tanner. They will raise her as their own."

Amanis's eyes closed for an instant. She turned to follow Othar.

"Wait," the old man called. He glanced nervously inside, then shuffled over to a corner of the hut. Amanis heard him shifting things about. A moment later he reappeared, holding a small bag.

"Here, take this. It isn't much, but you can probably use it." She heard the clink of coins as he placed it in her hand.

"What—? I don't—"

"For showing mercy to the fatherless. Now go," he said, motioning them away. "Before Hannah wakes up. She'll never let me hear the end of it."

With a final look at him, she stuffed the bag in her belt and turned to leave.

Just as they neared the corner of the Jewish sanctuary, Othar pushed her up against the wall with his forearm. A squad of soldiers marched past, and in the van of the patrol was Scaevolus's man. "Are you sure there are guards on every gate?" he was asking. "Scaevolus will be very displeased if she gets out of the city."

The commander of the squad gave a terse reply. They marched down the street and toward the harbor. Othar craned his neck to see the patrol, then held his alert position until the sound of their footsteps faded. He dropped his arm, and Amanis drew a deep breath. Othar looked up and down the street, then darted across to the alley where Tarquinius still waited.

"What was all that about?" the dwarf asked. "This is going to be touchy enough without you dashing off whenever the notion strikes you! And who was that fellow with the patrol? 'Scaevolus will be displeased if she gets out of the city.' I guess it's too much to hope he wasn't talking about you?"

Amanis said nothing.

"What have you done to attract the attention of the biggest slave trader this side of Athens?" he demanded.

"I don't know, I swear. Here—" She fumbled in her belt and fished out the money bag. "The old man over there—he gave me this."

Tarquinius poured the money into his palm. He cocked an eyebrow up at her. "Well, at least your little side trip was worth something. Have you got something you can wear over your head?"

Amanis untied the sash at her waist. She poked the sikhimi into the top of the pack, then unfolded the sash and draped it over her head.

"Yes, that'll do. Keep your head down and it'll be hard for anyone to recognize you." He took another long look up and down the empty street. "All right, let's go. And no more running off."

They moved into the street—Tarquinius leading the way, Amanis behind him, and Othar bringing up the rear. They kept to the right, close to the edge of the street. The dwarf led them along side streets and down alleys in a route that roughly paralleled the main road leading from the harbor district to the city's northern gate. Now and then, they passed single men or groups of two or three: early morning laborers on their way to work. No one seemed to notice them.

As they neared the gate, however, the foot traffic grew heavier. They paused at the edge of the open square before the gate. A squad of legionaries was stationed there. They held torches, and their commander was peering closely at everyone who approached.

In the orange glow of the brands, Amanis could see the dark-bearded man in fine robes who stood near the commander, carefully scanning faces in the crowd. Amanis had a sick feeling: This was Scaevolus, come to oversee the diligence of the guards at this gate.

The gate had apparently been closed all night; travelers were complaining of the delay in their departures. There was no trouble this far south in Asia Province, they said. Why had the gates been locked in the first place? The soldiers didn't seem to be listening to them.

Tarquinius gave a signal, and the three of them edged slowly back around the corner of a building. He pointed across the square, at a short stone edifice a few paces from the soldiers' position.

"There—see that lararium?"

Amanis nodded.

"We'll work our way around the square and get behind it.

That's where we'll wait for the others."

"But how are we going to get past the guards?"

"You'll see."

They took a circuitous route and finally arrived where the shrine stood. They were able to keep the shrine between them and the guards' scrutiny, though Othar had to curl into a ball to conceal his bulk behind the lararium. They leaned against the back of the shrine. They might have been three traveling companions, catching a final nap before the soldiers opened the gate.

The lararium felt hard against her shoulder blades. The *lares augustales* were supposed to protect travelers. Did that include a fugitiva? She would soon find out; the sky would begin to lighten anytime now.

Six

*J*ust as the light enabled Amanis to make out the seams in the masonry of the buildings across from the lararium, she heard a faroff ringing. Tarquinius jabbed an elbow into the ribs of Othar, who had been snoring softly for a while.

"Wake up. They're coming."

Othar's eyes opened, and he stared down the street that emptied into the gate plaza from the west. The ringing was growing louder, and Amanis could now make out the sound of singing.

"They'll come down that street," Tarquinius said, pointing. "When they come past us, slide out from behind here and get into the middle of them. Do whatever they do: sing, dance, clap your hands, whatever. Just stay in the middle. They'll see you with me and they'll keep themselves between us and the uglies at the gate."

Amanis threw him a confused look, but by now the noise from the procession had halted the conversations of the guards and those waiting for the gate to open. Amanis imagined that everyone in the plaza must be staring past the lararium to the street beyond. How could their exit from this hiding place possibly be concealed with everyone looking toward them?

When they rounded the corner, she saw. The jangling came from two young women, one vigorously plying a tambourine, the wearing finger cymbals on both hands, skillfully weaving her arms in patterns above her head, in front, to either side, and behind. They were scantily clad; their skirts were mostly strips of cloth, and their waists were bare from just below the bustline to the navel. They smiled and flashed their eyes at the men in the square, and their anklet bells created a merry accompaniment to the instruments in their hands.

Behind the girls came a motley crowd of jugglers, acrobats, and other performers whose specialties Amanis couldn't begin to guess. They were singing a raucous song about youth and love and the enjoyment of wine. Groups of them engaged in impromptu dances; there didn't seem to be any fixed number of participants. They filled the plaza like a colorful, noisy flood.

They swept around the lararium. Amanis felt Tarquinius nudge her. She slipped into the throng and burrowed as deeply as she could. Looking back, she saw that one of the acrobats—a woman wearing the outlandish breeches of a Scythian rider—had grabbed Othar's hands and was spinning him round and round in a dizzying jig. In the morning light, Amanis had her first clear look at Othar. Two thick, blond braids twirled behind him. He must be German, she realized.

Someone had linked an arm through hers and was singing in her ear. She looked at her partner, and realized it was the juggler she had seen in the agora the day she went to fetch dates for her mistress. He smiled as if they were on a holiday outing. "Sing!" he yelled.

"I don't know the words!"

"It doesn't matter! Make up your own."

The two dancing girls had moved beyond the gates. The soldiers' eyes were glued to them and the commander of the patrol scolded his men. Still, some of the more daring ones would risk a moment or two of flirtation when they thought he was looking elsewhere.

The crowd of travelers now formed a loose circle around the dancers, smiling and tapping their feet in time to the tambourine and cymbals. Some of them even tossed a few copper lepta in the dust at the girls' feet. A child appeared from somewhere in the mob of performers and scurried between the girls, collecting the coins each time they were tossed.

The troupe gathered before of the girls, clapping and singing in time to their dance. Amanis looked through the swaying bodies and located Tarquinius. Like her, he was taking care to keep as many bodies as possible between him and the patrol at the gate.

After an exhaustingly long time, the dance finished in a flurry of cymbals, tambourines, and twirling skirts. The crowd gave them a sustained ovation.

The juggler next to Amanis pressed his way to the front of the troupe.

"Friends! You see before you a poor band of traveling entertainers! If you've appreciated the dance of Tarisia and Tyche, won't you give a little something to help us on our way to Smyrna?" He swept off his round, floppy hat and held it in front of him, passing through the crowd. A few dropped coins; most didn't.

Some of the travelers began to remember their need to be away. They surrounded the commander of the guards and demanded that he open the Koressos Gate.

Amanis could see Scaevolus craning his neck this way and that, trying to see everyone in the square. She tried to make herself as small as possible. She felt someone move in beside her. It was the juggler.

"Disappointing," he said, peering into his hat. "The way they were grinning and tapping their feet, I thought we might do a little better this time. Oh, well." He took the coins from the hat and dropped them into the waiting hands of a child, who had appeared from nowhere. He settled the hat back on his head and looked at Amanis. "You must be desperate indeed to fall in with the likes of Tarquinius." His eyes settled briefly on the watchers by the gate and moved back to her. "The fellow standing near the commander?"

She nodded.

"Well, don't worry. We've got to get our small friend safely away, and we might as well manage for you, too. Just stay close to me when the gate opens, and all will be well."

He was tall, and his beard had a sandy hue. The broad, shapeless brim of the leather hat drooped down over his forehead, nearly blocking his eyes from view. Vaguely disturbing those eyes were: such a light brown as to seem almost yellow—amber, maybe. And when he fixed them on Amanis, she had the sense they were judging and measuring.

His skin was pale and lightly freckled. He carried a large leather bag over his shoulder, and he reached into it now, withdrawing two painted wooden balls, each about the size of a plum. He started tossing and catching them with one hand. He didn't look at the balls, didn't even seem to be paying attention. His motion was habitual and unerring.

The constant harangue from the travelers had its effect on the commander of the guard detail. He barked an order to someone behind him, and two soldiers applied themselves to the winch. The gears creaked, the lines—nearly as thick as Amanis's wrist—stretched and groaned, and the bronze-clad gates slowly opened.

The travelers pushed through the opening, some of them with their wares and possessions loaded onto shoulder packs, others driving ahead of them donkeys laden with panniers. Amanis watched as Scaevolus pressed himself forward into the exiting crowd, frantically moving from figure to figure.

The troupe also moved toward the widening gate, and Amanis allowed herself to be swept along in the crush of bodies. The juggler was beside her for a few paces, then the pull of the crowd forced them apart. Amanis was close to the gate when she saw, with a stab of fear, that Scaevolus was standing directly in her path. She lowered her head to let the covering hang as low as possible, but felt sure he would see the dark skin of her hands and feet.

Nearer and nearer the human tide pushed her. She was maybe five or six paces away when someone shoved past her right shoulder, nearly knocking her down. She glimpsed two blond braids as the burly figure surged through the crowd like a runaway ox passing through a milling herd of sheep. Othar bore directly down on Scaevolus, pushing the slave merchant roughly. Knocked off-balance, he was pressed aside by the throng of performers until he was nearly pinned against the hinge stanchions of the gate. Amanis passed by him, safely hidden among the crowd.

Once through the gate, the company thinned out along the northern road. Now Amanis could more easily observe her traveling companions. She heard several languages spoken within earshot. One man was dressed like a Bedouin from the deserts beyond Syria. On straps crisscrossing his chest and back clattered a shining collection of daggers and knives of various shapes and sizes. Walking next to him was a fellow with the fair skin and blue eyes of a Circassian from the far north. Besides the pack on his back, he carried an unstrung bow and a large quiver of arrows fletched in bright red. There were young women and grandmothers, some with bright scarves covering their heads. There were small groups of men and women, unaccompanied persons of both sexes, and family groups with ragtag children of all ages and descriptions racing in and out among them. A few of them had their belongings packed on donkeys, and the father and boys of one family group took turns trundling a handcart piled with bundles. One bandy-legged old fellow carried across his shoulders a pole strung with four cages aflutter with small, noisy, brightly colored birds.

The juggler strode up to Amanis. "Good thing they shut the gates last night. Without that big bunch of grouchy peddlers, it might have been ticklish to get you out of town."

"Nonsense," came a familiar voice from waist level. "Othar and I could have gotten her out by ourselves, if we'd had to." Tarquinius grinned up at her. Just behind him, the big German grunted and shook his head.

"One of these days, Tarquinius, your luck is going to run out," said the juggler.

"Damon, you worry too much."

"About you, I don't worry at all."

Othar gave a low chuckle.

"Why were you hiding back in Ephesus?" Amanis wanted to know.

The dwarf shrugged. "Hazard of doing business. I run a fair game, but sometimes those who lose don't see it that way."

"Fair?" said Othar. "Why do you need me around if it's so fair?"

"I've paid out plenty of times. And besides, maybe I *don't* need a muscle-bound blockhead hanging around now that I've got Amanis here."

"Tarquinius," said Damon in a low voice, glancing sideways at Amanis. "I'm not sure she's—"

"She'll be spectacular," Tarquinius insisted. "I'll teach her all there is to know. We'll make twice as much money as before."

"Well, since she's traveling with us, she'll have to contribute something at least. But take care, Tarquinius. She's in trouble already, and keeping company with you isn't likely to improve that if the past is any indication." Damon looked up and quickened his pace to catch up to a group of the grandmothers.

"You were talking to the old man at the Jewish temple about a baby," Othar said after Damon left. "What was that about? Is that why you had to get away? Did you steal someone's child?"

"No!"

Tarquinius and Othar trudged along on either side of her, and Amanis could feel the weight of their gazes.

"My master's wife bore a girl-child. He would not pick her up or name her. She was taken to the mountainside. I—I could not allow it."

"Couldn't allow? Since when does a slave allow or not allow?"

"Let her finish, Tarquinius."

"I...just couldn't."

"I understand this," the big German said after a long moment. "Among my people babies are never abandoned."

"Why was the slaver after you?" Tarquinius asked.

"I don't know. One of his men tried to take the baby from

me. But I fought him, and he ran away."

Tarquinius gave a low whistle. "Scaevolus's man, I guess."

Amanis nodded.

"But…babies are exposed all the time," said Tarquinius. "What difference did it make if Scaevolus got this one or the next one?"

"I don't know. That's what I can't understand—why he so wanted to find me."

"But it wasn't Scaevolus that made you run from your master's house," said Othar.

"No. My mistress died."

"You killed your mistress!"

"No, no. She came down with childbed fever. My master consulted the magicians. They told him someone in the household had violated the customs. They told him Fortuna was affronted, that his bad luck was because of that."

"And you were the one the blame landed on," Tarquinius said.

"Not exactly. I ran before they settled all that."

The three of them walked along in silence for a while.

"Damon was right about me, Tarquinius," she said. "I am in trouble. And if you take me on, my trouble could become yours. Are you sure you want to take the chance?"

"Damon worries about everybody," Tarquinius said after a few paces. "He has to, I guess. But you stay with me, Amanis. You'll be fine. Besides, I'm sort of partial to lost causes."

"You are a lost cause," Othar said. He muttered something else in German, shaking his head.

The troupe made camp that night in a rocky ravine just off the highway. Amanis stood to one side by a tumble of burnt-ocher rocks near the ravine wall, trying to absorb as much of the routine as she could. It was fascinating to watch them prepare for the night.

The old man with the birds took each of his feathered charges from their cages. The birds perched on his forefinger and pecked at the seeds in his palm. He talked to them gently, then put them back inside. When all of them had eaten, he reached into a satchel and came out with four small clay cups. He filled each cup with water from a skin and placed them inside the cages. He draped each cage with a sheet of sailcloth; then he tied each at the bottom with twine.

The Arabian took off his knives and stropped them on a piece of thick leather. He took out a small jar and poured something from it onto a cloth, then wiped the blades before rolling them in a larger cloth. She heard the muffled clanking of the metal as he stowed the bundle in his pack. The Circassian had a small fire going, and the two men talked as he carefully fed it twigs.

The grandmothers huddled in the center of the camp, pulling baskets from packs and filling them with provisions. To Amanis, it appeared that the responsibility for transporting the foodstuffs was distributed among various members of the troupe, but that only the grandmothers knew exactly where everything was and how much of it to put in each basket. Every so often, one of them would carry one or several baskets to the groups of people forming around the open fires among the sheltered places in the ravine. The old women wasted no motion.

Tarquinius strode up to her. "Come over to our fire. They just brought out some cheese and dried fruit."

They walked into the purple nightfall. Othar hunkered in front of a smoking fire, frowning as he poked sticks into it.

"I told you not to use that goosefoot weed for kindling,"

Tarquinius said. "It'll smoke like that all night long."

"Maybe it'll keep the flies away," Othar said. He got on his hands and knees and blew along the bottom of the blaze. He straightened quickly, fanning his hand in front of his face and coughing.

"Mind your beard," Tarquinius said. "I'd hate to have to douse you. I might just let you smolder. That'd keep the flies away for sure." He picked up a basket and offered it to Amanis. Inside were cakes of hard cheese with a strong smell. The basket also held a mixture of raisins, dried plums, and cherries. She scooped a handful into her lap and passed the basket to Othar.

"Do they have to sneak you out of every town they visit?" she asked the dwarf, who lounged against a rock at the edge of the firelight.

"No, not always. Only in the larger towns. I don't know why it is. In Smyrna or Thyatira there's scarcely a bobble—at least nothing that Othar can't handle. But you put me in a place like Ephesus or Pergamum, and the sorest loser in town will always find my game. And he'll be the magistrate's brother-in-law every time."

"What is this game you run?"

He reached into his satchel and brought out a flat square of poplar wood, rubbed so smooth it shone in the fire's glow. He put the board down on the ground and placed on it three walnut shell halves. He held out a cupped palm to Amanis. In it was a dried bean. She watched as he put the bean beneath one of the walnut shells, then lined them up on the board. He tapped the shell covering the bean, then began shifting the shells around on the board.

His pudgy hands moved deftly, keeping the shells in constant motion. Then he halted and looked up expectantly at her.

"Which one?"

Amanis blinked. "That one," she said, pointing at the middle shell.

Tarquinius picked it up; it concealed nothing.

"Try again," she said. "I'll watch closer now that I know what you're doing."

"Oh, you know what I'm doing, do you?"

He showed her the bean, then began sliding them again. When he stopped and looked at her, she had no inkling which shell hid the bean.

"That one," she guessed, stabbing at the shell on the left.

He picked it up. Nothing.

"Here," he said, tapping the center shell. He picked it up and showed her the bean.

"Again," she said, straightening and locking her eyes on the center shell as if it contained all the secrets of her future.

Seven

*H*is hands swirled over the board for a moment or two, then stopped. "The left."

Nothing.

"Try again," he said, without moving the shells.

She bit her lip. "Center?"

Nothing there. He picked up the right shell, showing her the bean.

They played four more times, and once she guessed correctly. She knew it was nothing more than blind luck.

"So if I take from you two lepta for each wrong guess and give you back three for the one right guess, I make a profit of eleven. I might even offer you a second guess on a single shift for another three, in which case my profit is fourteen." He grinned at her. "Not bad, eh?"

"Were you hiding the bean in your fingernail?"

"Certainly not! Less skillful players sometimes do that, but I don't need to."

"So…what is it you want me to do?"

"Enough time for that tomorrow." He yawned. "I'm tired. Today started early." He stowed the board and shells back in his pack and scooted closer to the fire. "You'll need to keep one eye over your shoulder, you know."

"Meaning what?"

His face was serious. "It'll occur to Scaevolus, sooner or later, that you aren't in Ephesus anymore. And he'll probably figure out that you must have gotten out with that crowd at the gate. If he wants to find you as badly as it seems, he'll be along behind us. Or some of his people."

She stared into the dying fire. After a while, she nodded.

The camp settled for the night. Amanis sat beside the coals with her blanket spread over her lap. The midsummer night was warm; the heat of the day still breathed from the ground. But by morning, she guessed, the breeze from the sea would cause the blanket, snug around her, to feel good.

She listened to the fretting babies and the gentling voices of their mothers. Somewhere someone was whistling through his teeth. Men's voices carried to her, sounding almost as if they sat beside her as they talked. The language was strange to Amanis, but the tone was familiar: low and lazy, like two children lying in the dark and telling each other their idle wishes. Maybe they were talking about a woman. Maybe they were wondering how free the purses of Smyrna would be when the troupe arrived there for the festival. The voices drifted in the night air, the words coming slower with longer pauses between. Then quiet. From somewhere overhead sounded the burring trill of a male nightjar looking for a mate.

Amanis thought about Scaevolus, the way he looked in the flickering light of the torches as he stood with the commander of the soldiers by the gate. His dark eyes were everywhere about the square, flashing with the intensity of a man jealous for the return of a stolen prize or watching for the face of a dearly hated enemy. Again she tried to imagine what spite could cause him to care so much about one infant taken away, or the woman who denied the child to him.

He couldn't remember her, could he? She had been a mere slip of a girl the day her father hauled her into his courtyard, the day her father sold her to Scaevolus for a hundred denarii. Untold scores of men and women, boys and girls had stood in the unadorned room where Scaevolus met his buyers. Hundreds had stood like dumb cattle, listening as their attributes were discussed between seller and purchaser with the same detached, offhand tones they might use to talk about a vase or a pair of sandals. "She knows how to work," Amanis's father had told Scaevolus that day. "And she is strong for her age." He had invited Scaevolus to squeeze her arms, told her to make a fist. "She learns quickly, and she won't talk much."

"A hundred," the slave trader had mused, looking at her. "And yet, Lucius, I have in mind a citizen of this city, a wealthy man who will buy your daughter for his wife, and he will pay at least two seventy-five."

Amanis had looked at her father, hoping to see at least the flash of satisfaction from a higher reward than he had expected for his efforts, a ghost of the smile he had worn on the day he placed in her hands the money for the gate and told her to show it to her mother.

But no. He avoided her eyes, shrugging off Scaevolus's words as if they made no difference. "That is your business, not mine. I'm a metalsmith, not a trader. A hundred is all I want."

That was the moment Amanis turned her face forever from her father.

She heard the scuff of feet on stone. She raised her face to see Othar, hugging himself and shifting from one foot to another on the sloping surface of the rock where Tarquinius had rested earlier.

"Aren't you tired?" she asked the German.

He gave a terse shake of his head.

"Why not? You were awake long before me this morning."

He gave a low grunt and stared off into the darkness.

A dry, skittering sound, like the tiniest twigs brushing against gravel, came from the rocks by where Othar stood. The big man wheeled about, peering at the ground. Amanis heard him whisper an abrupt obscenity.

"What was it?" she asked, standing quickly and gathering her blanket from the ground.

"Rock lizards. Hundreds of them around here. I hate 'em." He grumbled into his beard and hunkered slowly onto his haunches, hugging his knees and keeping a suspicious eye on the ground around him.

Amanis settled herself for sleep with her back to him so he couldn't see her smiling.

In her dream she was looking down at the road from above. She saw Scaevolus hurrying along, the tops of his shoulders hunched forward as he peered into the dust beside the paved roadbed. Her father ambled along behind the slave trader. Amanis could see the bald spot on the back of her father's head, the way his forearms angled out as he walked.

Scaevolus saw something and scurried to the side of the road. He got down on his hands and knees and put his nose to the tracks in the dirt. He beckoned her father to do the same. The tall black man bent down beside the road. He peered at the other man, who pointed insistently at the ground. Amanis's father put his face to the dust.

From somewhere, Scaevolus produced a board and placed on it three walnut halves. He shifted them about for a moment, then stopped. Amanis's father tapped the middle shell, and Scaevolus raised it to reveal a shiny black stone. He looked at Amanis's father and nodded as he put the board away. Then the two men got up and hurried down the highway.

The baby was crying. Amanis went to the rock tumble near the ravine wall and took the tiny girl from the scarf-draped grandmother who rocked her and tried in vain to hush her. The infant's eyes opened and looked into Amanis's face. She stopped crying, and the focus of her look sharpened; she was trying to tell Amanis something, to push some thought into her mind.

Damon was calling them back to the road. But just as Amanis was swinging her pack onto her shoulder, everyone froze. Beside the road, his nose to the ground where they had left the pavement for the camping place in the ravine, stood a lion. The big animal's breath came quickly as he smelled the scent in the dust. Then the lion raised his head and his eyes bore straight in on Amanis. The lion tilted his muzzle slightly upward, sniffing at the wind for her scent.

They were looking at her, waiting to see what she would do. Othar stood on his rock, arms crossed in front of him. "It's your lion," he said. "You decide."

Amanis woke in the rose-gray light of sunrise. Her right arm was numb, and as she struggled to sit up she grabbed her right sleeve and hauled the dead arm into her lap, waiting for it to prickle back to life.

Smoke from a dozen morning fires drifted around her. Othar was poking twigs and pieces of bark at a coal he had uncovered in the ashes. Tarquinius lay on his back on the other side of the fire, snoring up at the brightening sky.

Amanis unwrapped her parcel of parched grain. She tossed a fistful into her mouth, then handed the packet to Othar. He nodded his thanks and poured himself some, then gave the dwarf's outstretched foot a great thwack with the back of his hand.

Tarquinius snorted, then sat up and rubbed his eyes. "Are we going?"

"I wish," said Othar. "Ought to leave you here sleeping and let the jackals have you."

"Any more of that?" Tarquinius asked, leaning over Othar to retrieve the grain packet. He tilted his head back and dumped the remaining grain into his open mouth. He chomped like an ass at the feed box.

"How about letting us see that tickler?" he said, jutting his chin toward the bone handle of the sikhimi, which protruded from Amanis's pack. She handed it to the dwarf, who drew it from its scabbard. He ran a thumb along the edge of the blade. His eyebrows arched in appreciation.

"Plenty sharp." He hefted the knife in one hand. "Sits well in the fist, too. The one who made this knew what he was about."

Amanis nodded, looking away. Yes. Her father was a skilled metalsmith, no question.

Tarquinius handed the knife to Othar, who put it to a similar test. "And you know how to use it, I guess," the dwarf said to Amanis. "You could take care of yourself in a pinch?"

She looked at him silently, her eyes harder now.

"I thought so. And that's where you and I need to talk business. See, somebody like me is always at a disadvantage. My mind is on the game, on the money at stake, on the eyes of the other player, on my moves, on the pattern of where the bean gets left—it's complicated, and it has to move fast, but I'm good at it.

"But I can't watch everything that needs to be watched: the crowd, the talk over my shoulder, the side betting that goes on. Everything that's happening around the game is important. And that's why I need a spotter. I need someone to be my other eyes and ears…and sometimes my protection."

He jerked a thumb at Othar. "Now, not many people are going to get fresh with this fellow. But the other problem is that a spotter works better when no one knows who it is—just another face in the crowd. When Othar's around, even the blind beggars know where he came from.

"But you…" He nodded, assuming a sly expression. "You'd attract a lot less attention. And if you can use that thing half as well as I suspect, I don't think I'd have to worry about some bully boy getting the wrong idea."

"May I see that?"

The voice came from behind Amanis. It was the Bedouin. The Circassian stood beside him, and both of them were looking at the bone handle protruding from Amanis's pack. She gave Othar a doubtful glance, but he nodded. She retrieved the sikhimi once more, then stood and offered it to the wiry Bedouin.

He took the sikhimi from its sheath and balanced it on his palm. Then he flipped it in the air high above his head and caught it by the handle at the last moment. He twirled it from hand to hand, the blade flashing dangerously in the early morning light. He parried and thrust with it, made wide, slashing arcs in the empty air, and whirled the blade above and behind and from hand to hand.

When he was finished, he held the blade at arm's length and gave the Circassian an appreciative nod. He sheathed the sikhimi and handed it back to Amanis with a little bow. He and the Circassian walked away toward their fire, talking in low voices.

"Harim likes your little toy," said Tarquinius. "That's high praise."

The troupe seemed in no great hurry to break camp. Some of the boys began running up and down the ravine. Amanis smelled bread baking. Some of the grandmothers had steaming iron pots hanging over their cookfires. They stirred and tossed in grain or herbs now and then, making some kind of savory stew which they decanted into clay vessels and distributed among the few carts belonging to the band.

Finally, when the sun had climbed two handbreadths into the sky, Damon made his way around to each group, urging them to gather up and move toward the road. As the day before, they strung out along the highway, clumped together in parties.

They hadn't gone far when there was a commotion near the front of the march. Amanis craned her neck this way and that, trying to see the source of the confusion. Soon Damon came back down the line, ordering them to the side of the road. The troupe had scarcely shuffled aside when the clack of hobnails was heard from just beyond the next rise in the highway. Soon a forest of javelin points sprouted from the rise, closely followed by a column of imperial infantry regulars. The soldiers came over the crest jogging in crisp double time, their bullhide cuirasses creaking and their scabbarded gladii slapping their thighs. They hurried past with not a glance.

The column appeared to be a full cohort. They hustled down the highway, the one-two, one-two of their armored steps fading behind them. As the troupe ventured back onto the highway, some of the young boys found sticks for swords and javelins.

Well before midday, the heat began to bother Amanis like an unwelcome visitor. The road from Ephesus to Smyrna wound through a series of rocky ridges and hillsides, separated by stream-cut valleys. The highway followed the shoulders of the country up and down and across mostly dry stream beds. Copses of scrub juniper clung to the slopes and scattered across the ridge tops; stunted poplars and elms stood in clumps along the watercourses. But there was nothing available that could really be called shade, and even in the swales at the bottom of the valleys, not a cool breath stirred. There was only the heat, the glare, and the need to stay with the others and continue moving forward.

They came down into a wide valley drained by a stream that still ran clear, though in a meandering, narrow channel far from the cut banks marking its fullest width. Damon called a halt to refill the water skins, and Amanis nearly fainted with relief when the word came back from the front of the line. The hill that lay ahead of them looked to be the highest one yet, humped up like a sow's back. The notion of a rest before attempting the steep climb seemed like a good idea to Amanis. With Tarquinius and Othar, she staggered over to a small grove of hackberries. They crawled in beneath the low-lying eaves of the trees, their feet scuffing through the fallen leaves of seasons past. Amanis shrugged her pack from her shoulder and folded limply onto the ground beside it.

When they had passed around the water skin, a grandmother appeared holding out one of the clay jars Amanis had seen that morning. Tarquinius took it and swigged down some of the brew, then handed it to Amanis. The pungent smell of the herbs reminded her of green, growing things, but the heat of the day seemed like an odd time to be drinking broth.

"Go ahead. We don't eat at midday when we're on the road," Tarquinius told her. "This will give you strength without making you sluggish."

The broth was still warm, and to Amanis's surprise it was bracing, just as the dwarf claimed. She took a few large swallows, then passed the jar on to Othar.

"I'll go fill the water skin." She left the shade and picked her way through the knee-high grass and half-parched crown vetch that ran down to the cut bank. She slid down the pebbly bank to the rocky stream bed.

A handful of troupe members were already at the channel filling skins and jars. One of the girls who had danced at the gate in Ephesus was straightening after filling a canteen made from the stomach of a goat. She tied off the opening with a rawhide thong and looked at Amanis as she slung the bulging container over her shoulder.

"So you're the one who's taken up with Tarquinius and his giant." Her dark eyes looked Amanis up and down. "I hope you're up to it."

Amanis gave her an uncertain look.

"Oh, don't worry too much. You can outrun the dwarf, if nothing else, and the German is mostly afraid of women anyway."

Amanis stared as the girl flounced away.

"Pay her no mind," came a soft voice at Amanis's elbow.

An old woman stood beside her. She was short and stooped, and she looked up into Amanis's face with a faint smile.

"Why would she say—?"

"She's a dancer. They generally take in the most money, so they think they're entitled to say whatever comes to their minds."

"But Tarquinius and Othar—"

"Are harmless. You don't need to worry. Besides, I'd guess Tarisia might be a little jealous. It's been a while since we've had another unattached woman in the troupe who had the where-withal to turn a man's head." She chuckled at Amanis's shocked expression. She started to turn away but stopped and studied Amanis's face a moment. She asked her to hold out her hand. She took Amanis's palm and turned it this way and that, tracing its creases with a forefinger.

She appeared to be thinking. Then she dropped Amanis's hand and gave her a quick smile. "Never mind, dear. Just an old woman's fancy, nothing more." She bent to pick up a full skin and grunted as she took its weight onto her back. "And don't worry about Tarisia and her prattling," she said as she turned to walk away.

Eight

*A*manis filled the skin and made her way back toward the grove. When she reached the hackberry trees, Damon was there, sitting between Tarquinius and Othar with his long legs drawn up and his fingers laced across his shins. His floppy hat was on the ground beside him.

For a long time he looked at her with a frank, measuring gaze. Amanis squirmed, thinking about what the old woman at the stream had said.

The thought came to her that in the life she had just abandoned, it would be unthinkable for a proper woman to sit so informally in the company of three men, none of whom was her husband. Of course, slaves were subject to a different measure. A stable boy might grope a kitchen drudge with impunity, but a household manager and a matron's body servant might be indistinguishable from their masters in their behavior. Indeed, in Amanis's experience, the upper echelons among the slaves sometimes upheld their propriety more than the citizens who owned them.

There seemed no such rules among the troupe. Amanis had seen men and women visiting back and forth among the campfires the past night, and Damon moved easily among them all. No one seemed more free to her than this band of entertainers. And yet they approached one another with the familiarity of the lowest slaves. It was confusing.

Amanis kept her eyes on the ground beside Damon as he studied her. "Well," she said finally, "have you seen enough yet?"

The juggler laughed. "No, not by a long stretch, Amanis of Ephesus. Not yet."

"What's that supposed to mean?"

"Only that each of us in this troupe has a job to do. Even the children. And it isn't yet clear to me what you're fit for."

"Yet you were willing to help me past those who watched for me at the gate."

"Yes. We've all—or most of us, at least—been in and out of trouble of some kind or other. We've all had to depend on the rest to save our skins. And besides, we couldn't very well have taken Tarquinius without you; the way things stood, it was a trade for both or none."

"I tell you, Damon, she'll be a real help to me," said Tarquinius.

"So you say." He smiled as he said it.

The three men fell to talking about Smyrna, about how best to make the troupe's presence known there. Tarquinius was of the opinion that the best plan was to go straight to the agora and to deploy the dancers and possibly Harim and Turash—the Circassian, Amanis guessed. The knife throwing and stunt shooting always drew a big crowd, the dwarf said. They ought to make noise and gather enough onlookers to make their money quickly and move to the next town up the road.

But Damon was having none of it. The best way was to spread out all over the town as they always did, he insisted. Work Smyrna slowly and gently, sleep in the same place a few days before taking to the highway again. The midsummer festival made folks jolly, the juggler said. Why not take advantage of it?

"Why not hit them quick and move on?" Tarquinius shot back.

"You're talking about training a new spotter. How is she supposed to learn the business if you're raking in games hard and fast all day long?" Othar asked.

Damon spread his palms on the ground behind him and leaned back. He smiled at Othar and then at Tarquinius.

"He makes a good point, Tarquinius. Another incentive for the gradual approach, I'd say."

Tarquinius shook his head and mumbled something about the brevity of life and the scarcity of coin.

Damon sighed, then rose and dusted the dried leaf fragments off his seat and the backs of his legs. "We need to get moving pretty soon," he said. "Take another drink or two and then load up."

Amanis took a pull from the skin. The water had a chalky, alkaline taste. She wrinkled her nose as she swallowed.

"At least it's wet," shrugged Othar as he put his shoulders through the straps on his pack.

They found themselves at the front of the column when the march resumed. The only person ahead of them was the old man with the birds. "Hey, Horatius," Tarquinius called, "want some company?"

The old man waited, then fell in step with them. Tarquinius introduced Horatius to Amanis.

"How did you get mixed up with this crew?" the old man asked her.

"She had a little trouble back there in Ephesus," Tarquinius said. "Decided she needed a change of scenery."

Horatius laughed. "Not much different than most of us then."

"What kind of birds are these?" Amanis asked.

"Oh, I don't know. I take in all kinds really. I'm not prejudiced—as long as they're willing to work."

"Tarquinius wouldn't last long with you," said Othar.

"What do they do?" Amanis asked the old man.

"Little bit of everything—retrieve small objects mostly. That one there—the middling fellow with the black bands on his wings? I'm trying to teach him the difference between a lepton and an obol."

"Making a banker of him?" Tarquinius said with a grin.

Horatius shrugged. "Making something. He'd be far happier with the meat of a pistachio."

"How did you become interested in birds?" Amanis wanted to know.

Everyone was interested in birds, Horatius told her. Everyone watched them fly and wondered what it would be like to just spread a pair of wings and go anywhere. He said that birds made people think of freedom. And their songs created a way to measure cares. When you couldn't find some small pleasure in the fluting of a lark, he said, you were living with too much weight.

"Then why do you put them in cages?" Othar asked.

Amanis turned around to look up at him, her eyes wide. Even Tarquinius looked surprised.

Horatius didn't say anything for a long time. Finally he turned his face toward the big German. "I'm a simple man," he said with an apologetic smile. "My love isn't perfect."

Amanis considered the birds. They rode quietly in the swaying cages, fluttering only enough to stay balanced on their perches. She remembered watching Horatius remove each of them from their cages the night before. They had perched on his finger and eaten from his hand. "Have you ever lost any of them? Don't they sometimes fly away?" she asked.

"Not often—once or twice. After they've been with me a while, they usually don't leave."

How long, she wondered? How long after this old man caught a bird until it accepted him and the cage? What happened in the soul of a bird to cause it to quit the sky? And what about the few who didn't? What was different about them?

Maybe what held the birds to him was something like love. He fed them, talked to them, and treated them gently. He protected them, shielded them from the night air. He placed them among their fellows for companionship. Maybe the few who abandoned him suffered from a lack of whatever passed for devotion among birds.

Did birds have luck, she wondered? Or were they beneath the notice of jealous Fortuna? She tried to calculate whether those who left Horatius or those who stayed had the better lot.

"What's that?" Othar asked, stopping and staring ahead.

Only a javelin's throw ahead of them the road curved away to the left, down a small slope. It passed through a copse of oaks; they could see the tops of the trees above the shoulder of the downslope. Amanis heard cries coming from the copse. Othar started running toward the disturbance.

Amanis shrugged off her pack. "Here," she said, pulling the sikhimi from it and flinging the bundle at Tarquinius's feet. She set off after Othar.

As they got nearer, she could see several rough-looking characters grabbing at a man on the ground. The victim was trying to find a way out of the ring of his attackers, but there were too many.

"*Lestes,*" Othar hissed and charged forward, bellowing like a bull.

Amanis jerked the blade from its sheath and followed him toward the fray.

The bandits' faces whipped around when they heard Othar's battle cry, and they quickly formed ranks, brandishing knives and cudgels. Othar flew into them like a boulder crashing through a thicket. He spread his arms and took three of them to the ground.

Amanis found herself facing a wild-haired man with a pink scar on his cheek. He held a rusty blade with a reach half as long as a man's arm.

"What's this? A girl with a little toothpick come to teach me a lesson?" He moved in on Amanis, then lunged toward her.

Amanis stepped just beyond the reach of his blade and kicked at the outside of his knee. Her heel caught him squarely, and the leg crumpled inward. As he fell, she swung her other leg around and up, kicking the side of his head. The robber fell in the roadway and lay on his back without moving.

Harim dashed up, unsheathing two wickedly thin, curving blades. He wielded them in either hand, twirling them like deadly toys. The remainder of the thieves' band took to their heels at the sight. Turash, standing just behind the Bedouin, fitted an arrow to his bow and put a bolt into one fleeing man's shoulder and one into another's thigh. Their fellows seized them and dragged them along on their headlong retreat.

Harim was looking at the bowman with a scornful expression.

Turash answered him with a shrug. "I did not shoot to kill."

Othar walked over to the man Amanis had downed. He seized the bandit by the front of his shirt and hoisted him off the ground. The bandit hung limp, like garments stuffed with wet straw. Othar peered into his face.

"He's alive," pronounced the German, dropping the bandit like a sack of grain. "He'll wake up about the same time these do, I guess," he said, jerking a thumb toward the three he had felled.

Amanis kneeled beside the man the bandits had attacked. A thin line of blood trickled from a corner of his mouth. He was holding his belly and moaning.

"Let me see." The old woman from the stream squatted beside Amanis. She ran her hands down the side of the man's head and neck. Gently, she pried open his jaws and peered into his mouth. "The bleeding is coming from here," she said. "They kicked out one or two of his teeth."

Amanis nodded in sympathy.

The old woman looked at her. "Better that than bleeding from the belly." She loosened the man's robe and lifted his tunic, looking closely at his ribs and his stomach. She probed carefully with her fingertips. "He's bruised, but he'll live, I believe. Get one of the carts over here."

Turash turned and trotted away.

The injured man groaned something, a single word he repeated several times.

"What's he talking about?" the old woman asked.

"How can I know? I've never seen him before."

"It sounds like a name." She put her ear close to his lips. She looked up at Amanis. "Paul?"

Amanis shrugged. She could hear the others coming up behind. One of the donkey carts was wheeled alongside the injured man. Bundles and supplies were shifted to make a place for him. Four of the men got on either side of him and lifted him, under the old woman's watchful eye, into the back of the cart.

"What do we do about them?" Harim asked Damon, who had just arrived at the scene of the conflict.

Damon spat toward the three bandits who lay in the road. "Let them lie there till they come to or die." He walked to the cart, looking over the old woman's shoulder. "Can he travel, Thyrsis?"

"I think so. He's badly bruised, and his head may feel like it's been used for a pestle when he comes round, but he'll live."

"We'll take him to the next town and find a place for him to stay until he's stronger. All right, everyone," Damon announced to the troupe gathered around the cart. "Let's move on. We can still make Leucadiae before dark if we don't lose any more time."

Tarquinius came huffing toward Amanis and dumped her pack on the ground beside her. "Next time you go off to save the day," he said, glaring up at her, "find somebody with longer legs to carry your stuff."

Thyrsis perched herself in the cart beside the hurt stranger. She poured some water on a rag and daubed at the dirt on his face. Sometimes she leaned over him and dribbled a few drops from her water skin between his swollen lips. The cart started off, and Amanis looked around for her walking companions.

"You were pretty good back there," Othar said.

"In my father's native country, the girls learned to fight alongside the boys."

Othar arched his eyebrows. "That is so in my land, too. Some of our greatest queens were warriors." They trudged on a few more paces. "How did you come to be in Ephesus?" he asked.

"The men of my father's village were captured in a raid by a Roman patrol. The ones they didn't crucify on the spot were sold as slaves. My father was one of the lucky ones."

Othar gave a little chuckle and shook his head.

"What?"

"Again, another likeness," he said. "But they took me, not my father. The legionaries thought my size would be a novelty in Rome. They wheeled me down the Via Flaminia in a cage, mounted on a cart. Like a circus animal."

As the sun neared the tops of the hills to the west, they came upon a village tucked in among the folds and creases of the country as it fell from the central highlands toward the sea on the west. Leucadiae it was called, they told her. The surrounding hillsides were littered with pale stones; Amanis guessed that they were responsible for how the place got its name. It would take longer to say the name of the tiny town than to pass through it, she thought. There were a few houses clumped to one side along the highway and a handful of others farther back, as if trying to hide among the clefts. A small river flowed out of the hills, where the ridges and uplands gave way to a broad valley that was bound in the distance by yet another range of creased highlands. Amanis could see the road stretching out like a flat ribbon into the valley. Good. At least the next day's walking would be flat.

No smoke rose from the houses; nothing moved. The only sound, other than the shuffling feet of the troupe, was the sighing of the wind among the white boulders and the far-off skree of a harrier. Damon looked around with a puzzled expression. He looked at the sky, which was beginning to darken. He took a few steps toward the nearest mud brick house. Like most of the others, it was small and square with little windows set high on the walls. There was no outer gate or wall; its front door was the only barrier to visitors. It looked well-set in its place, though, and when Damon knocked, Amanis could tell the wood was thick and solid.

"Hello?" Damon called. "We're on our way to Smyrna for the festival. Can you shelter us for the night?"

No answer.

He walked behind the house. In a few moments he was back. "The ashes in the oven pit are warm, and there are leavings of fresh-ground meal in the hand mill," he said. "They're here, but they're hiding." He turned to some of the old women. "Get everyone off the road and behind these two houses. Hide the animals and the carts as best you can. Harim, Turash, Othar—place yourselves to see, but not be seen. The rest of you men, stay with the women and children. Amanis, you come with me...and bring your blade."

The band quickly dispersed. As she turned to follow Damon, Amanis saw the Circassian stringing his bow and running a hand along the notch ends of the arrows in his quiver.

"This village knows us well," Damon said as they strode quickly toward the hills above the settlement. "Whatever they're afraid of, we aren't it."

They moved up along the base of one of the ravines. At intervals, Damon would stop and cup his hands around his mouth. "Cleanthus! Artemion! It's Damon the juggler!"

"If they're here, they aren't going to answer," Amanis said. "Why do you keep shouting?"

"I don't want anyone to drop a rock on my head. Best they know who's tramping through their undergrowth."

They came to the head of the ravine and climbed out on a narrow shelf at the top of the ridge. Below them they could see the flat thatched roofs of the village houses. In the dim light they could barely make out the forms of the troupe, huddled against the rear walls of the two houses.

Damon cupped his hands and shouted again. They listened and watched. After a long silence, Amanis heard the faint sound of one rock against another. Then, moments later, she heard slow footsteps crunching in the soil of the hillside. A man's voice, low and flat, hailed them in the settling dark.

Nine

*H*e was climbing slowly toward them, making his way up a slope on the far side of the ridge. There were others: Men stepped from behind trees and climbed out of thickets, women carried children in their arms, young boys quietly drove small herds of goats.

The man arrived at the place where they stood. His face was drawn, his shoulders stooped. He had a long knife stuck in his belt. Each of the men slowly approaching them carried some form of a weapon: clubs, grain forks, scythes, swords.

"We heard you approach," the man said, "but the situation being what it is, we didn't dare hesitate in order to identify you."

"What do you mean, Cleanthus?"

"Bandits. They came yesterday, twenty or thirty of them."

Damon nodded. "We came upon a handful of them beating a lone traveler. We drove them off and brought the man with us."

Cleanthus looked grim. "I remember the man. He came through here yesterday morning. We warned him to turn back, but he claimed he had to get to Ephesus. Someone there he had to see, he said."

Another man stood beside Cleanthus. "They came right into our village, into our houses. Took all the food they could find."

"Do the proconsuls know of this?"

Cleanthus shrugged. "We're a small village; we have no money, not much land. Who knows if they'd do anything?"

"We saw a column of regulars on the morning of our second day out of Ephesus," Damon said. "But they were going toward the city, not this way."

"We're not warriors," Cleanthus said. "We know about herding goats and trading cheese and wool, not about fighting."

"Can we sleep in your houses tonight?" Damon asked. "We have our own provisions. And several of us know how to use a sword."

"We'll come down with you," Cleanthus said. "The extra swords will be welcome."

Damon and Amanis turned to go back toward the ravine.

"Not that way. There's an easier path over here."

When they got back to the troupe, the injured man was sitting on the ground, leaning against the back wall of one of the houses. Thyrsis was holding a cup to his lips. Cleanthus called for torches and lamps, and when Amanis brought a clay lamp out to the old woman, the man looked up at her.

"You're one of the ones who drove off the robbers," he said. "They told me one of you was a woman, an African. I owe you my life." The words hissed through the new gaps in his teeth.

"I could have done no less," Amanis said.

"Don't pay any attention to her," scoffed Thyrsis. "You're lucky she's such a good fighter."

"I believe it," he said. "What do they call you?"

"I am Amanis."

"Then I thank you, Amanis. If I can ever repay you, I will."

She inclined her head gravely toward him.

Despite Damon's protests, the villagers brought food from the caches hidden around the village. There was good cheese and bread with a hard crust hiding a chewy center. When the troupe had eaten, Damon insisted that they provide some diversion as payment. Soon a circle of torches was staked into a clearing near the center of the village, and Tarisia and Tyche beguiled the onlookers—mostly men—with one of their clanging, arm-waving, foot-stamping dances, accompanied by the tambourine, the finger cymbals, and two of the older boys playing reed flutes. Before long the men were clapping and chanting in time to the dance.

When the dancers finished, Damon leaped into the ring of light, juggling three of his painted wooden balls. He gestured, and one of the flute players tossed him a clay bowl. Someone else pitched him a smooth stone from the ground. Soon the villagers were tossing him cups and bowls and whatever hand-sized objects they could find. For each object the crowd threw at him, Damon would toss one back. At one point, Amanis was pretty sure the juggler had eight objects in the air.

Next came the acrobats, two men and a girl. They stood on one another's shoulders and catapulted through the air to the ground. The men linked arms and tossed the girl into the air; she performed breathtaking flips and twists on her way down. They turned handsprings, balanced one another on hands raised high above their heads, and performed intricate vaults. At the end the two men gripped each other's shoulders and performed a double cartwheel, flying around the perimeter of the circle as the girl tumbled beneath and vaulted between them. When they made their final flourish, the villagers gave them a loud ovation.

Amanis felt an upwelling of pride, seeing the way the troupe had transformed a frightened, cowering community. For a little while at least, the villagers had forgotten their fear.

"Too bad we're moving on in the morning. I could make some money here." Tarquinius stood beside her, his hands on his hips.

"Is that all you think of?"

"What?"

"Money."

The dwarf looked up at her with a sour smile. "What else is there to think about?"

The screams of women jerked their attention back toward the circle of torchlight. A handful of fierce-looking men stood in the flickering light. One of them, a huge fellow with a shaved head and a matted, dark beard, had Cleanthus by the front of his clothes. He shook the villager like a rag doll.

"What's all this racket?" the bandit yelled. "Who told you to make all this noise when working men are trying to sleep?" He shoved Cleanthus, and the headman fell heavily on his back.

Amanis backed slowly into the shadows, her fingers wrapping around the haft of the sikhimi. There were more outlaws coming out of the darkness from the direction of the hills.

The bandit chief stood glaring with his hands on his hips. "For bothering my rest, I'm going to need a lot more than the sorry pickings I took from here yesterday." He walked slowly toward the cowering villagers. Amanis saw the man who had stood beside Cleanthus earlier, on the ridge above the village. A girl hid behind him. She looked to be no more than fourteen. The bandit grabbed her wrist.

"Yes, this is something I might like." He grinned, pulling the struggling girl toward him. "What's your name, girl? With you in my bed, I might forget about your pitiful village—for a night at least." Some of the men laughed as their leader leered at the whimpering girl.

The girl's father started toward the chief. He had taken only two steps when one of the robbers stepped into his path and plunged a blade into his belly. The man crumpled to the ground. He crawled forward, reaching toward his screaming child. The bandit chief watched in amusement as the dying man came nearer; then he kicked him in the face.

Amanis heard a strangled yelp. One of the robbers lay face down in the dust, and Amanis could see the feathered shaft protruding from the back of his neck. As she watched, two more of the bandits crumpled to the ground with red-fletched arrows buried deep in their vitals. The men began yelling at the darkness and at one another. Some of the village women screamed. The robbers ran and crouched, trying to put something between themselves and the death coming from the darkness. Two more of them fell and didn't move.

The bandit chief shoved the girl aside and grabbed Cleanthus. He clamped an arm around the headman's throat and twisted him about so he was facing the direction the arrows had come from. He brandished a knife. "One more arrow and I'll slit your leader from gullet to navel!" Several of the other robbers grabbed fleeing villagers and faced them toward the darkness.

"Douse those torches!" the chief said. The robbers ran toward the torches and kicked them over in the dust, stamping until the flames were extinguished. For a few moments everything was draped in darkness. Then, as Amanis's eyes adjusted to the moonlight, she could see the robbers dragging their captives toward the nearest house. She ran her thumb nervously over the handle of her blade, feeling the likeness of the lion god carved there.

From the road behind the bandits something flickered silver, and there came a sound like the chopping of a melon. One of the bandits screamed. He twisted as he fell, trying to reach behind him for the dark-colored haft of the dagger sticking out of his back. His captive ran for the safety of the shadows.

The desperate robbers spun in frantic circles as they pulled their human collateral toward the house. The chief was about to back through the doorway when a dark figure stepped around the corner of the building. A hand gripped the bandit's wrist and wrenched it away from Cleanthus's breast, then slammed the hand, still holding the knife, against the lintel of the house. The chief released his captive and turned to face this new threat.

Othar's fist smashed into the robber's face. The bandit's head snapped back and he staggered, but he didn't go down and still didn't release the knife. Instead his free hand grabbed for the German's neck. Othar grabbed at the chief's wrist. The two big men staggered in the dust before the hut's entrance. They looked like giants performing some silent dance in the moonlight.

Men from the troupe, now armed with clubs and knives, charged across the moonlit clearing. They came noiselessly, like hunting cats; they gave no battle cries. They engaged the robbers fiercely and were soon bolstered by some men of the village. Amanis saw the two male acrobats fling themselves into the fray; they bobbed low to avoid blows and sprang up to strike. They whirled among the fight like four men instead of two. Then Harim strode into the melee, swinging his two curved swords and singing a high, terrible song that sounded all clenched teeth and no quarter.

The bandits fled toward the hills, chased by the villagers.

Othar and the bandit chief were still locked in their deadly embrace. The German was smashing the bandit's wrist against the lintel, trying to dislodge the knife. The bandit leader kept clutching at Othar's throat. The two stared at each other, their faces frozen in grimaces of pain and fierce effort. It was fearful to see them, like watching two bulls batter each other.

Finally, Othar was able to wrench the robber's hand from his neck. He pulled his opponent off balance and landed a kick to his chest. The chief staggered back and Othar seized his knife hand in both fists and twisted violently. Amanis heard the snapping of bone and the scream of the bandit. Othar twisted the arm behind the bandit's back, forcing him down on the ground. He put a knee in the middle of the robber's back and raised the knife above his head. He roared something in German.

"Othar! Hold!" It was Damon, running quickly to the huge man and putting a hand to his upraised arms. "Don't. He's beaten. Let Cleanthus and the villagers decide his fate."

The German stared wild-eyed at the juggler, and the expression on his face made Amanis gasp; he looked like a beast, not a man. Then, with an effort, he lowered the knife and stood over his enemy's form. He gave the robber a kick in the ribs before dropping the knife at Damon's feet and walking away.

Amanis looked down at the bone handle of the sikhimi, still clenched tightly in her fist. She hadn't even removed the blade from its scabbard. She watched as the women of the village ventured into the moonlit clearing, calling in low voices to their menfolk, trying to measure the damage of the ordeal.

Why hadn't she entered the fray? Amanis asked herself. The ball of her thumb was still caressing Apedemak's lion face. Not fear. She looked at the stricken expressions of the women. She saw the crumpled figure of the dead man, his daughter keening over him. No, it wasn't fear that stayed her. She wasn't needed; more than enough mayhem had happened without her aid.

The men came back from the hills and ravines a little later, shoving three robbers ahead of them. The thieves looked so badly beaten they could hardly walk; one held his middle and bubbled pink froth down his chin. The village men wore grim faces. Amanis saw the blood on their clothing and arms. They had learned something about fighting tonight, she guessed. Anger and fear were efficient teachers.

Amanis went into the hut where they had stationed the wounded man. Thyrsis sat beside him, wringing the water out of a cloth into a shallow bowl. She put the wet rag in the man's hand, and he held it to his forehead. His eyes opened slightly when Amanis's feet scuffed on the bare earth of the room; then he closed them with a sigh and laid his head back on the bundle Thyrsis had placed for his pillow.

"They must have used my head for a kicking ball," he said.

Amanis squatted beside him. "The headman said he warned you about the bandits."

The man moaned and gave a slight nod.

"What's so important in Ephesus that you'd risk your life to get there?"

He breathed heavily. She thought he was asleep. "Paul," he said finally.

"Who?"

"He speaks words of life. He is a servant of the Almighty God."

"Which god is that?"

The man raised himself up on one elbow. "There is but one God. He made all things, and He has given life to all the world through His Son, Jesus, the Christ."

Amanis eyed Thyrsis. "What talk is this?"

The old woman shrugged. "He's been at me about it, too, between the pains."

"You must listen to me, Amanis." He had a wide-eyed expression. "God has offered salvation to all humankind. I learned about all this from Paul. I was the first in all of Roman Asia to believe. I must reach him while he's in Ephesus. I'll take you to him. He can teach you, too—" He moaned with pain and clapped the wet cloth to his forehead, then fell back onto his pallet.

"There's nothing good for me back in Ephesus," said Amanis. "If you're so determined to find this Paul, I hope he's there when you arrive. But I won't be coming, I can tell you that much." She stood. "Thyrsis, do you need anything?"

The old woman shook her head. "I'll stay with him until he can sleep."

Amanis turned to go, then turned back. "What do they call you, anyway?"

"Epenetus," he said. "You should come with me, Amanis. Paul can teach you the words of life."

Amanis shook her head. She gave Thyrsis a sideways grin and left the hut.

The troupe left Leucadiae the next morning under a sky streaked with long, low clouds that looked like banks of combed wool. Damon stood in the middle of the highway, impatiently tossing two walnut-sized balls with one hand, glaring at the grandmothers as they methodically checked and rechecked every bundle in every cart.

Amanis had to drag herself upright; Tarquinius had talked away half the night about the strategies he used in plying his game. Each time Amanis would feel her eyelids drooping, the dwarf would jostle her elbow. "Listen to me now," he'd say, "you'll need to know this when we get to Smyrna." She had finally wrapped herself in her cloak and stretched herself on the bare earth of the hut they occupied, turning her back on him. Her sleep was not restful, though; she had dreams of the girl weeping over her father. The victim's face and form kept changing: now Damon, now Patroclus, now Amanis's own father, now Epenetus. Sometimes Amanis leaned over the crumpled, bloodied form, and sometimes she watched the scene from concealed shadows. She woke with the sour taste of fatigue in her mouth, bits of a song running on an endless loop through her mind. It was a song she used to hear her mother sing. The words were in the tongue of Nubia. Amanis had never learned what they meant.

Cleanthus was walking toward Damon. The headman's face showed fatigue. "I thank you, Damon. My people thank you."

Damon shrugged. "They attacked us, too. We're used to taking care of ourselves. I'm glad we were here."

More of the troupe were straggling toward the road. They were almost ready to leave.

"You will always be welcome here," Cleanthus said, spreading his arms as if to embrace them all. "We will never forget."

They moved off down the slope into the plain between the ranges of hills. At the edge of the village was the bandit chief's head, set atop a pole driven into the earth at the side of the road. Carrion birds spiraled into one of the ravines behind the houses, black against the rising of the morning.

Ten

*A*manis felt the muscles in her belly tense as Turash sighted down the shaft of the arrow. For what seemed a very long time, the Circassian's blue eyes focused on his target, some twenty paces away: a large wooden board, scarred from many uses, propped up in the center of Smyrna's main agora. Standing in front of the board was Harim, his arms outstretched, waiting with closed eyes.

The arrow flew. *Thwock!* It struck the board, quivering less than a finger's width below Harim's left elbow.

The crowd gasped as three more arrows struck the board, one on either side of the Arab's neck and another beneath his right armpit. None of them missed by more than the width of a child's wrist. By the time Turash had finished, the Bedouin's torso and head were perfectly outlined by red-feathered shafts.

From where Amanis stood near Turash's shoulder, the scarlet fletching looked like blotches of blood dotted all about Harim: It was as if someone had tossed a double handful of death at him and managed to miss by the narrowest of margins. The Bedouin held the pose, arms outstretched, for several moments, so still he might have been a painted statue of himself. A hush fell over the onlookers. Then he sprang forward and held his arms in the air, laughing like a man who had cheated death a hundred times over.

Turash bowed as the children moved among the cheering crowd, holding out baskets and pouches to receive the tossed coin. Turash shrugged off his quiver and handed it to Amanis with his bow.

"What am I supposed to do with these?" she asked.

"Hold them for me. It's my turn now."

"You mean Harim's."

He smiled at her. "Same thing."

He walked to the board and stood in front of it. His shoulders and head extended past the place where Harim's had been; his arms stretched beyond the edges of the board.

Harim sauntered over to Amanis. On the ground beside her lay the shoulder harness with all his throwing blades. He donned the gear, the blades shimmering in the sunlight. She heard some among the crowd make reference to the shining steel. He reached over both shoulders and gripped two of the daggers. He flipped them into the air and caught them as they came down. A ripple of excitement stirred among the bystanders, then subsided as he studied his target.

Holding the knife by the blade, Harim took a long, arching step forward, pitching the dagger like a boy hurling a stone or a ball. The blade whistled through the air and thudded into the plank beside Turash's chest. Harim tossed the blade from his left hand to his right and sent it hurtling toward the plank. It embedded itself just above Turash's head, close enough to part his sandy brown hair.

Harim was a better showman than Turash. He chattered to the

crowd as he threw; he hurled playful taunts at his target, hinting that he might miss this time or the next. He turned his back on the board, then suddenly spun around and threw, causing young boys in the crowd to grin in appreciation. He even threw two blades with his left hand; they found their marks as securely as the others. Finally, when the plank all around Turash bristled with steel, Harim sent his last dagger into the board between Turash's breeches-clad thighs. The shocked expression on Turash's face brought a loud guffaw from the crowd along with enthusiastic applause. Coins clinked loudly into the children's baskets and pouches.

The two marksmen stood together, acknowledging the crowd's ovation. "You startled me with that last blade," Amanis heard the bowman say from the side of his mouth as they bowed. "I'll have to think of some little surprise for you next time."

Harim chuckled. "Be glad I didn't sneeze."

"How's the crowd?" asked a voice at her waist.

Amanis looked down. Tarquinius stood there, his gaming board held under one arm and his shells and bean cupped in the other palm.

"They seem friendly enough. They were pretty free with their coin for Turash and Harim."

The dwarf peered around the agora with a critical eye. "Over there," he said finally, pointing with his chin toward a small fountain. There were stone benches grouped nearby. Tarquinius made his way to one of these and placed his board in the center of it. He squatted cross-legged at one end of the bench, placing the shells on the board in front of him. He reached into a purse and retrieved three lepta, then stacked the copper coins on the right edge of the board.

Amanis drifted around the edges of the crowd as Tarquinius had coached her, keeping him in the corner of her eye without appearing to pay particular attention. She knew Othar was somewhere around as well and would come quickly if a situation appeared to be getting out of hand.

A temple fronted the agora near the fountain, and Amanis realized the blindfolded figure in front was a representation of Fortuna. The goddess stood balanced on a globe the size of a large cooking pot, and she held a cornucopia in her upraised hand. A chill went down Amanis's spine. Hadn't Tarquinius noticed? He was plying his game under the nose of the very deity Amanis had offended.

"Who'll play? Who'll play? Guess where the bean is, that's all you have to do. I risk three lepta, you risk two." Tarquinius was calling in a singsong voice, shaking his money bag for accompaniment. A few men gathered about him, and soon one of them sat down on the bench, across the board from Tarquinius. He put two coins on the board beside the three Tarquinius had stacked there, and the game began.

Tarquinius lost the first two shifts. His forehead wrinkled with worry as he saw his opponent drop the six coppers into his purse. Then Tarquinius won the next shift, and the next, and the next. The other player's smirk faded, and he watched the stubby fingers flying over the board with an expression that reminded Amanis of a cat watching the hole where a mouse had just vanished.

Amanis began to relax and enjoy the show. The other man grew more and more befuddled as Tarquinius's fingers circled faster and faster. The dwarf kept the game going, kept the shifts coming, never giving the other player a chance for pause. When he finally hesitated in confusion, Tarquinius had won sixteen lepta from him. The man shook his head like someone coming out of a trance and staggered from the bench.

"I've been watching you, dwarf, and I think I've got your

system figured out," said another fellow with a broad grin, sitting down across from Tarquinius. "Here's your two lepta. Let's play."

But Tarquinius baffled them all with his quick hands and constant banter. He let them win enough to keep their interest, but his purse bulged more and more with the coin he made in a steady trickle.

What made them keep trying? she wondered. They watched their fellows fattening Tarquinius's wallet, but somehow each one thought that he alone held the key to Tarquinius's pattern. Perhaps it was the deceptive simplicity of the setup: an unmarked board, three walnut shells, and a bean. What could be so complicated in that? Or maybe it was Tarquinius's appearance. How could a waddling dwarf possibly outwit a clever fellow of normal height and build?

Whatever it was, the dwarf knew exactly how to play them, how to hesitate just enough to let them persuade themselves they had discovered his weakness, when to rotate the shells in patterns that no one could follow. His eyes never left the board, it seemed, but Amanis could tell he studied each player as carefully as a perched hawk studies the meadow below his roost. Sitting at his gaming board, Tarquinius was like a charioteer driving a racing tandem, or like the helmsman of a coaster sailing along a narrow channel.

An aulos skirled loudly at the main gate of the agora, closely followed by the sounds of singing and hand clapping. A festival procession wound into the marketplace. Bystanders, both old and young, ran from all over the square to join the dancing line of revelers as it snaked among the stalls and colonnades of the agora.

Many in the procession wore flowers in their hair and garlands of flowers around their necks. Close to the middle of the cortege, four stout-looking young men carried a flower-bedecked litter, on which sat a young woman completely covered in blooms and greenery. From the joking and shouting, Amanis surmised she might be wearing no more than that. More than a few of the marchers carried skins which they tipped to their mouths and squirted on those along the path of the parade. There was a great deal of rowdy laughter.

The procession wound all about the agora, spawning little impromptu eddies of dancing and laughter that whirled before dissipating into the ebb and flow of the festival crowds. Amanis watched as the celebrants moved toward her, then turned toward the temple of Fortuna.

The marchers crowded onto the raised pediment on which the temple stood. They gathered around the statue of the goddess, singing the last refrain of a hymn in her honor. The litter with the girl on it was passed over the heads of the crowd until it arrived in front of the image. The girl gathered the trailing vines of her raiment and stood. She gave a little squeal of fright and fought for her balance as those holding the litter allowed it to tilt. She spoke sharply to her bearers and there came a loud burst of laughter from the gathering. Finally she steadied herself, facing the statue of Fortuna. She saluted the image:

> *Hail, Fortuna, bringer of prosperity!*
> *Changeable as the moon.*
> *Bound by neither man nor god,*
> *You regard poverty and power alike:*
> *as but two spokes of your wheel;*
> *Ever turning, ceaselessly you stir the heavens and the earth.*
> *You renew all things, and cast all things down.*
> *May we, who revere you, be granted your favors;*
> *May all who flout you taste the dregs of dismay.*

The celebrants gave a loud cheer as the girl sat down on the litter. They gradually dispersed, leaving at the base of the image a pile of blooms and other votive offerings.

The words of the ritual made Amanis feel exposed and vulnerable. Surely it was an omen—why else should she be here at this place and time? The goddess would pursue her, would never let her be at peace. She had disturbed the order of things. She had altered the rhythms of chance, usurped the goddess's prerogatives.

"Amanis! Over here!"

Tarquinius was standing on his bench, waving at her urgently. She put her hand on the haft of her blade and made her way through the crowd toward the dwarf.

"What's the matter?" she asked. There were no players gathered around him, nothing to threaten as far as she could see.

"I've been trying to get you over here for the longest time," Tarquinius said with a scowl. "You were standing over there, mooning about like a sleepwalker. Didn't you see me signal?"

"No—I'm sorry."

"You've got to keep your eyes open. I'm depending on you."

"I'll do better."

"We can hope." Tarquinius looked around, then made a veiled motion toward his wallet. "I've got too much money in here to keep with me; I'm a walking invitation to some bully. I need you to get two or three runners to come around and pick it up."

"How would I do that?"

"Just walk through the middle of the agora and do this." He made a peculiar motion with his left arm. "They're all around. They'll see you and know you're working with me. Now go."

She started toward the center of the square.

"And pay more attention from now on," he called crossly after her.

By the time she had taken thirty paces into the crowded marketplace, she had seen at least four of the older boys ducking through the throngs, heading toward Tarquinius's station. She circled back through the agora, and when she reached the dwarf again he was already shifting the shells. A hump-backed old man with no teeth sat across from him, nervously fingering the coins lying on the board. Tarquinius's wallet was slack, and Amanis had little doubt it would fill again soon enough.

From all appearances, the Smyrneans were thoroughly enjoying their midsummer festival. People of all ages roamed the agora: Children chased one another through their elders' legs; small groups of young men and women circled with carefully contrived randomness; citizens and their wives strolled contentedly, some hand in hand. Amanis could hear, through the happy din, the ring of the dancers' finger cymbals. Tarisia and Tyche must be working the other side of the square, she realized.

And there were many others besides the troupe trying to harvest the currency of the festival crowd. The colonnade surrounding the agora was jammed with stalls. There were old women selling amulets and charms. There were men hawking small cult images. Some of the grandmothers from the troupe were reading palms and casting fortunes with dice of painted bone. One family had a stall with a clay firepot, and now and then the smell of spiced meat wafted toward Amanis.

A young girl and her older sister strolled through the agora selling candied figs from baskets they balanced on their heads. Amanis found a coin and bought a handful of the sticky treats. She had just popped one in her mouth when she heard shouting.

"You're a cheat, you deformed runt!"

Amanis moved quickly toward Tarqunius's bench. A young man with a scraggly beard was standing over the bench. His face was red, and he held the bunched front of the dwarf's blouse in his right fist.

Tarquinius had the man's wrist gripped in both stubby hands. "I don't cheat! You guessed wrong, that's all. Now, let me go before something bad happens to you."

"And what are you going to do to me, dwarf? I've a mind to feed your cheating little hide to my hounds, not that you'd make much of a meal."

A circle had quickly formed, though no one would lift a hand to interfere. Amanis wrapped her hand around the haft of the sikhimi, took a deep breath, and stepped into the ring toward the bench.

"Leave the dwarf alone. He doesn't cheat."

"And how would you know this, woman?" the man said.

"Leave him alone. He won fairly."

"And what will you do if I don't?"

"Just leave him alone. I warn you."

"You warn me? Is that what you said, woman?"

He shoved Tarquinius, and the dwarf fell backward off the end of the bench, sprawling on the packed earth. The tall man swung an open hand at Amanis's face. She ducked and drew the sikhimi. The blade flashed in an upward arc as the man's arm passed over her. The blade's tip drew a thin line of red along the inside of his forearm.

He let out a yelp and cradled his arm with his other hand. Blood sheeted down the arm, soaking into his clothing and dripping onto the ground. She stood with her knife at the ready, waiting for his next move.

"You cut me, you wench! You sliced open my arm!"

She said nothing. Her eyes never left him.

"You all saw!" he yelled, turning to the crowd. "She cut me!"

"She cut you all right, Diamedes," said one fellow. "Maybe that'll teach you to think twice before picking on dwarves and women." Several laughed at this, and some of the onlookers began to walk away.

Diamedes whirled back to Amanis. He jabbed a finger at her face. "And now I warn *you*. I'll find you again. And next time I won't be caught by surprise." He stalked off, gripping his injured arm to his side.

"Well, at least you were watching that time," said Tarquinius, dusting off his clothes. "And you made a good example of him for the crowd." Nodding to himself, he looked in the direction the fellow had gone. "Well done."

Amanis started to smile at Tarquinius, but something made her turn her head. The last of those who had watched the confrontation were drifting away; one of the faces seemed eerily familiar.

Scaevolus's man.

Eleven

*A*manis fought the urge to bolt. Perhaps it was her imagination; maybe it wasn't the man from the hillside. She scanned the noisy market-place—nothing. If she had truly caught a glimpse of the man, he had already disappeared into the sea of strange faces.

Tarquinius had another victim seated across the board from him. Amanis sauntered around the far side of the fountain, careful to keep the dwarf within sight. She sat for a moment on the fountain's parapet, dipping her fingers in the cool water. From where she sat behind Tarquinius, she could trace the progress of the game in the face of the other player. It followed a predictable course: elation at first as Tarquinius gave him an easy shift or two to gain his confidence, then increasing frustration as the stubby hands flew and his coin disappeared into the dwarf's purse.

She stood and strolled around, coming closer to Tarquinius's bench. She began to notice people peering with queer expressions at something behind her, then hurrying on their way. What was happening at her back? She turned quickly.

Othar was coming toward her, the crowd parting before him

like water divided by a ship's prow.

"What's he doing here?" Tarquinius demanded, alerted by the staring of his opponent. "He's scaring away the crowd."

"You must come away," Othar said to Amanis in a low voice. "Now."

"Why?" Tarqunius said. "She can handle herself. You there," he said, turning back to his game. "Are you going to play or gawk at that overgrown barbarian?"

"The tall fellow with the beard, the one by the gate back in Ephesus," Othar said to her. "I saw him talking to another man just now."

"Scaevolus? Here?"

He nodded.

"But...I can't leave Tarquinius—"

Othar made a hand signal. A youth stepped out of the crowd, nodding at the German.

"Come on." Othar moved past Tarquinius toward the other side of the agora.

"Where are we going?" she asked.

"Not back there. Unless you want to chance running into them."

They reached the encircling portico, then the western gate. The crowds thinned considerably outside market square. They moved quickly down side streets and alleys. Othar seemed to be heading for the harbor, the small bay that sheltered Smyrna's docks and quays from the Aegean Sea.

They came to a line of low wooden buildings along the waterfront. Othar pushed at the doors of several until he came to one that rattled slightly on its hinges. He looked up and down the way, then heaved a shoulder against the door. Amanis heard him grunt softly, then the sound of splintering wood. He pulled the cracked door to one side, and they stepped into a dark, dank-smelling space.

"I don't think anyone followed us," Othar said. "Wait here until evening. Someone will come back to take you safely to camp."

There was a quiet scratching sound in the back of the shed. Othar flinched, then hurried toward the doorway. He propped the broken door into something resembling its original shape. Then Amanis heard his footsteps going away.

She stared at her surroundings. Daylight seeped in from numerous cracks in the walls and ceiling. There were piles of goods, some covered by pitch-coated canvas, some just mouldering on the ground where they sat. Dust motes swam in the light that leaked through the planking; Amanis could make out cylindrical objects stacked atop one another like firewood—parchment sheaths, by the look of them. Rats and mice had chewed them and their contents. Curious, she lifted the corner of one of the canvas covers—another stack of parchments. The shed was full of parchments in leather cases.

Amanis had never learned to read, but her master had jealously guarded his store of books. Who would transfer such expensive cargo to this leaky shed, then leave it here to rot? She thought about how long it had taken someone to copy the words on a single one of the scrolls. What if the men who had labored over these writings knew their work was slowly turning into dust in the dark of some forgotten shanty?

Gradually the scratches grew louder; the vermin came back to their feeding among the scrolls. Amanis kept herself still. Why interrupt the feast?

Scaevolus had tracked her to Smyrna; it was hard for her to believe. He had come himself—not even trusting an agent! This merchant who bought and sold men and women could not tolerate the threat posed by an unruly chattel; like a potter who cannot abide a defective vessel leaving his shop, Scaevolus was bent on rescuing his reputation as a purveyor of obedient servants.

Amanis had once seen a slave crucified. He had stolen from his master, they said. His owner denied the poor wretch even the cruel comfort of having his legs broken. For an entire market interval the fellow had hung there, his wrists nailed into the crossbeam. Amanis wondered why he didn't just hang limp and allow himself to suffocate, but the instinct to breathe was more powerful than the need to die. The corpse hung on the stake until the birds and animals picked it clean.

The day wore on. Sometimes she could hear echoes of the festival merriment coming from the agora but little else. Othar had chosen well; no footsteps came down the path outside the row of sheds.

What would she do? Even if she were able to hide from the slave trader in Smyrna, he would follow her wherever else in Asia Province the band might choose to go. Doubtless Scaevolus had many friends among the provincial administrators. If he took a mind, he could probably have the entire company imprisoned for harboring a fugitiva.

Evening was drawing near. Amanis felt the gnaw in her stomach; she had eaten nothing but a single candied fig since breakfast that morning. She hoped that whoever came for her would bring bread or a few handfuls of dried fruit and pistachios—and a small skin of wine, perhaps.

Footsteps outside—a group, from the sound of it. Moving as silently as she could, she made her way to the back of the shed and crouched behind one of the larger bundles. She stared at the cracked door to her hiding place.

She heard voices. Men and women were just outside between the line of buildings and the water's edge. Women's voices? What were they doing here? Why weren't they at the festival with the rest of the town?

The voices quieted. Then came a man's voice singing. Amanis didn't recognize the language. It was neither Greek nor Latin, for certain. The entire group was singing now, then the man's voice, alone. It was as if he were speaking to them all and they were answering in song rather than speech. Was it some sort of religious rite? Amanis had never heard of any religion that performed in a nondescript place like this, between a row of ramshackle buildings and the backwater of Smyrna's seaport.

Amanis crept forward and put her eye to a crack in the wall. Fifteen people—ten men and five women—were seated in a semicircle and a man was standing in front of them. His eyes were closed and his hands were folded in front of him. As he sang he rocked his head slightly, as if he were saying yes to a question that only he could hear.

The song ended, and the man reached into a pouch and withdrew a parchment scroll. The leather of the pouch gleamed from recent oiling. When he had taken the scroll from the pouch, he kissed the parchment before unrolling it. He began reading, and Amanis was slightly surprised to realize the words were Greek.

"When the LORD your God has destroyed the nations whose land he is giving you, and when you have driven them out and settled in their town and houses, then set aside for yourselves three cities centrally located in the land…" He then read a strange suppostion, about two men cutting wood in the forest, and the head of an axe coming loose and killing one of the men.

The man whose axe killed the other would flee to one of the three cities, the man read, where he would be safe from any who might want to avenge the death of the other. He could take refuge there, the reading went, so that innocent blood might not be shed in the land this god was giving to his people. And as their territory expanded, they were to set aside three additional cities for the same purpose.

Cities of refuge—Amanis tried to imagine what they might be like. A place where the avenger couldn't follow, perhaps—would these cities be more peaceful than the surrounding towns? Would the safety found within their walls extend to all people?

She tried to imagine herself entering one of the safe cities. The shadow that had dogged her steps all the way north from Ephesus would be halted at the gates. She would go in, but Scaevolus would be prevented. He might glare after her and raise his fists and curse, but he would not be permitted inside. Not into the city of refuge.

But who was she deceiving? Her pursuer was but the agent of a greater force: blind Fortuna. What city wall could repel the goddess? What skill with stone or steel was proof against the blind force of destiny? Amanis could run and even hide, but the cosmos—the whole order of the universe—was against her. She could only delay the inevitable; she couldn't alter it.

The man was still reading. This god certainly had a lot of rules; how could anyone remember them all? There were instructions for legal proceedings. There were laws about the conduct of warfare, laws governing the absolution of blood guilt for an unsolved killing, laws about inheritance, laws about returning stray cattle or a lost cloak to the rightful owner. There were even statutes stipulating the type of cloth that garments might not be made from and the ways in which that clothing could be decorated.

There was a pause. "Here ends the reading of the Law," the man said, and the people responded with a word from the same language they had been singing in earlier.

The speaker sat down at the end of the semicircle, and a younger man took his place.

"My people, the day of the Lord is upon us," he said at last. "The Christ, the Holy One of God Most High, has come in fulfillment of the prophets. Jesus of Nazareth, in the land of our forefathers, offered Himself as a sacrifice for our sins. He was crucified and laid in a tomb. But on the third day, God raised Him up, just as He said through David,

> *O Lord my God, I called to you for help and you healed me.*
> *O Lord, you brought me up from the grave;*
> *You spared me from going down to the pit.*

"And through Jesus the Christ, son of David, God proclaims forgiveness of sins and eternal life to all who call on His name."

It was the strangest prayer Amanis had ever heard. How could anyone who earned a death by crucifixion have anything to do with the gods? She had never heard of any place called Nazareth, but if it was a place where humans were killed to pay for the wrongs of others, she intended to stay clear of it. And as for this business of rising from the dead—she gave a little shudder. To think of a decaying corpse leaving its grave and walking again among the living...

"These are strange teachings, Philomenes," the older man was saying, the one who had been standing before. "Where did you hear these things?"

"All the synagogues of Pisidia have heard this message: Antioch, Iconium, Lystra, and Derbe—Paul, the servant of the Christ, has taught people throughout Galatia and Phrygia the good news."

Paul—wasn't that the name that fellow Epenetus kept repeating?

"Who is this Paul, and why should we pay any attention to what he says?" the older man wanted to know.

"Paul is a messenger of the Almighty. God has confirmed his words by great signs and wonders. On Cyprus he struck blind a magician who was perverting the word of God. Even the proconsul there was amazed and believed. In Lystra he healed a man who had been crippled from birth. Many of the people there saw these things."

"How far away is Lystra?" the other man asked. "And Cyprus—who among us has ever been there? There are many places in the world where strange things are supposed to have been done and said, yet each day goes on for us as days have gone on before."

"I tell you, the God of Abraham is doing a new thing among our people."

"And I say to you, Philomenes, that for generations beyond count we have had the Law and prophets. As for this Paul, who is he, and who are his people that we should listen to these strange words they bring?"

"Paul is a Jew like us! More than that, he's a Pharisee who once sat with the Sanhedrin of Jerusalem itself! He is a man skilled in the Law—"

"This is enough about this, Philomenes. We shouldn't confuse ourselves with goings-on from places we don't understand. There are many things done, even in Jerusalem, that need not concern us. We have the Law and the prophets right here in Smyrna. Better to keep the traditions handed down to us than to chase after some strange new doctrine that leads we know not where."

They were singing again in their own language. When the song was finished, they dispersed. Amanis heard the voice of the young man fading away into the distance. He was still earnestly telling someone about the truth of his claims for the crucified god.

So this Paul business was an argument among Jews. Amanis thought of all the strange things she had heard of these people. Some said they didn't believe in gods at all. But these people were clearly concerned with their deity, even to the point of memorizing rules about the weaving of cloth. It seemed a great waste of time and energy to her.

But…the old crippled Jew in Ephesus had taken in the abandoned infant when no one else would have. Might there be something to a god who would cause his people to do such a thing? A god who cared enough about fugitives to provide cities of refuge?

Not long after the Jews had left she heard quiet footsteps outside, then a low voice calling her name. It was Damon.

"Here." She pushed against the damaged door, and it fell outward. Damon stood in the darkness, his wide-brimmed hat pulled low over his face. "Othar gives good directions." He handed her a small loaf of bread. She eagerly tore at it.

"Most of the people are still in the center of town, waiting for the torchlight procession. We'll take another route back to camp."

He was clothed in his working attire, a close-fitting garment with strips hanging like fringe at his knees and elbows. The saffron-

and-purple bustle swished as he shifted his weight from one foot to the other. In the light of day, Damon was a rainbow-colored advertisement for his craft, impossible to ignore. How had he come to lead this ragtag band of people who had nothing in common but their oddities? They were much like his costume, a garish mixture that somehow blended just as it should.

"Maybe I shouldn't come back," she said between mouthfuls. "The man who's after me is wealthy. With powerful friends, most likely."

He reached into his bag and came out with the two small balls he habitually tossed and caught with the same hand. He was looking at her. Amanis wished he would say something.

"Tarquinius told me why you had to leave Ephesus," he said at last.

She swallowed and tore off another bite. "I did what I had to do."

"And so must I. Are you ready to go?"

She looked at him. "Are you sure?"

"Is anyone ever?"

They walked back toward the city, but stayed on the dark side of the streets, giving a wide berth to the agora and its noisy revelry.

"Why did you choose juggling?" Amanis asked.

He gave a soft laugh. "That's a different question than most ask. Usually they want to know how I learned."

She smiled to herself. "The how can be figured out once the why is settled. Don't you think?"

He was still tossing the two balls as they walked. She could hear the soft pop as they hit his palms and see the flick of his wrist as he tossed them: one, two, one, two—like the steady rhythm of raindrops falling from an overhanging roof.

"The toss is the main thing. Everybody thinks catching them is so important, but really, learning to toss is the hardest part. I used to toss one ball, back and forth, until I could see the arc in my mind, until my hand could find the ball without the guidance of my eyes. One ball, until it was as natural as breathing.

"Once you've got the toss, the only other trick is remembering to catch them one at a time. That's what throws beginners; they want to toss three balls before they're ready, and pretty soon they're trying to watch and catch and toss them all at once. They forget that your hand and eye can only attend to one at a time. Two balls, three, six…you still have to catch them one at a time." He flicked one of the balls to his other hand and began tossing them simultaneously. The balls crossed in an arc in front of his chest and landed at the same time in both hands.

"But now you're tossing and catching two at once."

"Not really," he said. "Each hand is still working with one ball at a time."

Three figures crossed the street in front of them and stood facing Amanis and Damon. She put a hand on Damon's arm. She turned around to see how far it was back to the nearest cross street, but two more men stepped from the shadows behind them.

The middle one of the three took a few steps forward. "Well, well. It's the African wench. Let's see how fancy her knifework is now."

Twelve

he man reached beneath his robe and pulled something from his belt. The two on either side of him began to advance. Amanis unsheathed the sikhimi and put her back against Damon's, facing the two assailants approaching from behind. She didn't know if the juggler carried any weapons. She felt her mouth go dry.

There was a shuffling noise and the sound of laughter from one of the side streets. Four men stumbled into the street, colliding with the two attackers. One of the drunkards fell, carrying one of the attackers to the ground with his weight. Amanis yanked on Damon's sleeve, and the two broke for the side street at a full run.

They dashed down the narrow corridor between the buildings. Amanis prayed that no unseen holes would send them sprawling. The sounds of pursuit were close behind them. They flew around a corner. The noise of the agora was closer; she could see torchlight flickering on the buildings. The gate of the marketplace was just ahead, and the two of them raced into the crowd.

A man grabbed Amanis's arm and leered drunkenly at her, his breath smelling of wine. She pulled away and ducked into the swaying mass of people. She had lost Damon. Her only thought was to make her way to the eastern gate of the city and the troupe's camp just outside the walls.

The celebration enveloped her. There must have been a dozen aulos players scattered around the agora, each accompanied by tabor and cymbals and each squalling a different tune. People were singing along with the impromptu orchestras. An old, fat woman was sitting on one of the benches near the Fortuna temple, her arms clasped around her knees. She was rocking back and forth and emitting a single screeching pitch, her head thrown back like a baying hound. No one around her took any notice.

There were large pots of smoldering, aromatic pitch scattered around the marketplace, and something in the smoke began to affect Amanis's senses, as it had apparently already affected everyone else's. Strange thoughts began to swim through her mind. She fancied that she saw, in a dark corner beside the temple of Fortuna, the eyes of a lion reflecting the torchlight. A moment later she could have sworn she saw the big, lithe shadow slipping past the base of a statue. Maybe it was Apedemak, come from the land of her ancestors to rescue her. She rubbed her thumb across his likeness on her knife handle and tried to think of an invocation, but nothing came to her mind.

The racket of the crowd was inside her head, and she felt herself carried along by it. Only a little while ago she had been trying to reach a certain place, hadn't she? The image of that need was already dim and was growing fainter. She knew she was trying to escape something, but just now she felt nothing other than a vague uneasiness.

Many people carried wineskins from which they were taking frequent drinks and offering them to everyone they passed. Much of the wine was spilled or sprayed with loud hilarity over the heads of those nearby. The smell of wine was nearly as strong as the smell of the burning pitch.

She looked up. The embers from the torches were climbing into the night sky and mingling with the stars. Amanis laughed, and the stars laughed with her, welcoming her as they welcomed their little sisters, newly freed from the torches. She knew now that the old woman had been singing to the stars, singing a high note that thrummed with the same life shining down on her from the darkness, the same life that glowed from the lion's eyes, the same life that vibrated in Turash's bowstring and birthed the buzzing flight of his arrows, the same life that danced through Damon's fingers and wrists and eyes, the same life that heaved inside a baby's chest until it cried for a rescuer. Amanis wanted to join the sound, that single, high cry, rising and falling like the wind on a rocky hillside. It was her cry mingling with the torches' sparks on their way to the stars. The cry of a newborn child. The cry for help, for rescue. For life.

She remembered: She had to get to the troupe. Men were chasing her—men who wanted to take the cry from her. She lowered her eyes from the laughing, dancing stars, and began to move toward the east side of the marketplace.

A man stepped in front of her. She moved to go around him, but he was still in the way—probably another drunken dancer who wanted her to join him and sing with the aulos. She looked up to say something to him, to explain why she couldn't take the time right now.

It was Scaevolus. Fear sent a shock along her limbs.

"You!" he said. His hand shot toward her wrist, and just as

quickly she pulled away and dove into the crowd.

"Come back!" she heard him shout. "You must come back!"

She plunged into the crowd, no longer caring about anything but getting to someplace where she could be safe.

She finally broke free of the mob near the agora's eastern side. She ducked among the columns and, after satisfying herself that Scaevolus's man was not lurking nearby, left the agora.

Amanis skulked along walls and in dark corners of buildings until she came to the eastern gate. Luckily for her, the wardens were busy letting revelers in and out, and she was able to slip outside into a group of fellows loudly announcing their need to perform some bawdy ritual outside the city.

She slipped from one tree to another, one rock outcropping to another, until she smelled the smoke of the troupe's campfires. The first person she saw was Thyrsis. The old woman squatted beside a dying fire, idly stirring the glowing coals with a switch. She looked up as Amanis emerged from the darkness. Quickly she leaned over and shook the foot of a sleeping boy. She said something to him that sent him scampering off to another part of the camp.

"Damon was worried about you," Thyrsis said as Amanis knelt by the glowing coals. "He told me to send him word as soon as anyone saw you."

"We ran into a little trouble."

"I'd say. Have you eaten?"

"Some bread. A while ago."

"Here." She handed Amanis a wooden bowl full of curds. Amanis cupped the bowl close to her face, scooping the food into her mouth with her fingertips. When she had finished, Thyrsis held out a skin of water.

Amanis told Thyrsis about their escape from the angry man. She looked at the ground for a time, thinking of what, if anything, to say about Scaevolus. Then she told, in slow words, how she had come upon him in the agora. She told of the infant on the hillside in Ephesus and of the trader's relentless pursuit.

"At least I think it was Scaevolus," she said slowly. "The fumes, the smell of the wine, the noise—maybe it was only a dream."

"No. It was no dream."

Amanis looked at her.

"I knew the day I read your hand by the stream on the road from Ephesus. You must go away. But be careful, because some-one *will* follow you."

"Why must I go?"

"I don't know. But you will. You must."

"The one who will follow me—"

"That is hidden from me. But your path lies over many hills and many seas before you find home once again."

The only home Amanis could remember was during that long-ago time when her mother's dark hands touched her, when her soft voice and easy smile hovered. When her father remem-bered how to have enough. Ever since those days had ended, there had been no home. Only shelter. Only a place to wait for the day to end and for another just like it to start.

"Have you said anything to Damon?" Amanis asked.

"No. I do not try to shape what must be. I only see the guise of it sometimes." She gave a sad little smile. "Much less often than I lead my customers to believe. Coin is coin, after all. But that day I knew. The force of the knowing made me a little afraid. At first, I thought it came from you. But I've decided it came from somewhere else."

Damon strode out of the darkness toward them. "Good, you made it back. I was worried."

Amanis shrugged. Damon squatted by the coals. Together

they watched the glow of the embers chase itself back and forth.

"If he followed me here, he'll follow me to the next place," she said finally.

"Maybe we hid you in time. Maybe he'll give up when he can't find you."

"No. I saw him in the agora on the way here. And he saw me."

Damon picked up a twig from between his feet. He stirred the coals with it until it burst into flame; he held it aloft until the flame faded to an orange nub, then to nothing.

"Where would you go?"

"I don't know. Stay here, maybe, and let you move on to the next town. He would follow you, most likely, thinking that I was still with you. He might even call the magistrates down on you." She looked straight at him. "Hiding a fugitiva is a crime against the empire."

"All of us are trying to get away from something. Don't you think?"

She stared into the coals, thinking about cities of refuge. "Where is Nazareth?"

"Never heard of it," he said. "Why?"

"Something I heard some Jews talking about while I was hiding in the shed by the docks."

"An odd people," said Thyrsis. "They don't fit anywhere and seem proud of it."

Damon nodded. "The strangest stories I've ever heard have come from Jews."

Thyrsis sat up straight, craning her neck to peer at something behind Damon and Amanis. "People are coming," she said. "With torches. Quite a few, from the look of it."

Amanis heard it then: the sound of men's voices coming up the ravine from the town.

"You'd better hide," Damon told her as he sprang to his feet. He put his fingers in his mouth and gave a piercing whistle, then dashed off into the shadows.

Amanis scrambled a little way up the ravine. She found a copse of scrub juniper and made her way into it. She squatted in the heavy darkness and tried to slow her breathing.

Angry shouts came from down in the ravine. A single voice rose and fell on the night breeze. Amanis strained to try to pick up some of the words. "...cheated!" she heard. Then, a little later, "—cut my arm."

There was more shouting and choruses of angry agreement, but Amanis heard nothing that sounded like an actual fight. After a long time, she dared to part the juniper boughs enough to see the line of torches filing back the way they had come, toward the eastern gate of Smyrna.

She picked her way back down to the camp and met Damon, Turash, Harim, Othar, and some of the other men. Tarquinius was nowhere in sight.

"What did they want?" she asked.

"Tarquinius's neck and yours," said Damon. "But mostly Tarquinius's."

"What kind of fool would keep playing after he'd lost a hundred denarii?" one of the men wanted to know.

"The best kind," said Tarquinius, coming out from behind the rock outcropping where he had been crouched. "Am I their mother? Am I supposed to tell them to go home when they've lost enough?"

"It might have been good if you had this time," said Damon. "That fellow's crazy as a goose, I'll grant you. But he's got a lot more money where that hundred came from, and he wants it back. And he says he'll follow us all the way to the Bosporus if he has to, to get his hands on you. He says we can't have someone watching you all the time, and he's right."

"I just don't understand it," said Tarquinius. "I never have this kind of trouble in the smaller towns. Only in Ephesus."

"Well, we can't afford to have this troublemaker tagging along after us wherever we go," said Damon. "And we can't kill him; he may be a hothead, but he's also a citizen of a town where we'll want to return someday." He looked long at the dwarf, then at Amanis. "I think you were right, after all. I think we need to part company. For a while, at least."

"I will go with them," said Othar.

"I assumed you'd want to," Damon replied.

"Go where?" Tarquinius said. "Why are we talking about this? Just because of one sour-tempered loser? There's money in this town! I was just hitting my rhythm. I could make four, five hundred here! You can't be serious!"

"You won't make any money if you're dead," Othar said. "Damon is right. You need to go away. And so does Amanis. You're putting the rest of the troupe at risk."

"Especially if they have Roman troops with them," Amanis said. "But where can we go? I don't think anywhere in Asia Province is safe."

"I wasn't thinking of your staying in Asia Province," Damon said. "I know a man with a ship that sails with tomorrow morning's tide. I was hoping we could get you on board."

"Where's this ship going?" Tarquinius asked.

"Along the coast to Miletus, then across to Athens," the shipmaster said. "Why? You got something that needs to get out of Smyrna quiet like?"

They stood on the wharf, but the seaman still swayed from his night at the agora. Damon had roused him from a sound slumber; it had taken several minutes for the captain to come to enough to understand anything the juggler said.

"Well, it's mighty late. Don't know…maybe we could fit three passengers in, maybe not. Space is precious during the shipping season, you know. Got a big load of wool to deliver to a very impatient merchant in Athens…"

"How much?" Damon asked.

"Who'd I be hauling?"

Damon jerked his thumb at Tarquinius, Amanis, and Othar.

"I might could find them a place in the hold. But it'll be cramped quarters for him," he said, nodding toward Othar.

"Never mind that," Damon said. "How much?"

"Fifty each."

Tarquinius sucked air through his teeth. Othar growled. The shipmaster took a half step backward. "You ship chancy cargo, you pay a higher price," he said.

Damon held out a fist to the seaman. Amanis heard the clink of coins. "There. All the way through to Athens if they want to stay with you that far. And I'll expect you to let them sleep on board tonight."

The other man gave a quick, single nod.

Damon turned to them. "Here," he said, reaching into his bag and holding something toward Amanis. He put three leather balls about the size of large plums in her hand. The leather was fine grained and perfectly smooth. "Start with these," he said, smiling. "When you drop one, it won't roll so far. Next time I see you, you'll be as good as me. Remember— one ball at a time."

The balls felt cool in her palm. She smiled at him.

"I don't suppose it's any good, advising you to find a different game?" he said to the dwarf.

"What for? I'll wager there's more silver to be made in Athens in a day than in a place like this in a month. I just can't believe you're so worried about one little misunderstanding."

"I am. And you should be." Damon turned to Othar. "Take care of them. Especially Tarquinius. He doesn't seem to care about his own hide."

Othar grinned. He and Damon clasped wrists.

Damon turned to the captain once more. "I'd take good care of them, Linus, if I were you. Especially the big one. He's a German, you know. If he gets hungry enough…"

The captain stared at Othar, who stood with his arms crossed over his chest, staring back. Amanis had to hide a grin.

"All right, aboard with you," the captain said finally, making an impatient motion toward the ship. "No sense standing out here all night, waiting for whatever's chasing you to catch up."

Thirteen

*A*manis squirmed around in the cramped space, trying to find a position that didn't involve being gouged by hard objects. The *Thermopylae* swayed with the swells, creaking and groaning like an old woman. It didn't help that Tarquinius was splayed against the bulkhead next to her, snoring with a sound like a taut rope being sawed back and forth across the edge of a thin plank.

Linus had told them they'd round Samos sometime during the night, arriving in Miletus by morning. As soon as they reached port, Amanis vowed she would get off this cursed boat and walk about on dry, steady land—even if for only a few moments.

Her mind was as restless as her body. She fell to thinking of the troupe. What was it Damon had said? "We're all trying to get away from something." Maybe the troupe itself was a city of refuge—a roaming city without walls, peopled by those who had something to hide, something to escape. Maybe that was better than walls or even strange words read from an old Jewish scroll.

Amanis suddenly realized that Damon had not answered her

question. She had asked him why, but he had told her only a little about how. Her fingertips reached into her bundle and found the three leather balls. She smiled in the darkness. Maybe she would find Damon again, when she had learned something about the how. Maybe then he would trust her with the why.

A bloodcurdling yell erupted from the darkness just beyond Tarquinius, followed quickly by thumping, thrashing, and a string of German curses. Tarquinius bolted upright and hit his forehead on an overhanging beam. He fell back like a sack of barley, moaning and rubbing his head.

"What is it, Othar?" Amanis shouted, scrabbling about for the haft of the sikhimi.

"A rat! It ran across my legs!"

"You big idiot! I thought someone was cutting your throat!" Tarquinius hollered. He moaned. "I think I cracked my skull."

"But it ran right across my legs!"

"Oh, shut up—this hold is full of rats. Amanis, lend me your tickler. Maybe I'll just cut his throat for him."

"I'm not staying down here," Othar said. Amanis could hear the German feeling his way toward the ladder to the hatch.

"You'd better go up with him, Amanis," the dwarf sighed. "In the mood he's in, he'll toss a sailor overboard, and the three of us will end up fish food."

"Aren't you coming?" she asked.

"I'd rather stay down here with the rats."

She felt the cool sea air on her face as she climbed the ladder. When she came out on deck, she had to remind herself to keep her eyes on her feet and not on the swells.

Clouds scudded past the quarter-moon. The mainsail snapped in the breeze. Two sailors were tending the mainsail lines amidship, and another sailor stood in the pool of light from

the aft lamp, talking in a low voice to the helmsman who han-
dled the huge steering oar. Amanis had to peer carefully to find
Othar, now huddled at the base of the main mast.

She went over and sat beside him, leaning her back against
the treelike mast. She could feel the vibrations of the mainsail.
"At least the air out here doesn't smell like soggy sheep," she said
after a while.

"In my land there are trees four times larger than this mast,"
Othar said. "Trunks so big that three men can barely reach
around them."

"I've never seen a tree that large."

"I used to sit in the forest when I was a boy, just like I'm sitting here now. All by myself. I wasn't afraid. I used to listen to
the wind in the leaves. I used to think about many things."

"Why did you leave?"

He was silent for a long while, staring out at the sea. The
swells looked like gray, transient hills in the light of the moon.
Now and then a whitecap would unfurl from the lip of a swell,
a sudden flash of silver against the dark sea. Amanis wondered
how far they were from the headlands of Samos. She let her eyes
drop. The night sea gave a feeling of vast loneliness, as if this ship
held the only people on earth.

"The Romans call my people the Marcomanni," he said
finally. "For as long as the oldest singers can remember, maybe
since the day Wotan and his brothers raised the land out of the
sea, my people have lived along the river valleys and in the
forests.

"When I was a boy, we raided cattle from the Chatti, and
they from us. Then one of our chiefs married his son to the
daughter of one of the Chatti headmen. That was when we
began raiding cattle from the Hermundari and the Helvetii.

"But some of the Helvetii were cozy with the Romans, and they started making trouble for us. They told the consuls we were raising an army and would soon be raiding the villages and farmsteads of Gaul. The Romans decided to punish the Marcomanni. They sent a few cohorts out along the Danube with Helvetii scouts. They burned the first three of our towns they came to and sowed our fields with salt.

"My people don't seek trouble. But when they are attacked, they don't run away. The horns sounded down the valleys and across the hills. The men of the Marcomanni mustered. My father forbade me to go, but I begged him, and finally he gave in. I went to the gathering place. We sang the songs of Tiu and sacrificed to him. We readied ourselves. My blood felt like fire running through my veins.

"We met them on a plain not far from Noricum. They were drawn up in battle formation, a solid rank of bullhide shields with the armored cavalry at the rear. We broke upon them with a shout of rage. We went at them like stones from a sling; we didn't care about their javelins and their gladii. We would have run straight into the teeth of the dragon of Niflheim, so great was our thirst for blood. Any one of us could have cut any one of them in half with a single stroke.

"But you don't fight just one Roman—you have to fight them all. We shattered on the phalanx of shields like waves crashing on rocks. I saw my father batter them with his axe, then I saw the gladius come through his back, just under his shoulder blades. He died with the battle song of Tiu in his throat."

He fell silent again. Amanis could see the muscles in his jaw clenching and unclenching.

"I don't know why I wasn't killed. I stood over my father's corpse to keep the Romans from desecrating it. I remember beating blindly at anything that came within reach of my axe, screaming my father's name over and over. There was a charge then; the Roman cavalry swept forward. The last thing I remember was a horse coming, the rider swinging a lance down at me. There was a dark flash, then nothing.

"When I woke up, I was bound hand and foot like a pig for roasting. They put me in chains and took me to Rome so that women and children could gawk at me like some strange beast."

Amanis listened to the boom of the mainsail, the whistle of the wind in the lines. One of the men at the helm gave a low laugh. "You loved your father," she said at last.

Othar nodded.

"I wish I could've loved mine. But I didn't—don't. He sold me to the slaver who's chasing me now."

He turned to face her.

"Is such a thing done in Germany? Do fathers sell their children?"

Othar shook his head.

"Take me there someday. Let me see your valleys and forests of huge trees. I want to smell the air of a land where sons are willing to die for their fathers."

He looked away. "It's too far. I don't think I'll ever be able to go back."

"How did you come to be in this part of the world?"

"Tarquinius," he said with a wry smile, remembering. Othar was supposed to fight in a show the next day at the Circus Maximus, he said. He would be given a small knife and sent into the ring against a bear. If he killed the bear he would be a free man. During the night he heard a voice from the shadows but didn't understand the words. He did, however, understand the strange dwarf's motion for opening the door. Tarquinius picked the lock, and they slipped away into the darkness.

They hid among the warehouses of the Transtiberium for the rest of that night, Othar said. The next morning they stowed away on an empty grain barge bound for Ostia. From there, getting to Africa Province wasn't too hard. They tramped across most of the province, saving enough money from Tarquinius's gaming to book passage on a trader bound for Athens. But there was a squall, and they were blown off course. The ship landed at Ephesus instead. It was close to midsummer, and the troupe was in town, making its way through the cities of Asia Province.

"Damon decided I looked to be of some use," Othar finished. "I told him Tarquinius had to come, too."

"You don't part easily with companions, do you?"

The big German shrugged. "I owe him a blood debt."

"So do I."

The ship took on three tuns of oil at Miletus and freshened its supply of drinking water and bread. Then the *Thermopylae* left for Ikaria, where Linus traded one of the tuns to the headman of the island for some coin and a pot of raisins. They sailed southwest to Delos, and Amanis breathed a sigh of relief when she heard Linus say he planned a layover in Delos harbor. The thought of another sleepless night held no appeal.

Close to sundown, the three of them wandered into the agora of the main village. Most of the shopkeepers had gone or were packing up their booths, but one old woman and her daughter remained. The woman sat cross-legged on the hard-packed earth; her daughter stood behind her. By her posture and expression, the daughter clearly wished to be somewhere else.

Arranged in front of the crone were small metal trinkets decorated with feathers or bone, painted clay figurines, beaded leather pouches, and various shriveled objects that probably came from some animal or another. The old woman's face was wrinkled and there didn't appear to be a tooth left in her head. She looked up at them with birdlike eyes. "Protection against the evil eye," she said, "love charms, potency, ague cures, good luck—and growth fetishes," she said, glancing at Tarquinius. The dwarf made an obscene gesture at her and stalked away. A chuckle rumbled in Othar's chest.

Amanis squatted on her heels. "Which are the good luck pieces?" she asked.

The woman flicked a finger at the feather- and bone-decorated baubles. Behind her, the daughter heaved a sigh and shook her head. "Mother, how much longer will you persist in this deception?"

"As long as we need to eat. If you aren't going to help, go away."

"Some new religion," the woman said to Amanis, shaking her head. "My daughter's husband came back from Athens talking craziness."

"The Christ is the Son of God," the daughter said. "He has conquered death."

The mother made a sound of disgust. "Lot of good it did Orestes. He's still in the ground, best I can tell. Where's this *Anastasis* he was always praying to?"

"Orestes will live again," the daughter said in a wavering voice. Amanis could see the tears glistening at her lower eyelids. The death of her husband was still raw in her heart, Amanis guessed. "The Christ will raise him and all the faithful when He comes to judge the earth."

"Well, until then, folk will need their charms and totems,"

the old woman said, turning back toward Amanis. "Now then. Can I interest you in this one here? It's been blessed by the oracles at Eleusis—good for games of chance, finding lost coins, and attracting aid in time of trouble. Only six obols, since I can see you're tired from your journey."

Amanis started to reach for her purse when the daughter stepped around her mother and knelt beside Amanis. She put her hand on Amanis's arm and looked up at her with a pleading expression.

"Don't put your trust in magic and superstition," she said. "Believe in the Christ, and He will save you."

Amanis started to shove her away, but something in the younger woman's face stopped her. "Why do you stay here with your mother if you don't believe in what she's doing?" she asked.

"The Christ commands us to care for our parents. His law teaches us to respect them. She practices sorcery and deceit, but she is still my mother. I can't abandon her."

Amanis studied her for several moments. "I've heard others talking about this resurrected god of yours. It sounds like nonsense to me."

"Hah!" barked the old woman.

"But you are right to care for your mother. You won't always have her."

"I know," the daughter said. "I hope that before she dies, she will come to believe in the Christ so she may have unending life."

"Who wants that?" the woman scoffed. "I've lived long enough. But I don't see any sense in starving to death. There are more pleasant ways to die. Now—how about the charm?"

Amanis gave the daughter a sad smile, then reached into her purse. She handed some coins to the old woman, who put the charm in her hand.

"You bought this from that old hag?" Tarquinius said when Amanis handed him the trinket.

"She said it was good for games of chance. I thought it might be of use to you."

"I don't go in much for games of chance. The people who play with me don't have a chance."

"She also said it was to bring help in tight places," said Othar. "You'll need that, for sure."

"Probably causes warts." Tarquinius rolled the talisman in his palm and eyed it balefully before dropping it into his pocket.

It was a pleasant night and sleeping on the deck seemed like a good idea. Tarquinius wanted to play his game with some of the crew before bed, but Othar wouldn't let him. "Better we get to Athens first. More places to hide."

They cast off the next morning beneath a sky so blue it made Amanis's heart ache. She stood on the deck and watched the shoreline of Delos drop away. Linus had said they would make a brief call at Andros, then cross toward the Achaean headlands. He hoped to make the harbor at Piraeus well before nightfall two days hence.

Just out from Delos they spotted dolphins running with the ship. Amanis had never seen them before, and it thrilled her to watch the way they leapt into the air, the sun glistening on their smooth skin. They looked for all the world like children vying with one another for attention. They dove beneath the hull and surfaced on the other side, sitting up in the water and chattering like gossipy little girls. She had never seen animals so brimming with joy.

"Good omen," said Linus, watching the display. "Dolphins

are friendly to sailors. I've heard they'll sometimes swim for days with a shipwrecked man, guiding him toward land."

The dolphins stayed with them for the rest of the morning and into midafternoon. Amanis was saddened as one by one they chattered at the ship, then disappeared beneath the surface into the depths. It was like bidding farewell to friends she had just met.

The sun was halfway down from the sky's zenith when they docked on Andros. There Linus sold the other two tuns of oil to an eager merchant. One of the crewmen, helping to raise the cargo over the gunwale, slipped beneath it, and the heavy barrel smashed his hand. Annoyed, Linus left the man on shore. Soon they were back at sea, crossing to the mainland.

Toward evening, just before they lit the fore and aft lamps, another ship came into view. It was also a square-rigged freighter, but the imperial standard was emblazoned on the main mast.

"Not pirates at least," Linus mused.

"Are you sure?" Tarquinius said. "Sometimes the official pirates are worse than the unofficial ones."

"True enough."

The two ships closed to within hailing distance. They exchanged greetings and identification. The imperial freighter was just out from Piraeus. She had taken on a cargo of Achaean wine for the proconsul of Asia Province and was bound for Ephesus to make delivery.

"Any chance of tossing us a cask or two?" Linus shouted.

The other captain's laugh carried across the water. "Fair winds and smooth water to you," he called as his men hoisted the sail to get back underway.

"And to you," answered Linus.

Dark fell. Amanis realized she was tired enough to sleep,

even in the cramped hold. But she wasn't ready to lie down—not quite. She went aft to the flickering circle of light cast by the helmsman's lamp. She settled herself against the starboard gunwale. She reached into her bag and fished around until she felt the leather balls Damon had given her. She held them both in her right palm and ran her fingertips over them. They felt like the cured bladders that water skins were made of. The stitching at the seams was small and careful.

Cautiously she tossed one into the air, watching its arc and catching it in her other hand. Again and again she tossed the ball, alternating hands until she could trace its flight in both directions without looking. Her catching hand found the ball almost every time. After a while she decided to try two balls. She tossed one, then the second. She caught the first, but the second bounced off the side of her hand and into her lap. She tried again. Time after time one or another of the balls fell into her lap. After a number of tries, she was able to toss and catch both balls, then toss again with barely a pause between. She kept at it until her wrists and shoulders began to stiffen and her eyelids refused to stay open.

PART TWO

Rescuer

Fourteen

he pomegranate arced through the air toward her. Amanis caught it and built it into the pattern with the two balls, the stone, and the ball of spun wool she was already juggling. "If I keep it in the air, can I have it?" she called. The fruit seller grinned and nodded. "Too bad it isn't a purse full of drachmae then," she said. The crowd laughed.

It was cool in the agora today, especially for the month of Scirophorion. The sky was overcast, and a breeze whispered through the columns of the Peristyle court. Right now it didn't feel too bad; this crowd had kept her busy for a good while, and she was starting to break a sweat.

Her hands and eyes moved constantly. It was just as Damon had said, she thought; she saw each of them separately, and yet had a sense of the whole pattern. It was just a different way of seeing.

She finished with a flourish: She let the balls fall into her wallet and tossed the stone at the feet of the old woman who had pitched it to her. She kept tossing the pomegranate in the air with one hand and threw the yarn back to its owner with the other. Then she ducked beneath the pomegranate to catch it behind her back. The crowd applauded her, and a few of them tossed coins at her feet.

As they dispersed, she counted the money in her wallet. Nearly forty lepta. Not bad for an afternoon's work; with what she'd collected before noon, she would have money for bread and maybe enough left over for some cheese.

The fruit seller grinned. "Now you've got enough to pay for the pomegranate." Amanis made a face and began tearing off the husk. He laughed and waved her away. The crowd she'd gathered hadn't hurt his trade any.

She walked across the agora. A crowd had gathered between the temple of Apollo and the Old Bouleterion. Amanis saw two men standing on the steps of the Hephaisteion; she could see the practiced gesticulations they used as their voices carried to their listeners. This crowd wouldn't be in the mood for her sort of entertaining. She'd learned that, at least, after these years in Athens: The only thing any Athenian citizen liked better than listening to rhetoric was listening to the sound of his own voice performing rhetoric. Even Tarquinius had to admit he couldn't wedge himself between an Athenian and a good argument.

Amanis strolled along the South Stoa until she came to the stall of her favorite baker. "Hey, Procyon, how much of that stale bread will you sell me for twenty lepta?"

The toothless baker laughed and rolled his eyes. "You again? I thought I told you not to bother me anymore."

"Well, if you don't want my money…"

"Here." He tossed a loaf to her, then another. He turned away with a dismissive motion as Amanis began juggling the loaves.

"Only two? Surely you can do better than that," she said. A few people were stopping to watch. "I can handle four at least."

Without turning around he pitched another loaf over his

shoulder. "Three then. Now get out of here, won't you?"

"Tell you what, Procyon. I won't charge you anything for the crowd I've gathered in front of your stall. You give me these loaves, we'll call it even."

"Someone call the authorities! This swarthy barbarian is robbing me of my livelihood."

Amanis laughed, catching the three loaves in midair. "Here you go, old man." She held out a handful of coppers. "Twenty-five. But only because I'm feeling generous today."

He looked over his shoulder at her. "Twenty-five? Well, all right then. I might let you have some of my leftovers another time." He put the money in his pouch and grinned at her. His naked gums were dark and shriveled.

She left the agora by the Heliaea, skirting the northwest slope of the Areopagus, then left the road and started climbing the Hill of the Nymphs. There she stopped to listen. Nothing. A part of her wanted to leave right now, to walk away with the fantasy intact: Because she heard nothing, no one was there.

Instead she began walking slowly back and forth across the rocky slope, carefully scanning the ground. Junipers and slender poplars clustered here and there on the hillside, and she peered into their shadows as she passed. Beneath a laurel bush she found what she had hoped against: an abandoned newborn too weak to cry. His deformed arm and club foot told her why the little boy had been brought here.

She went to the baby and knelt beside it. Its chest moved steadily up and down. Amanis reached into her pouch and found the piece of linen she kept there. She picked up the little boy and cradled him in the crook of her arm. She brought the small skin flask out of her pouch and dripped a little goat's milk on the baby's lips. The tiny tongue licked at the warm liquid.

Amanis wrapped the cloth around the baby and put a few more drops of milk in his mouth.

She tried not to think of the babies she didn't find, those the slavers and procurers got to first—or worse, the wild dogs. So far she had never found more than one at a time. Some days there were none. Was the Hill of the Nymphs the only place where Athenian babies were abandoned? Probably not. But she couldn't be everywhere. She did her best to keep her mind on the infants she found, not on the ones she didn't.

She dripped some more milk into the baby boy's mouth. He was getting the hang of it. She smiled down at him. "You're a quiet one," she murmured. "Maybe that kept you alive. Maybe that is why I found you instead of someone else." She gave him some more milk. He swallowed with a tiny, satisfied grunt.

Amanis made her way down the narrow street. Two- and three-story tenements lined either side. Pleasant smells wafted from the cooking fires inside the dwellings. A few lamps were lit. The room she shared with Tarquinius and Othar was further down this street and then a short way along the Avenue of Theseus, in a tenement near the western wall of the old city, close to the Salamis gate.

When the doorway to their building came into view, she saw Othar squatted on the ground beside the entrance, scratching between the ears of a scrawny, orange-striped cat. Amanis could hear the animal's rhythmic purring; it opened its eyes and blinked at her once.

"You found another one," Othar said, looking at the tiny bundle in her arms. "How many babies can the Jews take in?"

"I don't know. One more I hope."

He stood and came over to her. "Let me see it."

"A little boy," she said, pulling back the linen. As Othar

watched, she dripped some more goat's milk into the infant's mouth.

"This one's deformed."

"Maybe so, but he deserves a chance to live."

"He eats like he wants to live."

Amanis smiled. She looked down at the cat entwining itself between Othar's legs. "Looks like you found something, too."

He bent down and picked up the cat. Amanis thought she could count the poor thing's ribs through its hide. "I've been feeding it, trying to keep it around," Othar said. "I'm hoping it will catch rats."

"I think some of the rats in our building are as big as this cat. Maybe you'd better start it out on mice. And keep feeding it on the side. Is Tarquinius upstairs?"

"Yes. He had a good day today."

"Me, too. I'd better go up and get this little one settled in until I can go visit the Jews."

The tenement was a three-story building wedged into the delta formed by the joining of the small Avenue of Theseus and the busier Melite Street, which became the road to Salamis once it left the western gate. The first story of the building was built from dressed limestone blocks. The side that fronted on Melite had a colonnade with shops, a tavern, and other businesses. The top two floors were of baked clay bricks covered with concrete and plaster. Amanis went through the entrance and into the central atrium of the tenement, a large yard of bare dirt with a communal cistern in its center. A flight of steps wound up the inside wall to the second story where their room was located.

Trudging up the steps, Amanis listened to the murmur of life in the tenement as households of all colors and customs readied their evening meals. She passed the doorway of the dark-skinned family from the far reaches of the Parthian lands. The pungent smell of curry wafted to her. Amanis liked the Parthian family. Sometimes as she drew water from the cistern in the atrium, the older boy and his sister would stand behind her. They never spoke to Amanis, but they gave her shy smiles from time to time. When Othar was about, the boy followed him like a puppy, staring at his long blond braids and his pale skin.

A little way along the balcony of the second story, Amanis heard loud voices in the chambers of Tullius and his family. Tullius made a precarious living as a guide to pilgrims and tourists. He had a kind of crafty, catch-as-catch-can intelligence. He likely needed it to survive among the sharp-tongued women of his household.

She came to her doorway. Tarquinius sat on a tall stool in front of the brazier, his legs dangling as he leaned over a large pot. A savory aroma rose from the pot as he stirred. He looked over his shoulder at her. "Pork stew," he said, arching his eyebrows.

"Meat! You did have a good day, didn't you?"

"I was particularly brilliant, I must say."

"I didn't do too badly either. I've got bread and some cheese."

"We'll feast tonight." He looked at the bundle in her arms. "Boy or girl?"

"A boy. With a crippled arm and a malformed foot."

Tarquinius nodded, then turned back to his stew. "Found him in the usual place?"

"Yes."

"I've always wondered why my father didn't toss me out. Maybe I looked normal when I was born."

"Maybe your father loved you."

He stopped stirring, watching the white smoke from the fire climb the blackened wall and go out the small vent just under the ceiling. "If so, he had a strange way of showing it. The main thing I remember about him is the back of his hand."

She carried the tiny boy to her pallet. She sat down and began giving him as much of the remaining goat's milk as he would take. "At least he didn't sell you as a slave."

"He might as well have. 'Here, runt, get me my staff.' 'Runt, go tell your mother to come here.' Runt this, runt that. If my mother hadn't whispered my name at night, I wouldn't have known it. I wasn't sorry when he died."

"What did your mother do after his death?"

"She had a sister whose husband was willing to take her in."

"And you?"

"Oh, I could've stayed there, I guess. But I couldn't stand the way the others looked at me. I'd learned a thing or two by then about how to take care of myself. I decided these short legs were good enough to take me somewhere else. I thought almost any-where else had to be better."

Amanis put the baby over her shoulder and began gently rubbing his back. "And now that you've seen something of the wide world, how does your decision look to you?"

Tarquinius stirred the pot for a while. Without looking at her he said, "I wish I could have seen my mother one more time. But the rest of them can die forgotten, as far as I care."

The baby gave a loud belch, and a little curdled milk spilled onto Amanis's shoulder. She laughed. "Well, your stomach isn't crippled, is it?"

Tarquinius hoisted himself from the stool and came over to look at the infant. "Doubt this one will make much of a basket weaver or a messenger."

"Nor will he be food for the dogs."

"All of us will one day feed the dogs. Or the birds. Or the worms."

She set the baby on her pallet and went to the water urn. She wet a soft rag, brought it back to her corner, and began sponging away the dried birth blood. "You think I'm foolish to interest myself in these babies."

"I didn't say that."

"What do you think, then?"

He tucked his hands beneath his arms and looked out the doorway for a long time. "I don't know exactly. I heard some men talking today. They sounded like philosophers, and I didn't understand most of what they were saying. But one of them said, 'Better to die young. Better still never to be born.' That I understood."

"Has your life really been that bad?"

Now he looked at her. "All of us get crossways with Fortuna. Some earlier, some later, but we all fall out of her favor sometime." He nodded toward the baby. "Maybe you did a good thing for him. Maybe not. Perhaps it will be for him to decide. But you probably won't be around to see, one way or the other." He climbed back onto the stool and resumed stirring his stew.

Amanis wiped the last of the blood from the little boy's body. She covered him with some soft wool blankets and watched as his eyes fluttered shut.

Othar came upstairs carrying the gaunt cat. He set the cat on the floor, then strode over to Tarquinius. He leaned over and sniffed the pot. "Don't overcook it," he said.

Amanis took from her satchel the bread and cheese. Tarquinius ladled his stew into clay bowls. They handed the food around and ate without talking, scooping the stew into their mouths with the bread and cheese. When she had eaten, Amanis gathered up the sleeping newborn. "I'll be at the Jews'," she announced, and went out.

The Jewish family lived on the third floor of the tenement across the courtyard. To get there, Amanis had to descend to the atrium, cross it, and climb the three flights of steps that led to the rooms on the other side.

How long had they been in Athens before she began looking for abandoned babies? When they first arrived, she had thought of little beyond the necessities of daily existence: go out with Tarquinius and Othar; watch the progress of the gaming; protect the dwarf as needed; size up the crowd and be his eyes and ears; signal Othar if matters began to look ugly.

The children in the tenement had brought the need back to her mind. In the evenings the little ones gathered around to watch her practice with the leather balls in the courtyard. Their delight in her growing skill made her want to laugh out loud. Then one day she caught herself wondering how many of these children had brothers or sisters whose fathers had left them on the floor where the midwife had put them after their births.

Why did the thought remain lodged so firmly in her? She didn't know. But the next evening, as Tarquinius and Othar turned toward home, she chose a different path. She didn't find any babies that day or the next. But on the third day a tiny girl was lying near a myrtle tree at the base of the Areopagus. Amanis stood for a long while over the helpless figure, wondering if Fortuna was watching, if she would resent another intrusion on her authority. Finally she picked up the baby and brought her back to the tenement. She had found her just in time; the infant lived. Some of those she would bring back here would not. As she held the first of several babies that died in her arms, she thought her heart would stop beating from the ache. But the very next day she found the strength to go back, looking for more lives to save.

The first little girl had been very strong. Amanis cleaned and fed her, then took her to the room the Jewish children ran to for their evening meal. And the Jews did not turn her away. They found a home for the child—the first of many she would bring to them.

Amanis was approaching their doorway now. One of the boys stuck his head out the door and saw her coming. He ducked back inside. Amanis heard him calling his father.

Fifteen

tephanos was there when she reached the doorway. One of his younger daughters stood behind him, holding onto one of his legs and peering up at Amanis. They had just finished their supper; Herodia and the older girls were clearing the baskets and bowls from the low table the family had been reclining around. Amanis smelled the green canes Stephanos split to make his baskets. Bundles of cane and baskets of a dozen different shapes, sizes, and stages of completion were stacked in every corner of the dwelling.

There was an older woman there Amanis hadn't seen before. The youngest boy was curled up in her lap.

"Amanis, I cannot take this child to the rabbi just now," Stephanos was saying. "As you can see, we have a guest—"

"What do you have there?" the older woman asked, setting the little boy on the floor beside her. She stood and came toward Amanis. "Let me see."

Amanis folded back the cloth covering the baby's face. He was still asleep, his head to one side, his lips slightly parted.

"Ooh, what a beautiful child." The woman glanced at

Amanis. "But obviously not yours."

Amanis looked from the woman to Stephanos. A slight smile parted his lips. "Damaris, this is Amanis," he said. "She lives across the way. She—she finds babies that have been exposed."

Damaris looked sharply at her. "Why would you presume to do such a thing?"

Amanis replied quietly, "Because I must."

Damaris studied her for a long time. "I see. Come on. I'll go to the rabbi with you."

"But you said you were going to tell me a story about the Anointed One," whined the little boy who had been sitting in her lap.

She turned to him and kneeled. "Hush now, Artemion. I'll come again soon, and next time I'll tell you two stories. I promise. I have to help this nice woman take care of the baby. You do understand, don't you?"

Artemion stuck a finger in his mouth and nodded reluctantly.

"Good boy." Damaris pulled him to her in a quick embrace. "Thank you for the meal, Stephanos. Grace and peace to you."

He gave Damaris a little bow. "And to you, good sister."

"I didn't know Stephanos had a sister," Amanis said as they went down the stairs. "You don't look Jewish."

"What? Oh, that. He didn't mean 'sister' in the usual way. We are brother and sister in spirit."

"I've never heard of such a thing."

"No, I wouldn't suppose that you have," Damaris said, smiling.

"Well, aren't you going to tell me what you're talking about?"

Damaris laid a hand softly on Amanis's shoulder as they walked through the tenement's entryway. "I'm sorry, dear. You must think me a very strange old woman."

"I've seen stranger, I can tell you. I just don't understand the meaning of the words passing between you and Stephanos."

"Stephanos and I are both believers in the Christ, the Anointed One. This belief binds our hearts and minds to each other like members of a household."

"I heard you speak to the little boy about this Christ. I've heard other Jews speak of Him, but never a Greek."

"The Christ has come to save everyone: Jews, Greeks, Romans, Gauls—even odd old women like me."

"This is the one who was crucified in the Jewish country?"

"Yes! You've heard the good news then?"

"I don't know what you mean by that. I heard a story one time that sounded like something a drunk man might tell: gods killed in some backwater country, dead people coming out of graves…None of it made any sense to me."

Damaris gave a soft chuckle. "No, I'm sure it didn't."

"Do you think me a fool because I don't understand some nonsense you choose to believe?"

"You don't need to get angry, Amanis."

"I'm not angry! I just don't like it when people I barely know make sport of me. A crucified god! Why would any god allow such a thing? Crucifixion is for criminals and slaves."

"I'm sorry. Please forgive me. I've lived long enough in the faith of Christ that I suppose I've forgotten how strange it must sound to someone coming upon it for the first time." They walked for a time in silence. "Tell me then—why do you seek out babies like this little fellow here?"

"I already told you. Because I must."

"Ah, but that really tells me nothing. Here is where we turn, isn't it?"

"Oh yes."

They rounded the corner where Melite intersected with Northwest Way. Amanis glanced at the baby. He was still asleep.

"It tells you all I know how to say," Amanis went on.

"You say you go out and get them because you must. Why must you?"

"I…I don't know. I simply must."

"Someone forces you?"

"No, of course not."

"Or you sell them, maybe?"

"Would I be taking this child to the Jewish priest if I intended to profit from him?"

"No, certainly not. So this is something you choose to do, maybe even for reasons you don't completely understand?"

"Yes, I guess that's it."

"An inner need drives you? Some urge from within that you cannot disobey?"

Amanis gave her a thoughtful look. "Yes. It seems so, I think."

Damaris nodded. "Then you already understand something of the way of the Christ."

"What does this have to do with that?"

"We—all of us—were helpless. He came to save us because He chose to do so. He could have chosen otherwise, but He didn't." She looked at Amanis and smiled. "And that tells you all I know how to say."

"I haven't been helpless since I was a child. Who taught you such crazy ideas?"

"His name was Paul. It was quite a few years ago—ten or more, maybe. The elders of the Areopagus laughed at him when he spoke of the Christ's rising from the dead. They couldn't believe it any more than you can. Only Dionysius and I could."

They were approaching the synagogue. The last remaining glow had nearly faded from the sky. "Will anyone still be here?" Amanis asked.

"I don't know. Maybe not."

They went up the steps and pulled on the oak door. It opened into a dim entryway, lit only by a small lamp at the front of the main room. An old man stood between them and the lamp. His back was to them, but Amanis could see him repeatedly nodding his head. A shawl, white-and-black-striped with tassels at the corners, was draped over his head and shoulders.

"He's praying," Damaris whispered. "Wait."

He stood in front of an ornately carved cabinet, lit only by the lamp. The cabinet was set into an alcove and framed by a small portico. If he was praying, he was doing it silently; Amanis could hear no words nor any tune or chant coming from him.

"Is his god inside that cabinet?" she whispered.

"No. Our God cannot be seen by human eyes."

The old man was removing the shawl from his head. Damaris gave a quiet cough. The man turned, lamp in hand, and held it aloft, peering down the long room at them. "Who is there?" he asked.

"I am Damaris. I'm a friend of Stephanos the basket maker, who lives over on the Avenue of Theseus."

"Yes, I know him. Who's that with you?"

"This is Amanis, also a friend of Stephanos and his family. Is Rabbi Nathaniel anywhere about?"

"No, the rabbi has gone home long since. What do you want with him?"

"I found this baby," Amanis said, stepping forward. "I've brought others I've found to him before. He has taken pity on them and searched out places where they could live."

The old man took a slow step or two toward them, still holding the lamp above and in front of him. He was looking at Damaris. "You're one of those Christ people, aren't you? I've seen you with them in the agora, haranguing anybody who'll listen. You're the one who preached all that foolishness to Stephanos and his family."

"Please," Damaris said, "can you tell us how to get to the rabbi's house? Is it far?"

He moved another step closer. "It's dark outside. You ought to go to your own houses."

"Yes, but this child needs shelter."

"Then see to it yourselves. Go on with you both. I have to lock the synagogue for the night." He stepped deliberately around them, gathering his clothing as if to keep from brushing against them. He went to the door and pulled it open, motioning them impatiently toward the street.

Damaris gave Amanis a sad smile and a shrug. They went out, and the old man slammed the door behind them.

"I can't care for this child!" Amanis said. "But now, thanks to you and your crazy religion, I have no choice. I should have waited for Stephanos. We never had this trouble when he came with me."

"You soon would have. Stephanos has become a follower of Christ. That's why I was at his house."

"What am I going to do?"

"It seems to me you have two choices, at least for the time being: take that child home and care for him, at least until you can find someone else who's willing to take him in—"

"I don't have time to take care of a baby!"

"—or put him back where you found him."

The silence pounded in Amanis's ears. She looked down at

the little boy, half expecting him to be watching her with accusing eyes, waiting to see whether she would choose death or life for him. But he was still asleep. Unaware. Innocent of the choice being made.

She started walking, back down Northwest Way. "Curse me for a fool," she said under her breath.

"No," Damaris said. "There is deep goodness in you, Amanis. You have no cause to be ashamed."

"You would have let me take him back to the hillside?" Amanis said after they had walked a while. "You wouldn't have stopped me?"

"Maybe I would have followed you. Maybe I would have taken him to my house. That would have been my choice. But you had your own choice to make."

"I wonder. Sometimes I think my whole life is already decided."

"No, Amanis. Choices come upon us suddenly; they surprise us. Each is a gift, a chance to do better."

She looked at the older woman. "How can you be so sure?"

Though the dark hid Damaris's face, Amanis could hear the smile in her words. "Hope is stronger than fate, Amanis. And love is stronger than death."

They walked many paces in the darkness. "I know too much of death but very little of love," Amanis said.

"Yet your heart is full of love, daughter. The child in your arms proves it."

Daughter. Amanis let the word hang between her and Damaris.

"I'll help you, Amanis. I'll help you with the baby."

"Why should you do a thing like that?"

Damaris was quiet for a while. "I have heard it said that the

Christ loved little children. He once said anyone who wanted to enter the kingdom of heaven had to become like a little child."

"I remember hearing some Jews once," Amanis said. "Their god told them to make cities where fugitives might go and be safe. I've never heard of a god who cared about fugitives. Or children."

"It is the same God, the God of Abraham, Isaac, and Jacob. The God of the Jews is the one who sent the Christ to save us. The Christ is the only begotten Son of the Most High."

"These are confusing words." Amanis stopped. "Here is the door to my building."

"Well?" said Damaris. "Aren't we going in?"

"You mean—tonight? You want to come up tonight? To help?"

"What better time to begin than at the very beginning?"

"But…Othar and Tarquinius…"

"Interesting names. Shall we?"

If Damaris was shocked to find her new acquaintance living with a dwarf and a hulking German, she gave no sign of it. She held the baby, rocked him and cooed to him as Amanis improvised a place for him to sleep. As Damaris unwrapped him to change his swaddlings, Amanis saw her eyes rest briefly on the withered arm and the misshapen foot. Damaris stayed until the baby was changed, fed, and sleeping soundly once again. When his breathing was deep and even, the two women tiptoed out the door to the walkway.

"Shall I walk with you to your house?" Amanis asked.

"Oh no. I often go home much later than this. I'm quite safe."

"Damaris…thank you. You've been very kind to me. I'm glad you were at Stephanos's house."

"What will you call him?" Damaris asked as they started down the stairs.

"Oh. I hadn't even considered that."

"The boy should have some kind of name, don't you think?"

"I'll have to give it some thought."

They had come to the street gate. Amanis slid back the bolt and swung the door open. Damaris stepped through; then she abruptly turned back.

"Would you like for me to ask around and see if there's someone who can take the child in?"

Amanis hugged herself and looked back over her shoulder toward the dark room where the infant lay sleeping. She turned back toward Damaris.

"No. Not yet, at least."

Sixteen

*I*n the days that followed, Amanis was overwhelmed with assistance. It flooded the little room she shared with Tarquinius and Othar; it arrived in the hands of smiling strangers whose names she often failed to catch. This one brought a skin of goat's milk; that one carried a bundle of soft woolen blankets; another dropped by to visit and inconspicuously left a pouch containing enough money to purchase a week's supply of food for the entire household. Stephanos wove a shaded basket for the child so that she could take him with her to the agora without having to worry about leaving him in the sun.

The common root of this compassion was Damaris. Apparently she had spread word about the baby and Amanis among all her Christ-follower friends. Most of those who came mentioned Damaris in some way. And Amanis began to notice that most of them spoke of her with a smile.

She decided to call the little boy Daphnis, since—like the Sicilian shepherds in the old story—she'd found him near a laurel. Maybe he'd have a happier fate than the character in the tale. With his infirmities he wasn't likely to attract the jealous attentions of any vengeful nymphs, at least. He was an obliging baby; as long as his stomach was full and his bindings were clean and dry, he made little bother of himself. Mostly he slept and seemed happy whether he was on his pallet in the apartment or beneath his woven shade in a corner of the agora. He was seldom noticed, except for the sympathetic soul who now and then glanced at him and tossed two coins at Amanis's feet instead of one.

"That's the last of the milk, little man," Damaris said, smiling into Daphnis's upturned face. "You've drained it, I'm afraid."

The baby wriggled and cooed, his eyes never leaving Damaris's face.

Amanis rubbed her tired feet. "He knows you as well as he knows me," she said, smiling.

"He's about ready to break out in a big grin," said Damaris as she stroked his cheek. "He's growing and changing so fast."

"I don't know how I'll manage when he starts to move around. I have to make a living, and I can't watch him constantly."

"Why not let him stay with me?"

Amanis looked at her. "Do you mean that?"

"Of course. Why else would I have said it?"

"Damaris, you are too kind."

"Oh, nonsense. What could be more natural?" She bent over Daphnis and took his left hand in her fingertips. "We'll let this precious little fellow come and stay with his Mêmê, won't we?" She covered the tiny hand with kisses. Daphnis gave a loud gurgle and wiggled excitedly.

"In fact, why don't you come, too?" she asked, straightening to look at Amanis.

"Leave Othar and Tarquinius? Oh, I…I don't think—"

"They're very dear to you, aren't they?"

"I hadn't really thought of it that way. That is…well, we look out for each other, I guess."

"Is that all it is?"

"Do you mean Othar and Tarquinius and me?" Amanis looked at her, astonished, and then began to laugh. "Oh, no," she said, "no, no, no. Not like that."

Damaris placed Daphnis on her shoulder, patting and rubbing his back until he gave one of his resounding burps. She leaned against the wall and settled him in her lap.

"Tarquinius and Othar rescued me from—from a bad situation. I owe them much."

Damaris smiled at her. "Of course. Just know that the offer is always there. And please let me keep Daphnis during the days."

Tarquinius and Othar came in then and the sight of them set Amanis to laughing again.

"What's wrong with her?" asked Tarquinius.

Damaris smiled sweetly at the dwarf and shrugged.

"How's the little one?" Othar asked.

"He just ate. Do you want to hold him?"

The German's eyes widened. He took a half step backward. "I don't know how."

"Oh, don't be such a big coward," said Amanis, still giggling as she raised herself to a sitting posture. "You won't break him."

Othar stared from one woman to the other, then at the baby. "What do I do?"

"Well, start by sitting down, right here beside me," said Damaris, patting the floor at her side.

"Now bend your arm a little—like that. Yes. All right. His

head goes here in the crook of your—that's it. A little more under his neck. There. See? You're doing fine."

"What if he does something on me?" Othar whispered.

"Then you'll wipe it off," Tarquinius said from his place by the brazier. "Like as not, it'll improve your smell." He shook his head and returned his attention to poking through the ashes, looking for a live coal.

"How was the game today?" Amanis asked Tarquinius.

"Only fair. In this heat people aren't too interested in whiling away their time in the markets. If we don't get some cooler weather soon, I imagine we'll starve."

"A usual sort of day then," Amanis said. "Here." She tossed a purse at him. "Three obols, give or take."

"Not bad. I may have to take up juggling."

"Oh, that reminds me," said Damaris. "Amanis, can you hand me my bag?"

Amanis slid the satchel toward Damaris. She dug in it for a moment, then produced a bundle wrapped in gauzy linen. The yeasty smell of the round loaf reached Amanis's nostrils.

"One of my friends baked this for you," Damaris said. She went over to Tarquinius and handed him the bread. He nodded his thanks, inspected the loaf for a moment, then set it aside and went back to his fire.

"Well, I must be going," Damaris said.

Othar looked at her in panic. "Please, don't leave me here like this."

"The great German warrior," Amanis said. She raised herself from her pallet and went to him. "Here. I'll take him."

"You did very well," Damaris said to Othar. "You just need a little more practice."

Damaris left. Amanis stood holding the baby, watching

Tarquinius for a moment. He'd found a promising coal and was blowing on it, feeding it tinder.

"It's so hot, Tarquinius. Why not leave off the fire today? We've got bread, and I think there are still some dates and apricots left from yesterday."

Tarquinius shrugged. "Fine with me. Let's eat then."

Amanis put Daphnis down on his stomach in the corner. She placed a ball of brightly colored rags near his head. He turned his face toward the ball and began to kick and wriggle. He grasped the ball with his left hand and tried to raise himself, but the underdeveloped right arm failed to support him. Amanis smiled down at him and went over to join Othar and Tarquinius around the food baskets. Tarquinius was breaking the still-warm loaf Damaris had brought. He handed it around.

As they were eating, Tarquinius turned to Amanis. "Why does she do it?"

"What do you mean?"

"Helping you with the baby. Bringing us food. Bringing us money. Why?"

"She is…good. Kind. Why else would she do it?"

The dwarf held her gaze for a moment, then studied the apricot in his hand. "I've met very few people who did me kindnesses without wanting something in return."

"What could she want from me? She knows I have nothing." Amanis glanced toward the corner; Daphnis was still absorbed in his attempts to grasp the rag ball, kicking his feet against the mat on which he lay. She looked back at Tarquinius. "I think she just wants to help. I think that's all there is to it."

"I like her," Othar said. "Her heart is strong."

"And what would you know about her heart?" Tarquinius asked.

Othar tossed a handful of dates into his mouth and chewed, watching Daphnis.

Amanis heard Tarquinius snoring and saw Othar stretched out just inside the open doorway. She reached toward Daphnis's bed and laid a hand softly on his back, feeling the small, even breaths. The baby didn't stir when she touched him.

She rose from her mat and moved silently to the doorway, stepping carefully over Othar. She leaned against the frame, holding her shift away from her to let the breeze cool her skin. She stepped onto the balcony.

The stars hung immobile in the humid sky. Amanis picked out the lady in her chair and found the great bear and her cub. Higher up was the lion, its cub not far below. Tonight's sky was crowded with parents and children.

Amanis tried to remember some of the god-stories of her people, the stories her mother told her. She remembered the warmth in her mother's voice. She remembered the gentleness of her hands. She remembered the way her mother's smile illuminated her face, her teeth as perfect as pearls against the dark beauty of her countenance. She could even remember the spicy scent of her mother's skin. But she couldn't remember a single one of the god-stories.

What stories would she tell Daphnis? Amanis wondered. A child needed stories to make him strong, especially a child like Daphnis. But all he had was her. No—he had Damaris, didn't he? She would tell him stories of her Christ.

But how could stories about a god on a cross be of any aid to a child like Daphnis—or to anyone?

And yet...Othar was right: Damaris had a solid heart. She

had called herself Daphnis's *mêmê*—grandmother. A smile teased Amanis's lips. She had also called Amanis *daughter*. What story could ever explain such a strange family?

The moon had set; there was only the silent song of the wheeling stars. Until the great, sleek shape padded through the entryway.

Amanis caught her breath. Had the watchman failed to set the bolt? How else could the lion have entered the atrium? She watched, wide-eyed and silent, as the beast paced slowly around the perimeter of the atrium, now and then pausing to sniff the air. It stopped at the base of the stairway, smelling the ground, the steps. And it began to climb.

Amanis flattened herself against the wall and sidled into the room. She leaned down and shook Othar. "Wake up!" she hissed. "Where is your knife?" The German snored on. Cursing under her breath, she stumbled through the darkness to her corner. She grabbed at her bag, rummaged through its contents until her hand found the sikhimi. She stood over Daphnis, panting in the darkness with the blade ready.

She could hear the lion's pads scraping against the stone steps. She heard the balcony creak beneath the beast's weight; she heard the rough rasp of its breathing. Its mane and shoulders filled the doorway. The lion was looking at her, and its eyes glowed as yellow as lamplight. Amanis tried to scream, but no sound would come from her throat. The lion sniffed at Othar, then stepped over him. It was coming toward her. The baby awoke and began to cry. "Mother," Amanis croaked as the lion came closer. "Mother."

She sat up. The sun was already high in the morning sky. Why had she slept so late? Daphnis was fussing. No wonder—it was well past the time when he should have been changed and fed.

Her heart was still racing from the dream. She hadn't thought of the lion and his steady pursuit for years now—not since coming to Athens, in fact. Why had he returned to haunt her sleep with those eyes so bright with knowing?

She rubbed her face and looked around. A few crusts of bread and a melon rind lay on the floor near the brazier. The water basin stood on edge, propped against the wall. She took it to the urn and filled it, then splashed some water on her face. She went over to the fretting infant and gathered him up.

"Well, now, Daphnis. Did you think I was ignoring you?"

The baby quieted almost immediately, his eyes fixed on her face.

"Let's get you cleaned up and fed. Then I'll take you to Damaris...to your Mêmê." Amanis liked the sound of the strange word. She thought of the way Damaris had with the child. Yes, let him call her that if he would. It seemed appropriate.

She unwound his swaddlings and tossed the soiled wraps in a basket for washing. She soaked a rag in the washbasin and cleaned him, then rubbed his tiny body with olive oil. She put fresh bindings on him. He began to whimper again when she laid him on his pallet.

"Wait a bit, child, wait a bit. I'm getting it as quickly as I can." She poured some milk into a small bowl, then crumbled bits of the remaining bread into it. She carried the bowl to her corner and picked Daphnis up, settling him in her lap so that he leaned back against her.

She spooned the mush into the greedy little mouth. Daphnis fussed between spoonfuls and Amanis chided him for his impatience. As his belly began to fill, he grew calmer. She scraped the last of the mush out of the bottom of the bowl and spooned it into his mouth, then put him back on his pallet with the rag ball for company.

"Entertain yourself for a while until I get ready," she told him.

She splashed a little more water on her face and hands, then donned her chiton and himation. She tied her sandals on her feet and a piece of thin cloth over her head and shoulders; the thought of wearing her hooded robe in this heat was too miserable. She glanced inside her satchel to make sure it contained everything for the day's work: the wooden balls, her coin purse, a hollowed gourd for drinking, and the sikhimi. On a whim she put in a strip of cloth for a blindfold; she'd been doing some practice with it, and such a stunt might draw a crowd.

Amanis fashioned a cradle from a wide piece of cloth and draped it over her shoulder. She scooped up Daphnis and settled him in. With her satchel strapped across her other shoulder she pulled the door shut behind her and went down the stairs.

Seventeen

hat else did she tell you today?"

"She told me that not even a sparrow dies without God knowing about it. She said He cares for the grass and the flowers, but He loves us most of all."

They were almost to the tenement. Amanis moved slowly, matching her pace to Daphnis's. His halting gait was somewhere between a step and a hobble; she wished he would just let her pick him up, but the six-year-old insisted that he wanted to walk. Sometimes his determination broke her heart; sometimes, like now, it just made her impatient.

"I wonder where Mêmê gets such ideas," Amanis said.

"She says the Christ said it. She told me the Christ healed the lame. Can he heal me, Mother?" His eyes were on her in that way he had: watchful, serious.

"I don't know, Daphnis. You'll have to ask Mêmê."

"Well, I'm going to ask God to heal me. Mêmê says that if we ask God for something and believe in him, He'll do it. The Christ said so."

A sudden grief lodged in her throat. What was Damaris thinking? Kindling such foolish hopes in the innocent heart of a child! "Come, Daphnis, I'm tired. Let's get home."

"You don't believe in the Christ, do you, Mother?"

"Is that what Mêmê told you?"

"No. I just thought of it myself."

"What does she say about me?"

"She says how lucky I am that you found me on the hillside. She says your heart is good and you love me very much. She says what you did for me is like what the Christ does for everyone."

A harsh laugh escaped her. "Is that so? Well, in that case, I'm going to pray to this Christ, too. I'm going to ask Him to tell my little magpie to quit talking so much and move his feet toward home."

"Oh, Mother, you can't pray for things like that! Only big things—important, good things. Like being able to run. And having two good arms. What's wrong, Mother? Are you all right?"

"Yes, Daphnis. I'm fine." She forced a weak smile.

Othar and Tarquinius were just arriving from the opposite direction when they reached the tenement gate. Daphnis grinned and limped quickly toward the kneeling Othar, who hoisted the boy onto his shoulders and stood. The fingers of Daphnis's sound hand gathered the two thick braids like the reins of a horse.

"Well, Squirt," Tarquinius said, peering up at the boy, "did you make any money today?"

"Not today."

The dwarf shrugged in mock apathy. "Tomorrow then," he said, completing their ritual.

Daphnis sat cross-legged in the light of the doorway with his clay tablet in his lap. The tip of his tongue crept back and forth across his upper lip as he concentrated on the words Dionysius had drawn in the clay for him to copy.

Hecate roused herself from where she lay at Othar's feet and moved to Daphnis, arching her back as she leaned against him. He ran a hand idly down the cat's spine. Othar had originally christened the animal some unpronounceable German name that Tarquinius refused to attempt. The dwarf had spitefully named her Hecate, after the queen of darkness. To Othar's disgust, the name had stuck. She preened and purred, then strolled through the open doorway.

Amanis checked Daphnis's work. The boy's imitations were nearly as concise as his teacher's. His mind seemed to her like a clay tablet, still moist from its making; everything passing over it stuck and held fast. Sometimes, to her amazement, he would repeat entire conversations from months earlier. And once his prompting had reminded her of the event, she would see that his recollection was practically word perfect. Damaris had told her that old Dionysius had already started the boy reading some of the simpler passages in Homer. This didn't mean much to Amanis, but the pride in Damaris's manner made it evident this was a good thing.

What was it all for? she wondered. Let him learn everything there was to learn, and what would it matter? He would still be lame, with only one useful arm. Such thoughts shamed her, but she couldn't help worrying. In her experience sooner or later the unprofitable or unlucky were cast aside or eliminated altogether. Shouldn't she try to prepare him for that? To warn him somehow?

But as she watched his rapt face, these questions faded. Daphnis was fascinated with learning. If mastering his letters and numbers gave him pleasure, why not let him have as much of it as he could get?

She considered what he had said about being healed by Damaris's Christ. She couldn't deny Damaris's love for the boy— nor that of her Christ-follower friends, for that matter. Damaris's sponsorship had opened to him—and to her—all of the aid and goodwill the group had to offer. Damaris and her friends had not stopped with those early gifts of food, money, and clothing. Any time one of the boys of the Way outgrew a garment, it arrived, freshly cleaned and mended, at Amanis's doorstep. One of them, a leatherworker, had fashioned a special boot for the boy's deformed foot; he had worn out three of them already. Dionysius served as the boy's tutor for no pay other than the enjoyment of teaching one so eager to learn.

But with the gifts came the stories. Would these strange beliefs make him strong? Or would they only teach him to hope for what he could never have? Maybe she should have a talk with Damaris.

The next morning she waved good-bye to Daphnis as he hurried through the gate into Damaris's small courtyard. As usual the older woman stood just inside her doorway, arms wide open and welcoming. As the boy reached her, she kneeled and pulled him into her embrace. She gave Amanis a smile and a quick wave, then pulled the gate shut behind them.

Amanis stared at the closed gate. Over the wall she heard Daphnis's voice chattering happily to the older woman, heard the step-drag, step-drag of his progress across the courtyard. Later, Dionysius would come to give Daphnis his lessons. Behind this gate was everything he needed. Behind this gate he was discovering life.

She turned to go, but her feet wouldn't carry her on down Melite to the agora. For some reason she was walking back the way she had come, until she arrived at Melite's crossing. The east was still red-rimmed with the sunrise, but already the thorough-fare hummed with carts, pack animals, porters, and merchants. Amanis let herself be carried along by the flow.

In a little while she was walking southwest on the road between the Long Walls. The traffic around her gradually changed as she neared the Piraeus Gate and entered the road to the harbor; there were fewer merchants and peddlers, more drays and donkey carts. The voices were gradually becoming coarser, too, as longshoremen and wharf slaves replaced the merchants and their agents. She didn't know why she was going to the harbor. She knew only that behind her lay many voices, all speaking to her at once. Damaris, Tarquinius, Daphnis, Fortuna, the Christ and his people, even those who watched her juggle in the agora and tossed their coppers—all of them were beckoning to her, needing something, asking questions and accusing and giving and smiling and leaning in on her and watching to see what she might do. They pulled at her, jostling her in different directions.

Perhaps the air of the harbor would sweep the voices from her mind. Maybe the smell of strange places and the sound of unfamiliar tongues would keep her from drowning in uncertainty.

By the time she reached Piraeus, the sun was halfway up a sky the color of dusty brass. The heat's shimmering mantle swathed everything she could see. Black-headed gulls and terns swirled all about the Munychia pier, filling the air with their squawking.

Amanis had a sudden memory of the birdman from the

troupe. Horatius—wasn't that his name?

After they've been with me a while, they usually don't leave.

White feathers erupted just down the pier, as three or four gulls screamed at one another over some bit of offal.

Maybe I've got it all wrong. Maybe the best thing I could do for Daphnis would be to get on one of these ships and sail away to— wherever. He's better off with Damaris, probably.

She could see the square sail of a ship, far out in the harbor, passing through the neck at Kantharos. Idly, she wondered where it hailed from. What would happen if she found a ship bound for Africa? Maybe she would look for her people. She would display the knife until someone recognized Apedemak. She would surround herself with people whose skin was the same dark brown as her own. She would fill the empty place in her heart with their names, their stories. She would be free.

Her belly ached. It had been a long time since breakfast. Amanis ignored the pangs for a while, unwilling to leave her silent perch and reenter the world of choosing and being. Finally she had to admit her need.

She started walking. She reached into her bag and brought out the balls that Damon had given her years before. She tossed and caught them with the same hand as she walked. She smiled. If she ever saw Damon again, she would thank him.

She heard a noise from a nearby wharf. Men were shouting and arguing—and then there was the roar of a lion. Her hunger forgotten, she walked toward the sound.

A ship had just docked, and a crew was winching crates out of its hold onto the dock. The ship held a cargo of beasts. She saw birds with long necks and black-and-white plumage, their legs as big around at the thigh as a man's. There were great, spotted cats, snarling within their cages at the tumult around them.

There were striped, horse-like creatures that made yipping noises as they fretted in their confinement.

And dangling in the air from a winch was the crate holding the lion.

The man who was apparently receiving the animals didn't have available transportation for them from the dock to their final destination. It seemed, from the loud arguing, that he was demanding the animals be left on board until his wains arrived. Otherwise the dockmaster would charge him an outrageous fee for storing the animals. He had paid a ridiculous sum to the captain for bringing the beasts from Africa, he claimed, and he shouldn't be forced to incur more charges because the ship arrived earlier than anyone expected.

It was hardly his fault, the captain shouted, that the winds had been better than anticipated. Let the menagerie man look to his own troubles; the beasts were coming off his ship without further delay.

As all this was going on, the lion swung to and fro in the air, clawing frantically to maintain his balance in the crate. His eyes showed white, and fear lathered his jaws. All the beasts looked starved and ill-used from their voyage.

Amanis looked at the lion for a long time. She tried to find some connection with the beast that sometimes stalked her dreams. But this was only a pitiful, caged animal. Its eyes held no knowing, only brute terror. What swung in the air before her was no god, no omen. Only a frightened beast. With a strange sadness, she turned away.

The market in Piraeus was a bustling, squalid place. Not too far away from the entrance, a crone dispensed unwatered wine from a goat skin. The skin hung on a pole jammed into the ground, and she had a collection of clay cups stacked on the mat beside her. The line to her stall was long and growing. Amanis took the balls from her bag and worked her way to a place as near the wine seller as possible.

She had just begun drawing a small crowd when screaming erupted on the other side of the crowded market. Then she heard the roar. Amanis whirled around to see the lion, its flanks gashed and bleeding, running pell-mell through the market. The lion sent patrons shrieking right and left in its frenzied dash.

With a dozen or so others, Amanis cowered behind some large clay urns until the lion ran limping down a side street. A moment later a squadron of troops trotted into the market and were quickly pointed in the direction the lion had taken.

Soon the man who had purchased the lion dashed into the market, staring this way and that. Amanis went up to him.

"What happened? How did your lion get loose?"

He gave her a frightened look. "Shut up!" he hissed. "Are you trying to get me mobbed?"

The soldiers came out of the side street carrying the dead lion, its feet bound around a long pole. The lion's owner gave a cry of despair.

The commander strode quickly up to him. "This was your property?" he demanded.

The man nodded.

"Come with us. There'll be a heavy fine for this, like as not. You'll have to speak to the centurion."

Amanis felt a strong desire to see Daphnis, to look into his shining eyes and be certain that he was safe. She started toward the road back into Athens. Just as she was about to exit the market, she looked down and spotted a loaf of bread that had been trampled during the melee. She picked it up, dusted it off, and began eating as she walked back toward the city.

Eighteen

The image of the lion, its bleeding body hung upside down from the pole, haunted Amanis all the way back into Athens.

She guessed the crate must have fallen from the winch line and broken open on the docks. She tried to imagine the shouting, the scattering of dockworkers and handlers. She tried to picture the lion, dazed from its fall, perhaps for a few moments unable to recognize the destruction of its prison.

By the time she arrived at Damaris's gate, the sun indicated that it was midafternoon. It was quiet on the street; most folk were seeking shade from the heat of the day. Amanis raised her hand to knock but for some reason could not. What was this sudden fear that kept her from summoning a servant and rejoining Daphnis as she intended?

Suddenly the door opened and she jumped back, startled. A servant holding a basket and carrying a water jar on her head stood in the gateway. She stared back at Amanis with much the same expression Amanis was probably wearing.

"Is the boy still here?"

"Yes. With the mistress in her chamber." The servant studied Amanis with curious eyes.

"I'm sorry. I was just about to knock when you—it startled me."

The servant bowed her way around Amanis and left on her errand. Amanis went in, closing the gate behind her. She strode to the water urns along the far wall and dipped her hand into the fullest container, splashing a little water on her face and rubbing it on the back of her neck. She cupped her hand and drank a few swallows. She took one or two deep breaths and walked toward the doorway to Damaris's chamber.

She stood in the opening for some time before either of them saw her. Damaris was sitting on the floor, and Daphnis was in her lap. He was reading from a clay tablet.

"'For the message of the cross is foolishness to those who are perishing,'" he read slowly, "'but to us who are being saved it is the power of God.'"

"Very good! Daphnis, your reading is becoming quite good."

"Thank you, Mêmê. But where did Dionysius get this exercise? This isn't like reading Homer."

She laughed. "No, my little scholar, I daresay it isn't. But then, Homer didn't sound like Homer for scores of generations, or so some say."

He looked at her with a puzzled expression, then spotted Amanis.

"Mother!" He scrambled from Damaris's lap and made his way quickly toward her, hugging her fiercely around the waist. "You're here early. Wouldn't anyone in the agora pay you for your juggling?" He looked up at her, his forehead creased with worry.

"No, boy, nothing like that," Amanis said, kneeling and smiling at him. "I just decided to come a little before my usual time, that's all."

He looked at her silently.

"What's wrong?" she asked.

"Nothing." But his eyes never left her face. When she glanced at Damaris, the older woman was studying her, too.

"Daphnis, will you ask Eirene for some of those fresh apricots?" Damaris said. "Bring enough for me and for your mother."

The child rose and went out.

"Why are you looking at me that way?" Amanis asked in a low voice.

"I'm not sure. Something happened today?"

Amanis watched Daphnis's irregular gait carry him across the courtyard.

"I don't know," she answered finally. "I didn't go to the agora. I walked to Piraeus."

"Why?"

Amanis looked at her sharply. "I already said that I don't know! Something just—told me to. I thought about leaving—getting on one of the ships and going wherever it took me."

"Why?"

"I don't know!" She stood quickly and paced to the doorway, then back again. She realized that her fists were clenched. "Daphnis is so happy here with you. And his lessons with Dionysius—you can give him so much more than I ever could, things I don't even know about. Letters and numbers and Homer and—and whatever that was he was reading when I came."

"A part of one of the letters of Paul," Damaris said quietly. "He taught us about—"

"Yes, I know, about this Christ who died and came back to life." She continued to pace as she spoke. "Maybe I should just leave Daphnis to you and your Christ. Maybe he'd be happier."

She whirled around to pace back toward the doorway and saw Daphnis there, holding an armful of apricots and staring at her.

"Mother? You're leaving?"

Amanis looked at his stricken face and was on her knees in an instant, holding out her hands to Daphnis. "No, child, no. I was—I was upset, just now. Come here. Let me hold you."

He ran to her as quickly as his deformed foot would allow. Apricots scattered along the floor as he reached for her. Amanis inhaled the smell of him, felt the softness of his hair against her cheek. His good hand clutched her as if he meant to never let go. Then, all at once, he released her and rocked back, peering at her with those eyes that missed nothing. Could a woman who produced a child from her own body possibly feel a bond any stronger?

"Daphnis, why don't you give your mother some apricots? And I think I'd like some, too," Damaris said.

He gathered the fallen fruit and handed each of them a portion, keeping one apricot for himself.

"Mêmê, can I go play with Hector?"

"Of course, dear. Mind you wash your hands after."

He went out to find the old dog Damaris kept in place of a night watchman.

"A bright one, he is," Damaris said when he was gone.

"Maybe his mind makes up for what his body lacks," Amanis said.

Damaris nodded. "God has blessed him."

Amanis stared at the fruit in her lap. "Your god has an odd idea of blessing, then."

"You're doing all that can be done for him, Amanis. When all is said and done, Daphnis is in God's hands. He will appoint your child's days, as he does for each of us. Just don't spend so much energy worrying over him that you forget to love him. He's a very smart boy. He'll manage."

Amanis looked out the doorway. "If his days are appointed, then maybe I should have left him on the side of the Hill of the Nymphs, to whatever awaited him there."

"No! God has placed this child in your path for a reason. He has some purpose for him. Never doubt that."

"Purpose? What purpose? How can a god care about a crippled baby? Or about the one who picked him up off the ground?"

"What are you afraid of, Amanis?"

Amanis swung around. Damaris's eyes were fastened on her. "What do you mean, 'afraid'?"

"Fear is an old adversary of mine. I've fought the long war with him, and I can always recognize a fellow-in-arms."

Amanis stood and began pacing again. She took a vicious bite from an apricot and waved the fruit at Damaris. "What do you know about fear? You're a free woman. You've got friends to look out for you and money to buy what you need. What do you have to be afraid of?"

"You aren't free?"

Amanis clenched her jaw and said nothing. There was a long silence.

"As I watched my husband and child coughing out their lives, I asked again and again for the gods to take me, too," Damaris said finally. "I didn't want to live any longer in a world devoid of the two people I loved most. My husband was a good man, a kind man. He treated me gently and cared for me genuinely. And our little boy was such a darling—as bright as Daphnis and just as patient. Why were they taken and why was

I left? I asked this over and over.

"No, I didn't have to worry about starving like some widows. Xenocrates's family was well to do, as was mine, and with the dowry I'd brought and what his father willed me, I was far from having to beg for bread in the agora.

"But what good is money in the face of grief? What difference does it make if you can buy the richest sweetmeats but have to eat alone in a house fallen silent?"

Amanis stopped pacing. She watched Damaris, who kept her face down as she spoke, almost as if she had forgotten Amanis was present. Her voice sounded like something coming from far away, from a place of hurt and remembering.

"The anger was what brought me out of grief. When you hurt so much that you think you can hardly breathe, you either despair or you get angry. I railed at the heavens. My heart clenched like a fist until I was as dry and bitter as wormwood. I demanded an answer, and received none. That was when I decided to give myself an education."

Damaris chuckled and shook her head in amusement. "I decided if the universe wouldn't yield its secrets, I'd take them by force. I bought papyrus and vellum like an Alexandrian. I read Socrates, Plato, Aristotle, Epicurus, and Zeno until the third filling of the lamps nearly every night. I went to the agora and listened to the debates. I even became a regular at the meetings of the religious council of the Areopagus. They weren't too impressed by the surly woman in their midst. They ignored me when they could. All except Dionysius, bless him.

"And then one day when I was at a session of the Areopagus with Dionysius and the rest of them, some of the advocates and teachers from the agora brought in a man who called himself Paul. He was a Jew, and he was well educated. He even quoted

Aratus and Cleanthes. I'll never forget what he said. His words were like arrows aimed at my deepest pain, and every one struck true. When he told about how God made the Christ alive again, I knew I had to find out more."

"This sounds crazy to me, Damaris."

"That's what most of the teachers and lecturers said on that day in the Areopagus."

"But how can something dead become alive again? The spirit world I understand. Shades and ghosts and apparitions I've heard about since I was a child. Less than alive, lacking something—that makes sense to me. But you say your Christ was alive—in this world. That he even cooked food and ate it. How can that be?"

"I don't know." Damaris smiled. "And that's exactly the point of all this, Amanis."

"I don't understand."

"I was angrily demanding answers for my hurts, not knowing my anger was just a thin disguise for my fear: fear of being alone, fear of death, fear that my search was useless—that no answers existed. And all the time the cure for my fear lay in another direction, one I never suspected until I heard Paul. What I needed was something better than knowledge or answers, better even than safety. What I needed was hope. And that's what Paul gave me. As long as I have hope, I don't have to know. And I don't have to be afraid. Of anything. Ever."

Amanis stared at her for a long time, then turned away. She couldn't afford the risk. And yet...

"This hope you speak of—can it be allowed even to those who have forgotten their place and shamed their superiors?" She walked to the wall beyond the doorway. She leaned against the white stone and slid slowly down to the floor. When she was able, she lifted her gaze to meet Damaris's.

"I was born a slave, but my father was freed when I was very small," she began in a flat voice. "He was skilled in metal work and made a good living, from what I remember."

She told Damaris what she remembered of her mother. She told about the songs, the comfort and laughter. And when she talked about her mother's final sickness and dying, a tear slid down her cheek. It had been a long time since Amanis had felt the moist track of her own tears.

She told of her father's despair, and of how he sold her to the slaver Scaevolus. She told of the years in the house of her father's former master and current patron, of the anger and despair that burned long and deep.

Damaris sat silently, watching her like a navigator might watch the approaching line of an unfamiliar coast.

But when Amanis began speaking of the birth of the girl-child and the master's spurning of her, when she tried to explain the unexpected outrage that would not permit her to remain compliant in her master's house while the baby lay abandoned on the side of Mount Pion, Damaris sat forward. Now she was not only the attentive recipient of Amanis's words, but the curator of them.

"And that's why I'm in Athens," Amanis finished. "This slaver pursued me, even to Smyrna. I still don't understand why he was so determined to catch me, but I couldn't go on endangering the rest of my friends.

"Then, just over six years ago—something came over me again. I started going out to find exposed infants. I took them to the Jews. But I have violated fate so often that I think I've made myself a stench to her. And I fear for Daphnis, just as I feared for my friends before I came to Athens. What if Fortuna hates him as she hates me? What if I did him a cruelty by barring his quick exit from a world that can never cherish him enough? What if your Christ won't take me? What if He can't shield me from the destiny I've brought upon myself and everyone around me?"

Amanis glanced up and was surprised to see Damaris's cheeks moistened with tears. For a long time Damaris looked at Amanis, shaking her head slowly back and forth. She went on for so long that Amanis began to be afraid Damaris would order her from the house, or that she would send a servant to summon the authorities.

And then Damaris got up and came over to Amanis. She sank down beside her and pulled her into a tight embrace. Amanis could feel the wetness of Damaris's tears in the hollow of her neck. And something in the embrace and its warmth released something within Amanis that she had held in check for so many years. Her own tears began flowing freely; the dark grief of her abandonment rushed out of her with a force almost violent. She wept and wept and wept. And still Damaris held her, mingling her tears with Amanis's and saying, over and over, "Yes, my child. Yes. It's all right. Yes."

Nineteen

"I still don't see why you had to start telling her where the bean was."

"Uncle, you'd have taken her last three lepta."

"What business is that of yours? And quit calling me 'Uncle.' Your mother's about as much kin to me as Othar's old cat is to a dolphin. I can't figure out how you knew, but I know enough to leave you at home next time. I can't afford to start feeding the beggars of Athens just because you feel sorry for them."

Amanis heard Othar laugh as the three of them came through the doorway. Daphnis was a full head taller than Tarquinius, she realized. When had he grown so? True, he was still smaller than most boys his age, but she continually marvelled at his development. At moments like this, the twelve years since that evening when she had found him lying beneath the laurel bush seemed to have passed so quickly.

"It's not that hard, Uncle," Daphnis was saying. "You have a pattern. Once you know the pattern, it's easy."

The dwarf made a disgusted sound and flopped down cross-legged against the east wall.

"The boy's got you," Othar said with a wry grin. "You'll have to pay to keep him quiet. Otherwise, I'll see to it that everybody who comes into the agora knows your game."

"No, Uncle Othar," Daphnis said quickly, "I wouldn't do that."

"You're too softhearted for your own good, boy, you know that?" Othar made a lunge for the giggling boy and grabbed him around the waist. He flipped him upside down and shook him, as if Daphnis were a sack he was trying to empty. "I'll dump that softheartedness out of you."

Daphnis shrieked with laughter until Othar set him back on his feet. He staggered dizzily before collapsing in the middle of the floor.

The pot on the brazier was beginning to boil. Amanis dumped in a heaping double handful of beans, then another. She tossed in a fistful of dried oregano. She pulled an onion from the string hanging from a ceiling beam, quickly chopped it into quarters, and added it to the steaming mix. Soon the savory smell permeated the dwelling.

"I'll need to buy some more spices tomorrow," she said. "That was the last of the oregano."

"You need to buy wine first," said Tarquinius, eyeing the slack skin hanging near the door. "We'll have to drink water tonight."

"I'll go draw it," said Daphnis, getting to his feet. He grabbed the large ewer and went out. Amanis heard the uneven thumping of his footsteps on the walkway.

"How were the crowds today?" Othar asked.

"Not bad," Amanis said. "I worked the Acropolis. There was a big band of pilgrims at the Parthenon. I tried the fire on them."

Othar raised his eyebrows.

"It looks better in the dark, of course, but I needed the practice. I think I got about thirty or forty from them. They sounded like they were from Phrygia or Mysia—from somewhere in Asia Province, anyway."

"I wonder how things stand with Damon and the rest of them," Tarquinius said.

"I was thinking of that just the other day," said Amanis. "Do you think Thyrsis is still alive?"

Othar snorted. "That old woman won't ever die. I traveled with them for nearly ten seasons, and she never changed a bit that I could see."

Amanis grabbed one of the braids that hung down the German's chest and held it to the light coming from the window. "She may not have changed, but you have. This and the gray in your beard tell me that time has noticed you, whether you've noticed it or not."

Tarquinius gave a small chuckle. "Did you see Damaris today?"

"No. Agrippina said she's sick again."

"Maybe you should drop by. See if there's anything she needs."

Amanis nodded as the dwarf turned away. She stretched her hands over the mouth of the pot, enjoying the comforting warmth. It was the month of Anthesterion, and each year the cold worsened the ache in the joints of her fingers.

Daphnis came in and set down the long-necked ewer with a grunt. A little water splashed out onto the floor. "That really smells good, Mother. How long until we can eat?"

"Patience, boy, patience. The beans are still hard. Let it boil a while longer." She gave him a fond look. "Why don't you read to me while we're waiting?"

Daphnis gave her a quick grin and turned toward the small chest at the foot of his pallet. He rustled among the things there until he came up with a packet of papyrus, bound with a leather string. "I copied this out after the last assembly. Dionysius let me look at one of his books." He settled himself in the pool of light from the lamp, unfolded the paper, and began tracing with his finger along the line of the writing.

"And he entered again into the synagogue; and there was a man there who had a withered hand…"

Amanis felt a heaviness settle in her chest. Daphnis read on in a clear voice, telling again of how the Christ had mended the marred body of a man in a Palestinian synagogue; how the teachers of the Law had hated Him for it and begun plotting His destruction. When Daphnis read the words "his hand was restored whole as the other," he paused, glancing up at her before continuing.

How well she understood the desperate need for hope. Had not the compassion of Christ, poured through the lives of Damaris and the other Christians, finally melted the icy place in her own heart? Had not the comforting promise of His Spirit's presence and His eventual return given her the strength to cast off the yoke of despair fate had settled around her neck all those years ago?

But even as Daphnis read of the healing of the man's hand, his own deformed arm hung at his side, as useless as ever. His club foot still confined him to a limping gait, so painfully at odds with the beauty of his heart and the agility of his mind. If anything about her new faith was troubling to Amanis, it was this apparent gap between the actions and words attributed to Jesus Christ and the tangible benefits they actually conferred on His latter-day followers.

As Daphnis read on, Amanis watched Tarquinius and Othar. Tarquinius tried to act as if he were ignoring everything; he turned away from them to fuss with his belongings. Yet Amanis saw how carefully he kept an ear slightly tilted toward the boy, the way his hands stilled when he forgot himself. Othar, on the other hand, made no attempt to conceal his interest.

Amanis sometimes thought it might not be long before they, too, went down to one of the public baths to receive the ceremonial washing.

She still remembered her own baptism. When she had risen from the tepid water her skin had tingled with newness, like the healed flesh beneath a burn. Damaris, standing in the water beside her, held her while Dionysius intoned a blessing. Around the perimeter of the bath, Christians began their hymn:

Awake, O sleeper; arise from the dead.
And Christ will shine upon you…

Damaris had draped Amanis with a new robe as the hymn filled the air around them. One life was finished; another had begun. That was a good day.

She dipped a ladle into the boiling pot. "This is ready. Bring the bowls."

They ate in comfortable silence. They tore off chunks of bread and scooped out beans, trying not to scald themselves. The heat felt good going down, though. When the meal was finished, Amanis rinsed the bowls and the cooking pot, then poured the rinse water over the railing into the courtyard. When she came back inside, the other three were already bundled in their robes and blankets, lying on their pallets. She stacked the bowls and the pot beside the brazier, banked the fire, pinched

the wicks on the lamp, and lay down to sleep. She hoped tomorrow would be a little warmer.

Amanis blew on her hands as she entered the agora. An old man
huddled in his robes, squatting on the ground with his back
against the Agora Stone. He glanced up at her briefly, then pulled
back into the meager comfort of his wraps. Not many here,
which wasn't surprising given the weather. She could always try
the Acropolis, though she doubted it would be much better
there on a day like today.

The sky was clear except for high traces of wispy cloud. The
wind sweeping down from the Pindus highlands had a frigid
snap to it that would have been refreshing if she could retreat to
a cheering blaze when she felt like it. But there would be no
warming fire for her until she reached home again, when the
day's work was done. Too bad Draco wasn't working today; the
fire-eater had to keep a little flame going to refresh his torches.
It would have been some comfort anyway.

A small crowd huddled on the south side of the Old
Bouleterion; Amanis decided to start there. When she drew near
enough to overhear, it became plain they were discussing the
new emperor. Ever since news had come of Titus's death and the
ascension of his younger brother Domitian, speculation about
the death of Titus had become Athens's most popular pastime.

She reached into her bag and took out the leather balls. She
blew on her hands a final time, set down her empty money basket, and began to juggle.

Two or three of the men on the perimeter of the group began
to watch her. When one of them flicked a coin at her basket, she
reached into her bag and added a wooden ball to the pattern.

Another coin, another ball. They kept tossing coins in the basket, trying to see how many she could keep aloft. The next time she added a ball, she also tossed one at one of her watchers. The fellow chuckled and tossed it back, whereupon she tossed another ball at a different man.

"Is that fair, juggler?" one of them asked, smiling. "You require our aid to keep the balls in the air, yet you don't offer us any coin for our troubles."

"I keep trying to reach for the basket, but you keep throwing balls back at me," she answered. They laughed. Some of the others turned to see the source of the merriment. Her crowd grew.

She noticed that the old man from the Agora Stone had wandered over. Still hugging himself against the cold, he watched as she bantered with her audience.

Soon they were elbowing one another to catch the balls she tossed at them. They made wagers among themselves over how long Amanis could go before she dropped. They passed the balls from one to the other, trying to trick her by having a different person return the ball than the one who had caught it. Passersby paused to watch, then found themselves drawn into the fun. They smiled and laughed and jested and tossed coins into her basket.

By the time the crowd began to break apart, Amanis calculated she had almost four denarii. She would have been pleased with that much for two days' work, much less for a single chilly morning such as this.

It was almost midday and Amanis decided to go buy foodstuffs. She whispered a quick prayer of thanks, gathered the coins into her purse, and walked toward the South Stoa. Yesterday, near the old Nine-Spout Well, she had passed the stall of a spice merchant. She hoped he was still there.

By the time she had haggled with the spice seller and the wine purveyor, then selected a fowl from the meat vendor, the sun was dipping well into the afternoon. She slogged up the steps of the tenement, chilled and wishing someone already had the brazier kindled. To her surprise she walked into the room to find Tarquinius, Othar, and Daphnis huddled around the flames.

"Why are you back so early?" she asked.

"We might wonder the same about you," Tarquinius growled. "I see you tricked some meat vendor out of one of his less promising carcasses."

"I took in almost four denarii this morning. I decided to quit while I was ahead." She handed the wine skin to Othar, who hung it from a hook in the ceiling beam.

"You had a better morning than Uncle then," said Daphnis.

"Quiet," growled the dwarf. "I can tell my own troubles if I want to, which I don't."

"Bad day?" she asked lightly.

Othar hid a smirk and looked away.

"Here, Daphnis. Find the little pot with the lid and put this oregano in it. I'll go outside and get the chicken ready to cook." She turned toward the doorway and froze.

A hooded figure stood there. She realized it was the old man she had seen earlier in the agora. Just as she was about to ask him his business, a puff of wind pushed the hood back from his face.

"Scaevolus," she gasped hoarsely as the chicken fell to the floor.

Othar sprang to the doorway and grabbed the old man's throat in one huge hand. The slave trader clawed at the German's forearms.

"You shouldn't have followed us," said Othar between clenched teeth. "Now you will die."

Amanis heard herself calling out, saw her hands gripping Othar's shoulders. "No. Othar, don't."

He gave her an angry look, then jerked Scaevolus inside and threw him onto the floor. Othar kneeled on Scaevolus's chest, his fist in Scaevolus's face. "What do you mean? Why shouldn't we put an end to him, once and for all?"

"Please, Othar. Get off of him."

The German glared at her for a long moment. Then, growling under his breath, he removed his weight from the old man's chest.

Scaevolus lay gasping for breath. Finally he was able to speak. "At last, I've found you."

"How did you trace us to Athens?" Tarquinius said.

"Did you hurt our friends?" Othar yelled, bending to grip the front of the old man's clothing. He shook him. "Is that how you found out where we were?"

Daphnis put his hand on Othar's arm. "Don't. He's old and weak. He can't hurt you, can't you see that?"

Othar looked at the boy, then at Scaevolus. Slowly he lowered the slaver to the floor.

"Mother? What does he want?" Daphnis asked.

For a long time she stared at the frail man lying on the floor.

"I don't know," she said.

PART THREE

Redeemed

Twenty

Scaevolus put a hand to his throat and rubbed his neck. With difficulty he raised himself to a sitting position.

"Why are you here?" Amanis asked him.

"Because I need your help. You're the only person who can help me find her."

"What's this crazy old fool talking about?" Tarquinius said.

Scaevolus glanced at the dwarf, then back to Amanis. He looked at her with an expression that made her think of hunger—or despair.

"My daughter," he said.

Amanis stared at him, her mind engulfed by a whirlwind of thoughts and half-forgotten images. "What daughter do you speak of?" she was finally able to say.

"A little girl, born in the house of Patroclus of Ephesus. Exposed by his command. I sent my man to the hillside to bring her to me. But you were already there," he said, his eyes boring into her, "and you prevented him. By the time I found out who you were, you were gone."

"Your—your daughter?"

"Yes, Amanis. My daughter. Conceived in the embrace of Eurydeme, wife of Patroclus."

"What?"

"I loved her. Had loved her for years. We knew it was dishonorable, but neither of us had the will to bring it to an end. She was careful, Eurydeme was, but this time the medicines didn't work. 'Don't worry,' she told me. 'Patroclus will think the child is his.' She thought that ended it. She thought avoiding discovery was all I cared about.

"My child—the child I had made with my beloved—would never know me. I would never see my child play, never listen to her repeat her lessons. The thought tormented me." He looked up at her. His eyes were raw with grief.

"I paid a Gaulish girl in the household to keep me informed. And when Patroclus refused the infant, my happiness soared. I would have the child! I would bring her into my house, raise her as my own. She would have everything." He looked at her again. "But you kept that from happening, didn't you?"

"I thought the child would die."

"I understand. Incredible and frustrating as it was, even then I knew you acted out of concern for the baby. And I was willing to forgive, willing even to let you be her nurse, to pay you handsomely. But I couldn't find you."

"I thought you would kill me—if Patroclus didn't."

"Yes, Patroclus. He mourned Eurydeme's death in admirable fashion, didn't he?" He shook his head, then wiped his eyes with the back of his hand.

"She died of childbed fever."

He nodded slowly. "Yes. Of course."

There was a long silence.

"Are you hungry?" Daphnis asked. "We were about to make some supper."

Scaevolus looked at the boy, then at Amanis. "You brought him here?"

She nodded.

"So my daughter wasn't the last infant you saved." He smiled a sad smile. He looked up at Othar, who still stood with his arms crossed in front of him. "My large friend, I beg your pardon for intruding. I assure you, I did not harm your friends in Asia Province."

"You followed us to Smyrna," Tarquinius said.

"Yes. When it became clear to me that Amanis was no longer in Ephesus, I concluded she was traveling with you or some other band going in the same general direction. Your departure was memorable enough. Had I not been so anxious to find her, it would have been rather enjoyable to watch."

"You could have had the officials detain the troupe," Amanis said. "You had the power, the influence. You could have plucked me at any time."

"You'd already eluded me once, when I thought I had every hole stopped. And I needed your trust, to persuade you to take me to the child. A mass arrest didn't seem the right way."

Othar gave a wry laugh as he half-turned toward Scaevolus. "So all this time you've been trying to find Amanis because you were trying to find your daughter." The German looked at her. "You've been running from nothing."

"I followed your friends up and down the western end of Asia Minor," Scaevolus said. "I hoped against hope you were still among them, that seeing me in the agora on Smyrna hadn't sent you underground. But when two seasons had come and gone with no sign, I decided you'd left them. I began to despair.

"I spent money on bribes, on spies. I hired agents in every city, as far inland as Apamea and Laodicea. I traveled constantly, neglected my business, my property, everything. And then, one of my factors had a chance conversation with the captain of a merchantman out of Smyrna." He gave Othar another glance. "He remembered a big barbarian who threatened to cook and eat him if he didn't give passage to Athens."

Othar snorted and rolled his eyes.

"Daphnis, give our guest some wine," Amanis said. "Tarquinius, see if you can keep the fire from dying while I get this chicken ready for the stewpot." She picked up the fowl she had dropped and started toward the door before looking back at Scaevolus, still sitting cross-legged on the floor. "You will eat with us, won't you?"

"It's more than I had a right to expect, but yes, if you'll have me."

Tarquinius grunted and shook his head. "None of this makes any sense to me."

"Quiet, wart," Othar said. "Mind your fire."

Amanis looked at them all for a moment, then went out to dress the chicken.

That night she dreamed again of the lion.

She was on her back, sound asleep, when the warm puffs of breath woke her. And she knew without opening her eyes that the lion was standing over her, watching her with those lamp-bright eyes, breathing into her face.

The breath of the beast was sweet, like the smell of mint and thyme crushed together, and she took deep draughts of it. It calmed her, and it made her see.

She saw the face of the lion, huge and furry in the semidarkness above her, and Daphnis was standing next to it, dressed as if he were leaving on a journey. His good hand rested on the lion's back, and his fingers stroked its tawny hide. The lion turned toward the boy, and he buried his face in the thick mane. The lion padded toward the doorway, carefully stepping over the snoring Othar, and Daphnis followed. The lion preceded Daphnis through the entry, and just as her son was framed in the door, he stopped and turned to her, an expectant look on his face.

Amanis realized she was wearing her cloak, that her satchel was packed and lying under her hand. She got up and shouldered her bag. She followed the lion and her son out into the moonlight. She wondered briefly where they were going, then realized it didn't matter so much.

Amanis awoke the next morning with an expectant feeling in her breast. When she sat up, Scaevolus turned to look at her from where he sat crouched beside the brazier. Flecks of ash dusted his sparse beard and the front of his robe. A small flame licked the kindling he had stacked.

"Some almonds are in there," she said, indicating one of the clay canisters beside the door. "I'll go draw some water." She got up, gripping the ewer in one hand and balancing the night jar in the other, and went outside.

When she came back, he was poking a stick into the small but brisk blaze. He looked at her as she poured water into a cup and handed it to him.

"Did you sleep well?" she asked him.

"An old man doesn't need much rest. Before too many more days, I'll sleep forever." He jabbed the twig at the base of the fire.

"I only hope I can see my daughter before I die."

"Spring won't be here for another two months. Can you wait that long?"

He said nothing.

"The crossing is hazardous in winter," she said.

"Yet some will try it if the price is right."

"How much do you have?"

"Enough," he said after a pause. "But I can't go alone."

"I know." She searched within herself. "I must bring my son."

He nodded.

By the time they had both eaten a handful of almonds and sipped their water, Othar was stirring. He sat up and rubbed his eyes, watching as Amanis folded her things and placed them in her pack.

"Going somewhere?" he asked.

"I'm taking Scaevolus to find his daughter."

"Back to Ephesus."

She nodded. Othar scratched his beard. "Finding a ship won't be easy this time of year."

"He says he has money."

"Enough, I hope," added Scaevolus, smiling weakly.

"Enough money for what?" Tarquinius was sitting up and blinking in the morning light.

"They're going back to Ephesus," Othar said. "Today, it looks like."

"Mother?"

"Calm yourself, Daphnis. I wouldn't leave you here with your rascally uncles."

"Who says his uncles are staying here? Othar, toss me my bag. I was getting tired of Athens anyway. Time for a change of scenery is what I say."

"I…I don't know if there's enough—"

"Don't worry, old fellow." Tarquinius reached behind him, snaking his stubby arm between an urn and the wall. He dug around for a moment, then came back out with a leather pouch. He gave it a small shake, and Amanis heard the muted jingling of coins. "I always put a little something back for special occasions."

"Like drowning," muttered Othar.

Amanis stood and reached for Daphnis's hand. "Come on. There's a place we have to go before we leave."

When Amanis and Daphnis came into the room, the young woman sitting beside Damaris's bed looked up at them. Then she smiled down at the old woman. "Someone is here to see you," she said. She put a hand under Damaris's neck to lift her head.

Amanis smiled. She felt a place tightening in her throat, but she managed to say, "Grace and peace, dear friend."

"Amanis," said Damaris. Then she began coughing in great spasms.

Amanis started to pull Daphnis out of the room, but Damaris shook her head and waved them back. The young woman held her shoulders until the coughing stopped. Then she eased Damaris back onto her bed.

Daphnis went to her bedside and took her hand. "Mêmê, I'm sorry you're…I wish you felt better."

She patted his hand and gave him a weak smile. "Don't worry about me, boy. Soon this cough will be no more than a memory, if that."

Amanis stood on the other side of her. She smoothed back a wisp of the white hair on Damaris's forehead. "We're leaving,

Damaris," she said. "We're going back to Ephesus."

Damaris looked up at her for a while, studying her face. "Good. But why?"

Amanis looked out the window. "Something I have to do."

She felt Damaris's hand patting her arm. The sick woman's touch felt as insubstantial as the brushing of a leaf. "Or finish?"

Amanis looked at her. A tiny smile twitched at the corners of her lips.

"Mêmê, I'll miss you," Daphnis said. "I hope I can see you again soon."

Another fit of coughing shook her. There were flecks of blood on her lips when she lay back.

"Don't hope that, child. Not yet. The day will come when my destination will be yours, but I pray not for a long time."

Daphnis's forehead wrinkled. Damaris smiled at him and reached toward his cheek. "Never mind, Daphnis. Just a silly old woman talking when she ought to be quiet. Come here."

She pulled him toward her. Daphnis laid his head on her chest as her arms went around him. She whispered something in his ear. When he straightened, Amanis could see the course of tears on his cheeks.

"We'd better be going," Amanis said, the place in her throat tightening again.

"Wait. Come here," Damaris said. She beckoned with her hands. Amanis hesitated, then put her ear close to the old woman's lips.

"The way of love, daughter. Always choose the way of love."

Amanis felt the arms encircling her. She let her face fall onto the shriveled bosom. She took a quiet, gasping breath, then another, and she raised herself to look into Damaris's eyes. "Good-bye, dear one. And thank you."

Twenty-one

The day was a trifle warmer, and the Long Walls prevented most of the wind. By the time they reached Piraeus, Amanis could feel sweat trickling down her scalp. "Shouldn't we buy food in the market?" she asked, tugging her hood back from her face. "We didn't have much in the house when we set out."

"At least you had breakfast," Tarquinius said. "I'm starving."

"I smell bread baking," Daphnis said. "Maybe they'll have some for sale."

"Either that, or they just want to torture hungry folk," said the dwarf.

"I used to know a man who bought shares in shipping concerns," Scaevolus said. "He traveled in Asia Province quite a lot, but I think he was from Athens. If we could locate him or one of his agents, I think I could persuade him to get us on the next ship across the Aegean."

"How did you know him?" Othar asked.

"I sold him galley slaves."

No one said anything for a few moments.

"Let's hope none of your stock is working whatever ship we land on," Tarquinius said finally. "They might not remember you fondly."

They found the market and located a stall selling bread and dried apples. At another place, they spotted a few oilskin cloaks, which seemed like a wise purchase. Then they wandered down toward the docks to see if they could make connection with Scaevolus's acquaintance or, failing that, anyone desperate or greedy enough to permit them to book passage to Asia Province as soon as possible.

The Munychia Harbor docks in winter presented a much different aspect than when Amanis had last been here. A few ships rode at anchor beside the quays. Several craft sat on blocks, having their hulls scraped and readied for the next summer's shipping season. Aside from that, it was a quiet, still place. Even the gulls were mostly absent. The loudest sound was the lapping of the waves.

"So where is this fellow you know?" Tarquinius asked.

"I've never been to Athens before," Scaevolus answered. "How would I know where to find him? I guess he must have some place near the docks."

"What's his name?" Othar asked. Scaevolus told him, and Othar walked over to the nearest dry-docked boat. He hailed the men scraping the hull, and several of them turned toward him. Amanis saw one of them point at some buildings up the way. Othar turned and beckoned to them. "We're in luck. This ship belongs to him. One of his stewards stays right over there."

The building was low and blocky, built of rough-hewn stones. It squatted in front of a row of long, ramshackle sheds built of planks. A crew of slaves was pushing a large bundle on a sledge into the nearest shed as the travelers approached the steps of the stone building. Square windows, crisscrossed by iron bars, were mounted on either side of the door. Othar knocked, and a face showed at the right-hand window.

"Who's there?"

"Someone to see your master. We want passage to Asia Province."

The face disappeared, and a moment later someone was working the latch. The door swung open with a squeak, and they went into the building. The interior was dark and smelled of new rope and pitch. The bowlegged man who had opened the door jerked a thumb toward a short hall leading away from the entry. Then he shuffled back to a low stool beneath the window.

They knocked on the first door down the hallway, and a voice told them to enter. They stepped into a room stacked from floor to ceiling with casks, pots, bales, and bundles of every size and shape. A space maybe a man-length wide ran down the center of the room to a massive, scarred oak table. Seated at the table with his back to them was a man in a robe of scarlet wool striped with brown and black. He sat with one elbow on the table, his head propped in his hand. He appeared to be scanning a papyrus folio; they could hear him muttering to himself.

"Piracy. Sheer piracy. Better off to curse them to their faces and take our chances."

Scaevolus gave a discreet cough and the man at the table jerked around to face them.

"Well? Have you brought them?"

"Brought what?" Othar asked.

"The vials! The vials of rhinoceros horn, you fools. Don't toy with me, I haven't the time."

"What are you talking about?" Tarquinius said.

The man's eyes bulged at them for a moment, then he gave

an exasperated sigh and turned his face to the ceiling. "Lepus! The fool! May Athena strike him with a plague."

"We told the man at the door we wanted to book passage," began Scaevolus.

"Yes, Lepus. Deaf as a stone. Can't hear thunder. Probably thought you were the people I've been waiting for all morning."

"Rhinoceros horn?" said Othar. "From Africa?"

"Yes, the plague take it. Is it my fault if some doddering landowner with more money than sense marries a girl young enough to be his granddaughter and then can't answer the call? Waste of a ship and a bigger waste of money, especially at the rates these local pilots charge."

Scaevolus gave a quiet laugh. "Ah, friend. To an old man with little time left, money means less than you think."

The man looked at him strangely. "Why are you here then?"

"We require passage to Asia Minor. I'm an old friend of Tryphimus."

The man's eyes widened, but he said nothing.

"We're interested in getting to Ephesus as soon as possible," Scaevolus went on, "but we'll accept berths on the first east-bound ship you have." He reached into his robe and brought out a pouch. "I'm prepared to pay."

They heard footsteps scuffing down the hall toward the door. Two men came in, and one of them held aloft two small bottles stopped with corks. "Here you are, Tryphimus," he called in a triumphant voice. "The purest ground horn in Attica. Enough to keep you and your new wife busy for a good while."

The man stalked across the room and snatched the vials from the other's hand. He jerked a purse from his belt and flung it, striking the other man in the chest.

"Well, don't thank me so extravagantly," the man said. "You'll make me blush in front of these good folk." With a last grin at Tryphimus, he and his companion left.

There was an abashed pause.

"Perhaps it would have been more correct to say I was once an acquaintance," Scaevolus said.

Tryphimus gave him a hard look. "Yes, I remember you. The slave trader, from Ephesus." He turned and walked back toward the table, eyeing the vials in his hand. "Never mind. The years have changed us both a good deal. You say you want to go to Ephesus?"

Scaevolus nodded.

"Well, as it happens, so do I. My—my new wife is waiting there for me. So. You say you've got money?"

"Go on with you, then! And may all your sons be redheads!"

The pilot turned as he climbed over the gunwale of the ship and made an obscene gesture toward Tryphimus. Then he dropped over the side into the smaller boat that would take him back to the harbor.

"A plague on all pilots," Tryphimus said. "Bunch of robbers, the lot of them. Well, what are you waiting for?" he shouted at the slaves standing near the mainmast. "Do you think we'll have favoring winds for the rest of our lives?"

The crew began hauling on the lines, and the yard climbed slowly up the mast, carrying with it the bleached expanse of the square sail. The wind billowed, the bow dipped slightly, and the ship was again underway.

Tryphimus watched critically as the crew made fast the lines. He strode back to the helmsman and talked to him for a moment, then disappeared into the cabin at the stern.

Amanis watched worriedly as Daphnis leaned over the gunwale. The boy had been in constant motion since they came on board, trying to miss nothing. Now he was peering excitedly at the prow as it cut through the water, throwing a white comb to either side.

"How long will it take to get to Ephesus?" he asked one of the crew who squatted nearby, coiling and tying down the surplus rope from one of the mainsail lines.

The grizzled old slave smiled up at him. "We'll be there tomorrow if this wind holds."

"Where will we sleep tonight, Mother? Can I sleep outside?"

"I don't know—"

"I'll stay out here with him," said Othar. "He'll be fine."

"If he doesn't freeze," said Tarquinius. "It's still winter, you know."

"But I want to see the stars. I'll wrap up extra warm, Mother. Can I stay out here with Othar? Please?"

"I suppose so."

He gave her an impulsive hug, then limped happily toward the bow. She watched him go, noting the way the pitch and roll of the ship forced him to take small steps to keep his balance.

"He'll be all right. I'll stay close," said Othar.

"You're just afraid of the rats," said Tarquinius, ducking under the backhand Othar aimed at his head.

"Secundus says we'll round Delos during the night, then turn east-northeast toward the tip of Ikaria. We'll coast north of there and Samos, and then straight on into the harbor at Ephesus," Daphnis reported with authority.

"And when is your watch?" Tarquinius asked Daphnis. "I'd

have thought Tryphimus would have you in the crew by now. Hand me the jug, Othar, would you?"

Daphnis grinned. "Secundus let me hold the helm—just for a little bit, and he kept his hand on it. He said the sea people might try to trick me and pull the helm away from me." He paused long enough to toss a handful of dried apples into his mouth. "I told him the Christ was stronger than any sea people, and He wouldn't let that happen. But he still kept his hand on the helm."

"Good for Secundus," said Tarquinius.

They were belowdecks where they could hear the rattle and groan of the ship's hull as it rode up and down the long swells. There was only a small amount of cargo in the holds; Tryphimus was transporting very little to Ephesus other than himself, his vials, and the five passengers who huddled together for a meal before retiring.

"I don't expect I'll sleep much," Scaevolus said. "I may as well come up on deck with you and Othar, Daphnis. I've never gotten the knack of the sea."

"You sure you're safe up there?" Amanis asked. "Some of— one of the crew might—"

"None of them are my stock," said Scaevolus. "I'd remember."

"Well, at least the ship isn't outfitted with oars," she remarked. "The crew get all the fresh air they could want."

"A little more than, I'd guess," said Tarquinius.

"Mother, I'm full. Can I go back on deck?"

She nodded, and Daphnis scurried toward the ladder. Othar got up, bending forward to keep from bashing his head, and shuffled after the boy.

"I never treated slaves badly," Scaevolus said, staring straight ahead. "I placed them in good households whenever I could."

"How many of yours went to the mines?" Tarquinius asked. "We already know you sent some to the galleys."

"Many of them sold themselves to me!" Scaevolus said. "Service in a household is better than starving."

"My father wasn't starving, and neither was I," said Amanis. "I really don't blame you, though. You didn't cause his despair or influence him to surrender to it. He did that on his own."

Scaevolus looked at her oddly. "And still you despise him."

"The Christ teaches us to forgive, even when we are ill-used," she said in a flat voice.

Tarquinius shook his head and gave a skeptical grunt. "I'm going up for some fresh air before I settle in for the night." He dusted the crumbs from his hands and the front of his clothes, then clambered up the ladder.

"Perilous, this business of loving," said Scaevolus after a long silence. He looked at her. "I am sorry, Amanis."

"You did me no harm."

"Perhaps not. And perhaps I'm saying to you what I wish I could say to someone else."

She met his eyes for a moment, then looked away. "And maybe I'm saying to you what I wish I could learn to believe."

The night passed uneventfully. When Amanis's eyes opened, she saw light leaking through the chinks in the planking above her. Scaevolus, true to his word, had gone up sometime during the night. Even Tarquinius had stirred himself early, she realized, looking at his empty berth. She pulled her robes around her and climbed the ladder to the deck.

The morning sky glowed pink and golden. The freshening westerly was at once chilling and bracing; the crew had crowded on all the sail the merchantman could hold. Amanis noticed a knot of people near the stern. She walked back to investigate.

"If we angle east-northeast, just off the wind," Tryphimus was saying, "we can probably come into the lee of Ikaria before it reaches us."

"I don't know," said Secundus. "It's come on apace since sunrise." He was still gripping the tiller as he had been last night. Did the man never sleep?

"A plague on this winter weather," Tryphimus said. "Turns on you like a spurned woman."

Amanis saw the dark on the southwest horizon. "A storm?"

"Maybe not," said Tryphimus, smacking his hand on the gunwale. "East-northeast, Secundus! And tell the rest of those louts to keep themselves ready. We've got to get Ikaria between us and that squall."

Daphnis looked at her, his eyes big in his face. "Mother? How far are we from land?"

"I don't know, child. Let's go below, out of this wind." Suddenly the breeze carried a threatening feel.

When Amanis came on deck a little later, the threatening clouds had marched nearly a third of the way up the sky. They were moving much faster than the ship, it seemed, and would overtake them before they could come to Ikaria. Othar, Tarquinius, and Daphnis all stood in the bow, gripping the railing and staring ahead.

The midday sun was hidden from them, and the wind shifted and curled down on them from the north, forcing the crew to tack instead of run before it. And then the storm was upon them.

First came the rain, driving like icy needles in the gust that lashed across the port bow. Then came a vast, sustained gale that piled the sea before it in swells as high as houses.

"Reef the sails! Reef the sails, you whoresons!" bellowed Tryphimus, holding onto a mainsail line with one fist and gesturing frantically with the other. "Secundus! Lash the tiller in place and help them reef the sails!"

Amanis stood on the ladder from belowdecks, gripping the sides of the hatch and watching in terror as the crew scrambled about the wildly tilting deck.

"Go below!" Tryphimus yelled at her. "Go below, and make fast that hatchway!"

She backed down the ladder, just as a huge wave slapped the sides of the ship. Her head was slammed into the side of the hatch, and she fell into the hold, followed by a deluge of frigid seawater. She felt hands gripping her, carrying her. She heard voices shouting.

Twenty-two

When her eyes opened, the hatch was shut, and Daphnis was leaning over her.

"Mother? Are you all right?"

"Not all right, but better than I might be." She sat up and held her throbbing head. She felt in her stomach the rise and sickening drop of the ship in the storm swells, heard the thumping of the sea, like the fist of a giant against the hull.

"Are we home yet?" she asked Tarquinius, who squatted nearby, holding onto some cargo netting.

He looked up at her, vomit dribbling down his chin. "Almost there," he said. "I hope we're not late."

Scaevolus was braced between two of the ship's ribs, his eyes closed and his jaw clenched. Othar crouched beside the ladder, holding onto it against the swaying and bucking, his eyes lifted to the deck above.

Now and then, above the howling of the wind and the booming of the waves, they could hear the shouts of the crew, the thumping of their feet. *Almighty One, Father of our Lord Jesus Christ, protect us,* she prayed.

"Mother, are we going to die?"

She reached out a hand to him, and Daphnis curled into her, gripping her like his last hope as he buried his face in her chest. "I hope not, child," she said, smoothing the hair on the back of his head. "I hope not."

The ship gave a huge lurch, then a sidelong shudder. Water came spurting through a joint above Amanis's head. Othar staggered to the place and jammed his hand against the brace of the planks. Amanis heard him grunting, saw the sinews popping out all along his arm. The flow of water slowed but didn't stop.

"Somebody ought to tell Tryphimus," Tarquinius shouted. "I'll go up." The dwarf crawled across the sloshing hold to the ladder and pulled himself toward the hatchway. When he was about halfway up, a wave slammed the ship sideways. Tarquinius held on and somehow continued his climb, then disappeared through the hatch.

He had been gone only a few moments when the hatch slammed open and Tarquinius half-fell through the opening, barely catching himself on the ladder. "Out! Hurry! We're going to break up on a reef!"

They scrambled for the ladder, Amanis pushing Daphnis ahead of her. Othar reached for the boy and hoisted him toward the top. Then he grabbed her and lifted her. As she started to climb, she saw Othar hold out a hand to Scaevolus.

When she came out on the deck, all she could see at first were sheets of rain, lit by lightning. She grabbed Daphnis's cloak between his shoulders. "Stay close to me!" she shouted.

"Get aft! Get aft!" Tryphimus was holding onto the starboard gunwale and wheeling his free arm toward the stern. "Let the bows take the shock."

Amanis risked a look foward. In the blue-white flash of the

lightning, she could see jagged rocks: the sea between them churned into froth. The rocks looked like the teeth of some beast that was trying to swallow the sea and the ship with it.

"What will we do?" she screamed at Tryphimus. "If we don't drown, we'll be beaten to death!"

"Grab something when she strikes the rocks," he said. "Try to get to shore."

"Shore? What shore?" she yelled, but he had turned away and the wind drowned out his answer.

They gathered at the stern railing. Daphnis was clinging to her, and Tarquinius had one hand on the boy's shoulder and the other on a deck cleat. Scaevolus stood braced against the rain and wind. Othar stood hindmost, stretching his arms as far around the group as he could.

"Hold on!" said Othar. And then they hit.

There was a deafening crash and splintering, and they were all thrown forward onto the deck. "Daphnis! Daphnis!" screamed Amanis. Then she was deep in the cold water, fighting with all her strength to climb back toward the air.

Something knocked against her shoulder. She flung out an arm and realized one of the casks from the hold had bobbed up beside her. She grabbed at it and managed to get a good hold with both hands. She tried to blink the seawater out of her eyes, but the tossing and frothing kept blocking her vision.

An arm came out of the water, and she grabbed at it, nearly losing her grip on the cask. The hand grabbed at her, then the other hand. It was Tryphimus. He coughed and sputtered. Amanis tried to pull him closer, to get his hands on the cask. And then a wave slammed them into the rocks. Tryphimus was knocked loose. Amanis stretched herself as far as she could, trying to give him an arm, a leg, anything to grab onto. But the waves pushed him away, pulled him under. He fought back to the surface again, then went under. She didn't see him anymore.

She began kicking feebly, having no idea which way she was facing. The rain pelted down so hard that at times she wasn't certain whether her head was above or below the surface. Then she heard, beneath the wail of the wind and the pounding rush of her own desperation, the low rumble of breakers on a shoreline.

With the last of her strength, she kicked toward the sound. She kicked until her legs felt numb, as heavy as stones. Her breath was a ragged whimper, in and out, one lungful after another. Then her feet scraped against the rocky bottom.

Amanis dragged herself forward onto the beach and fell on her side. She felt rocks gouging her ribs, but she couldn't move. The rain beat upon her, the wind tore at her, and her grip on consciousness dissolved.

Several times her mind tried to surface from the dark oblivion. She would feel hands lifting her or voices talking above her head. She wanted to see them, to speak to them. *Where is my son? Are my friends dead or alive? What is this place? Who are you?* Her mind could form the questions, but her lips would not obey her wishes. She couldn't drag her eyelids open. And the dark would seep into her again.

When she could finally force her will to the surface, she realized she was lying on a reed pallet covered with woolen blankets. Above her was a roof of woven straw laid over a crisscrossed framework of sticks. The walls of the tiny hut appeared to be of mud brick, but well fashioned and sturdy. A fire crackled somewhere in the room. And a young man squatted at the foot of her pallet.

She tried to sit up, but the splitting pain in her forehead quickly forced her back down. She felt the young man's hand on her shoulder.

"Gently, good woman. It's good to see you awake, but you musn't try to do too much just yet."

"Where am I?" Her voice was a hoarse whisper, but even this effort made her wince with discomfort. And something about her face didn't feel right.

"Patmos," he said.

"The prison island?"

"Yes, I'm afraid so. But you're safe enough here with us."

"Who are you?"

"I am called Demetrius. The brothers have asked me to care for you and the others."

"Others? My son—" Again she tried to sit up, and again her head would not permit it.

"Son?" He looked thoughtful, then solemn. "I…I'm afraid you were the only African we found—"

"No, my son is not— Is there a boy with a withered arm?"

"Oh, Daphnis!" His smile came back. "Daphnis is your son?"

"Is he all right?"

"Yes, yes. He and the German have come here almost every day to watch by your bed."

"How long have I been here?"

"Almost a week now, I guess. Which reminds me—" He got to his feet and went to one corner, where the small fire was. A blackened pot sat in the coals, and he carefully ladled something from it into a shallow clay bowl. He carried the steaming bowl back to her and seated himself closer to her head. He gently placed a hand at the base of her neck and helped her raise herself slowly. He rearranged some cushions to support her. Then he spooned something from the bowl into her mouth. Hot broth. It felt indescribably good and comforting as it slid down her throat into her stomach. With the first swallow, Amanis realized she was ravenously hungry.

"You haven't had much more than the little bit of water we could get you to take," Demetrius said as he fed her. "I expect you'll want to eat, but it's probably better to let your bowels have a chance to remember what they're supposed to do. And I imagine putting something in your belly might improve the pain in your head."

"A dwarf?" she said between mouthfuls.

"Tarquinius," he said with a wry grin. "Yes, he's well enough, though he was considerably disappointed to find out none of the brothers had the least interest in games of chance—or money to play."

Her hand chanced across a familiar shape, lying on the floor beside her pallet. Her satchel. Yes, she had been wearing it when they went on deck, just before the collision with the rocks. She was glad to have a few of her things at least.

"Scaevolus? An old man."

Demetrius's hand paused before bringing the spoon to her mouth. His face was serious again. "He's here, but he was badly hurt."

"Alive?"

"We're doing all we can for him."

There was a shuffling of feet at the doorway, and the hide covering the opening moved aside. Daphnis came in, followed closely by Othar, who had some difficulty squeezing his bulk through the small entry. She held out her arms to the boy, who flung himself on her. Pain shot through her bruised body, but she waved off the remonstrating Demetrius.

"Mother! I was so afraid for you." The boy reached up and gently touched her face. "You're still swollen. Demetrius says that'll be all right, though. Does it hurt?"

"Some. But it doesn't matter." She held him close, breathed in his smell. Gratitude swelled in her throat, stung her eyes. *Thank You. Oh, thank You.*

Othar had to stoop over in the tiny hut. He looked vulnerable and out of place. She tilted her head back and looked at him. "The sea didn't want you?"

He grinned and shrugged. "When the ship went onto the rocks, a big section of the deck broke away. I got Daphnis onto it, and we rode it most of the way to the shore."

"He pulled me out of the water by my hair," the boy said.

"I was trying to— I didn't mean to hurt him."

"Don't be foolish," Amanis said. "You kept him from drowning."

"You really need to rest," Demetrius said in a quiet voice.

"Come on, boy." Othar laid a hand on Daphnis's shoulder. "We'll come back after a while."

Daphnis gave her a final squeeze, then followed Othar out.

"He loves you dearly," Demetrius said.

"He's a good boy." The warmth and comfort in her stomach were making her drowsy; again her eyelids felt as if someone had placed drachma coins on them. From far away she heard Demetrius say something. "What?"

"I said, he learned from a good teacher."

"Damaris?" she mumbled.

"Who's that?"

She tried to answer, but the darkness drowned her words.

In a day or two she was able to sit up and eat without help. Her still-swollen face made chewing uncomfortable, but she soon discovered that Demetrius and his friends had many tasty ideas about soup. Before long she felt well enough to get up and walk around a little.

The settlement consisted of a cluster of mud-brick huts like the one she occupied, clumped together at the base of a rocky hill. On the other side of the hill was the westward shoreline of the island; the promontory sheltered the little community from the main force of the storms that came over the Aegean from the west.

The clump of hovels was located just south of the bight that bisected Patmos. Most of those who lived here settled near the bight, which served as the island's natural harbor. "Not that we get a lot of traffic," Demetrius had told her. "Nobody comes here willingly, not even the guards on the transport ships." They located themselves as they did mainly to avoid the criminals and ruffians in the main settlement, he told her. "Brother John and the rest of us try to live in peace. Of course, it also helps that no one on Patmos has much of anything to steal."

"Why are you here?" she asked him.

"We came because of Brother John. When the governor exiled him, we accepted the same fate."

"Why?"

Demetrius smiled at her. "Why did the German pull your son from the sea?"

"Who is this John, to be the object of such devotion?"

He told her, in a voice hushed with reverence, how John was the last man alive to have walked with Jesus Christ on the earth.

He told of John's goodness, his quiet courage. Amanis wondered out loud why such a saint should be under Roman censure.

Demetrius gave a sarcastic snort. "Since when is it a fault to bear Rome's ill opinion?"

Amanis ducked through the opening of the hut where Scaevolus was. When her eyes adjusted to the darkness, she realized an older man was seated by his bedside—a man she hadn't seen before.

"The Ethiopian woman," he said. She could see the lamp-light gleaming on his teeth as he smiled. "Please. Sit."

"I'm Nubian," she said, settling herself on the opposite side of Scaevolus's pallet and leaning over to look at him. His closed eyelids looked like crinkled papyrus. They fluttered, and he was looking at her. He gave her a weak smile.

"Amanis. You're all right." His voice was scarcely louder than a whisper.

"Yes, I'm here."

"John tells me the others are well. The boy. Your friends."

"Yes."

"Good." His eyes closed. She thought he was going to sleep. "Tryphimus?"

"No. I saw him in the water just after we hit. I tried to reach him, but he went under."

"Too bad. His wife—" He sighed; his lips formed a grimace. The old man leaned over him. "Again?"

Scaevolus nodded weakly.

"Go find Demetrius," the man said to her, his eyes never leaving Scaevolus's face. "Tell him we need some more of the poppy powder."

Amanis found Demetrius walking on the slope above the huts. He left quickly for his quarters as she returned to Scaevolus. When she ducked back through the doorway, John had a hand on Scaevolus's forehead. John's eyes were closed, and his lips moved silently. He didn't stir as Amanis entered. She sat watching for several moments. John's hands were broad, she noticed, with large knuckles that were nicked and scarred. Like the well-used tools of a tradesman.

John took a deep breath, opened his eyes, and sat back.

"Will he be all right?" she asked.

"I pray for it to be so. Sometimes the Almighty uses my hands to heal, sometimes not. I never know how it will be. But I keep asking all the same. Winter is a chancy time for voyaging."

"He has...a loved one. In Ephesus."

John nodded. "A daughter. To find her is his deepest longing, he says."

Demetrius came in, carrying a small jar. He knelt beside John and poured a small amount of white powder into his palm. He and John tilted Scaevolus's head back, and the younger man sifted the powder into the patient's mouth.

"Gently now, friend, gently," John said. "Hold it under your tongue as much as you can."

In a little while the powder had done its work. Scaevolus slept. John stepped to the door and motioned for Amanis to follow.

"He's hurt inside somehow," John said as they walked along the slope. "Demetrius says there's little to do but keep him as comfortable as we can and pray he improves."

"Will he be able to continue on to Ephesus?"

"Impossible to know. And there is no hurry to find out really. The prison ships don't come too often, and as a rule they don't take on any return passengers."

They stood on a bluff encircling the harbor, overlooking the disorderly rows of shanties that made up the town. John clasped his hands behind his back and rocked on his heels. He reminded Amanis of a man surveying a field or a flock of sheep.

"Do you ever have trouble with any of them?" she asked, nodding toward the town.

"Oh, not much. Once or twice when we first arrived, they came around. But when they found out we don't have anything of value, they soon lost interest." He winked at her. "That, and hearing about the crazy old man who talks to the gods in his dreams."

"Do you?"

"Sometimes I know I do. Other times I'm pretty sure. And sometimes they're just the dreams of an old man who's lived too long and seen too much." He was quiet for a while. "When it's important...that's when I know.

"But I was going to say, you'd best stay as far away as you can from that lot down there. They've got women, but not the sort I'd want in my yard, much less my bed—even if I were young enough and so inclined."

"I can take care of myself." She laid her hand on the pommel of the sikhimi. John's eyes followed the motion.

"With that?"

"If I have to."

"And how many times have you had to?"

"More than once," she said, keeping her face turned slightly away from him.

She heard his soft chuckle. She bridled at the sound but kept still.

"Well, then," he said. "I'm too old to stand out in this wind much more. I have some herb drink in my house. Demetrius makes it. Where on this barren little island he gathers such plants and roots as he does is a wonder to me, but he brews this, and it's quite good for knocking off the chill. You don't even notice the brackish taste of the water. Would you like a cup?"

"No. I need to go to my son."

"Oh yes, Daphnis. Delightful boy. But how did he come to be yours?"

She kept her eyes on the ground in front of her feet and made no answer.

"Well, here's the way to my hut, and yours is in the other direction." She turned to go.

"We've gotten off on the wrong foot, Amanis of Nubia," he called after her. She stopped but didn't turn around. "I don't quite know why, but there it is. Maybe things will mend with a little time. I'll just look in on our sick friend. Give Daphnis my greeting, won't you?"

She heard his feet crunch along the path away from her. When he had taken a dozen paces, she turned her head to watch him go. Just an old man, picking his way along a rocky trail. She watched until he ducked through the entry of the hut.

Twenty-three

Winter gradually loosened its grip. Somehow, Scaevolus held onto life and even improved a little. He needed the opium less and less often as the days lengthened and could sometimes be seen leaning on John, walking slowly up and down the paths near the community site. The two old men sometimes sat together near one of the wind-gnarled shrubs wedged between the rocks of the hillside.

The soil of Patmos was poor, but the inhabitants had scratched out a few small plots to grow enough barley and beans to supplement their diet of fish and crustaceans. Berries and grapes grew sparsely in thickets in the ravines. There was even a spot where a handful of olive trees—too scant to be called a grove by even the most optimistic—clung to the hillside.

Amanis, Tarquinius, and Othar decided to clear a small patch near their hut and try their luck at farming. Actually, Amanis and Othar decided; Tarquinius had to be dragged into the enterprise, complaining every step of the way. But even he had to admit, after a few forays into the settlement by the harbor, that the gaming on Patmos wouldn't feed a cockroach.

"How will we ever till this sorry soil?" Tarquinius asked one morning as they pried rocks loose from the tract. "This ground's so hard you can't drive a tent peg into it."

"We'll use you for an ass," Othar said as he unearthed a stone the size of a large melon. "We'll hitch you to a plow, and I'll drive you back and forth till your tongue hangs out." He heaved the rock down the slope and watched as it crashed against a boulder and split in half.

"Do better to use you for drafting, you big ox," Tarquinius said. "I'll sit on your shoulders and box your ears with a switch."

"It'll be easier after the spring rains," said John, who had come up from the huts to watch them. Daphnis held John's hand, and Scaevolus leaned on his other shoulder. The three settled themselves on large stones at the perimeter. John leaned over to Daphnis. "You'd better go help your mother, boy. Wouldn't do to have you sitting here with the old men when there's work to be done." Daphnis slid off the stone and slouched over to her.

"What do you want me to do?" he asked, sounding like a prisoner about to hear his sentence pronounced.

"Push down on this while I pull on the stone." She held the rod she was using as a lever. He leaned on the rod as she wrestled the stone back and forth. It moved slightly and she redoubled her efforts as Daphnis kept up a steady pressure. Finally, with a sound like a sigh, it slid up out of its place. "Help me push it downhill," she said. The two of them got it rolling and watched as it joined the others at the bottom of the slope.

John laughed. "If this keeps up, we'll have a plain where we used to have a gully. Scaevolus and I would like to help, but it looks like the four of you have a good start."

Othar straightened himself and gave John a wry grin. "I can see you're just itching to get out here and toss rocks with us. Have you put roots down into that boulder you're sitting on?"

Daphnis fell down laughing, his arm clutching his middle. Soon Othar was also chuckling. Tarquinius squatted beside the boy, tickling him and wringing more gales of laughter from him. Amanis smiled and shook her head.

"I'm reminded of a story I once heard Jesus tell," John said a little later, as they took a drink from the water urn.

"Oh, tell it, please, won't you, Father John?" Daphnis said.

"Stories won't get the rocks out of our bean field," said Amanis.

"Please, Mother? Just this one story, all right?"

John looked at her, his eyebrows raised in question. "Oh, all right." She wiped the sweat from her forehead and walked a little apart from the others. She stood with her hands on her hips and stared at the rocks still to be cleared.

"It's about a man who planted a field, a little like this," John began. Despite herself, Amanis listened about the seed that fell on the path, among the weeds, and into the good, fertile ground. She thought about what it might have been like to walk with Jesus—to be his friend. What was His voice like? Did He gesture as He talked, or pantomime the action in His stories? Did He change the pitch of His voice to match that of His characters? Did He watch His listeners to see which way the seeds of His words went as He scattered them? Did He have quick eyes like John that saw what one might wish to hide? He was a friend to children, Damaris had once said. Did He laugh at His own jokes? Did He ever tickle a young boy just to hear the sound of his mirth? Did He ever help a neighbor clear rocks from a field?

John knew. He remembered. He could tell her the details of

a day spent in the presence of the Nazarene: whether He was out of sorts when He woke up in the morning; what made Him smile; what He noticed and what He didn't; what, if anything, embarrassed Him or surprised Him or made Him wistful. Did the Prince of Heaven ever get homesick? And if He did, how might His friends have known? John could tell her, if only she could discover how to let herself ask.

"And now, I think your mother's ready to get back to work," she heard John say. "You'd better join her."

Amanis turned around to see John helping Scaevolus to his feet. "Come on, friend. Watching these good folk has made me tired. Let's go find a better place for two old men to spend their time." He glanced at Amanis. Their eyes held for a moment, and then he turned away.

As summer drew near, Scaevolus began to talk more and more of going on to Ephesus. "The next time a ship comes, I'll talk to the commander," he said. "I've still got enough money to buy passage to Ephesus, at least. I know people there."

"But the ships don't come to shore," Demetrius said. "They anchor in the harbor and put the prisoners in boats with guards. They row in to the beach, put the prisoners out, then row back to the ship. They get here about midmorning, and by noon they've weighed anchor and left again. I don't think you'll have a chance to do much negotiating with them."

What Demetrius was too kind to say, Amanis knew, was that Scaevolus was still far too weak for any kind of journey. There were still some days when he needed help to dress himself, to eat. How could he think of sailing to Ephesus?

And the fact was, the time she'd had for reflection here on

Patmos had made her uneasy about returning to Ephesus. Scaevolus might have nothing but the fairest intentions, but she was still a fugitiva. If Patroclus found her, he could reclaim her, or worse. And what about Daphnis? What would happen to him if his mother was forced back into slavery or executed?

Such thoughts troubled her on a spring day as she pulled weeds in the bean patch. The spring rains had been good. The soil was well turned and loose, ready for seeding. But the nettles and borage had also discovered the place and were striving to stake an early claim. As she straightened to ease her lower back, she spotted John walking along the crest of the ridge and looking out to sea.

If anyone could make Scaevolus see reason, it was John. After a moment's thought, she dusted the soil from her hands and her clothing and began the climb to where John stood. If he saw her coming he gave no sign. He stood above her in the posture he so often used: hands clasped behind his back and rocking on his heels.

"Grace to you, Brother John," she called up the slope.

"Grace and peace to you, Amanis of Nubia. What brings you up to my perch on such a fine morning?"

"I'm worried about Scaevolus."

He watched her, saying nothing.

"I know he wants to find his child. I don't blame him for that. And he isn't getting any younger; I know that, too. But wouldn't it be better to wait a while, even another season, until he has gained more of his strength?"

Still he made no answer. Those eyes were on her: sifting, weighing, inspecting. She had to fight to keep from turning away.

"Why don't you say something? Don't you see the sense of it?"

He nodded. "I do. He is weak; you're right about that. But I'm wondering, too, about something else. I'm wondering how it is that you're tied in so closely with this search of his. It brought you here in the first place. It concerns you, chiefly. The others are here only because of you, I think."

"Hasn't Scaevolus told you?"

John shook his head. "I haven't asked, and he hasn't offered."

"Maybe there are things you need not know."

"Oh, I have no doubt of that, Amanis of Nubia. A great many things I need not know." He looked away then, back out over the sea. "I used to be a lot different, you know," he said.

"What do you mean?"

"My brother and I were hot young men, Amanis. Hot of blood and hot of word. Jealous both of what was already ours, and of what we thought ought to be. Fiercely protective." He looked at her, and a smile crinkled the corners of his eyes. "They called us the Thunder Brothers."

"Who did?"

"Everyone. The other ten disciples, and some of the women. I can't remember who started it. I don't think it was Jesus, though He had just cause, more than once, to fret at our ignorant zeal." He fell silent for a while, and when she looked at him, Amanis was surprised to see tears trickling into the folds of his cheeks. He gave her a shy look and wiped his face on a sleeve. "Sorry. I can still remember like it was yesterday. Will you sit with me for a bit?"

They went over to a flat stone. Still peering out over the sea, he began speaking in a soft, faraway voice.

"It wasn't long before they killed him. And still we didn't see, couldn't see. None of us—" He struggled for a few moments, then went on. "My brother and I—James was his name, did I tell you?—we were on Him about how things would be, when…when He came into His kingdom. Wanted to get our bid in early, I guess, though anyone should have known…the women, maybe. I think some of them knew better than we did." He smiled a sad smile. "Well, anyway. There we were, James and I, asking to be His top commanders, His chief ministers. Oh, the others were furious. And do you know what He told us? 'This isn't going to be a kingdom like the ones you're used to.' He had His feet planted wide apart in that way He had when he was saying something He wanted us to remember. He had that unbending look to him. 'In my kingdom,' He said, 'the highest must be the lowest. If you want to be a master, you have to learn to be a slave.'"

He looked at her. "All my life since, I've been trying to puzzle out everything those few words might have meant."

After a long silence, she heard herself say, "I'm not just afraid for Scaevolus."

His attentive quiet made it easier, somehow, for her to continue.

"I am a…a fugitiva. I ran away from my master. In Ephesus."

"Ah."

"Before I did, I saved a child. A newborn daughter that my master had exposed."

"And Scaevolus?"

"The girl's father…by my master's wife."

"Ah. I see."

"I took the infant to some Jews. I don't know what happened to her. I fled my master's house a short time later."

"Daphnis," he said quietly.

"Yes. Abandoned. Later, of course. When we were in Athens."

"And all these years, Scaevolus has sought you? Sought his daughter through you?"

She nodded. "I want to help him, I really do. But I'm afraid."

"How many other exposed infants have you rescued?"

"I don't know. A few. Maybe twenty or thirty."

"A mother of nations," he whispered.

"What?"

"The name of our most ancient mother. Of the Jews, I mean. Sarah. God called her that even though she was barren until old age. But out of her came the entire nation of Israel."

"What made you think of that just now?"

His eyes shone with kindness and compassion. "Because you have given life to so many children. True, someone else bore them. But they owe their lives to you. Why should you not be called 'mother'?"

She looked away. "I'm a mother to Daphnis. That's enough."

She felt his hand on her shoulder. He was standing now. "I'll talk to Scaevolus. Likely he needs more time to mend. And you need more time to consider."

He picked his way down the hillside. She watched him go, turning his words over and over in her mind. Highest must become lowest, master must become slave…and a barren woman becomes the mother of a nation. What other matters might the kingdom of God turn on their heads? She wasn't sure she wanted to know.

The rain fell softly. That was good; the last thing they needed, with the seeds freshly planted, was a deluge. No, this rain was just right: slow in starting, before first light, and falling gently still. It was pleasant this morning to be awakened by burling thunder, followed by the rhythm of the rain.

Amanis sat just inside the doorway of the hut, feeling the cool, rain-sweetened air on her face.

She heard the sloshing of footsteps. A figure, hunched and hooded, trudged uphill through the drizzle toward her doorway. It was John. He paused just outside the entry and shrugged off his thick wool robe, then ducked through the door.

"Good morning, Amanis of Nubia. May I offer you some fresh bread?" He held out a round loaf. "Demetrius is a pretty good baker. I'd take it if I were you."

She smiled and broke off a small piece. John sat beside her and looked out at the bean patch. "Good thing you got them in the ground when you did."

"Some of the men from the ship say if we get a warm sun in a day or two, the sprouts will fairly jump out of the soil."

"Could be. Don't know much about farming myself."

"Mother?" She turned around. Daphnis was sitting up, rubbing his face. "Is there anything to eat?"

John broke off a hunk of bread and tossed it at the groggy youngster. "Little bit of bad luck, this rain. In one way, at least. I was going to show the boy there a thing or two about fishing. But I don't fancy wading out in the water with a casting net in this muck."

She looked at him, startled. "What do you mean? Daphnis using a casting net?"

"Why not?"

She gave a worried glance back at the boy. He was chewing the bread with a slack expression, staring straight ahead at the nearest wall. She turned back to John. "His arm," she whispered. "Do you think he could—"

"Oh, that," John said, his voice sounding too loud in her

ears. "I think he'll be all right. What do you think, Daphnis? Want to learn to fish?"

He looked at John and gave a sleepy smile and nod.

"There. It's settled then. But no sense thinking about it today. This rain looks like it's staying on a while." He grunted to his feet and reached for his cloak. "Good day for farmers, maybe. Bad day for fishermen."

Amanis found herself a little dismayed the next morning when she awoke to a clear sky. She sat up and looked at Daphnis, still breathing softly on his pallet. He slept in his usual position: on his left side, with his good arm curled around his head and his withered arm cupped close to his body. Such a good heart this child had. Somehow his limitations seemed not to have corroded his enthusiasm for life. She hoped John knew what he was doing. No doubt the kind old man intended all for good, but...

"Wake up, boy! Best to get at 'em before the sun heats the water too much."

John ducked through the doorway and strode over to Daphnis's pallet. He grabbed the nearest shoulder and jostled it. "Come on, shake those lazy bones. Learning to cast is much easier before the wind gets up."

John had a net slung over his shoulder and a wide-brimmed straw hat on his head. "Got any lamp soot or a piece of charred wood? The glare from the water can be a bother. Good idea to rub a little black under his eyes if you can find some."

By now, Daphnis was sitting up, yawning and stretching. "Is there anything to eat?" he asked.

"Eat? A fisherman eats what he catches, boy; didn't you know that?" John said. "Come on. We'll snag some nice, fat bourri and smoke 'em over a driftwood fire before the rest of the world is awake. You never tasted anything so good in your life, I promise you that." He half dragged Daphnis from his bed, threw the boy's robe across his shoulders, and hustled him toward the doorway.

"Your shoes," Amanis called.

"Oh yes. Better get some shoes," John said. "Some of the rocks have got an edge or two on 'em."

"Where will you be?" Amanis asked as they started out the door again. "Down at the harbor?" She handed Daphnis a small piece of charred wood.

"No, wind's all wrong down there today," John said over his shoulder. "I know a little place the other side of the bight, on the western side. Just over the hill." He stopped and looked at her. "Don't worry. He'll be fine."

Twenty-four

*A*manis wanted to go after them. The old fear rose in her, the sense of disaster, hovering and making ready to stoop upon her.

Her mind tossed her back and forth until a little while after breakfast. She got up, intending to go out to the plot and pull weeds. Instead, she followed the dull roar of the surf toward the western side of the island.

She crested the hill and scanned as much of the shoreline as she could see. No sign of John or Daphnis. She picked her way down the switchbacked path toward the sea's edge. On the western side of the bight, just over the hill, John had said. When she reached the shoreline, she turned north.

· Patmos rose out of the sea at a steep angle; on most of its coastline there was very little beach. But when she reached the narrow neck connecting the island's northernmost end, she saw a little cove with a tab of shingle at its eastern edge. And there she found John and Daphnis.

The two of them stood in the water just out from the shingle.

The water was up to Daphnis's waist. He saw her coming down the bank and waved at her.

Amanis found a rock and sat, watching them. John's hat brim bobbed up and down as he earnestly explained something. He still had the net draped over his shoulder. Now and then he would make wide arm motions. Daphnis gave him quick nods, sometimes doing a one-handed imitation of John's movements. Then John reached up to the net, found the center line, and tied it to his belt. He gathered the net in both hands, swiveled his body once, twice, then flung the net into the air.

The net opened out into an almost perfect circle. It splashed into the water, and John played out the towline, letting the net sink to the bottom. Then he tugged at the center rope to cinch closed the mouth of the net, like a purse. He began hauling it in, hand over hand. He reached beneath the surface and raised the pursed end. He handed it to Daphnis, then pulled up for inspection as much of the rest of the net as he could. He took the pursed end of the net from Daphnis and pulled it apart. Amanis saw a few small, silvery shapes spilling back into the water. Then John handed Daphnis the net and gestured at the water.

Daphnis laboriously gathered the net, using his withered arm to wedge the gathered portion to him while he reached for the next loop with his strong arm. John helped him a little as he arranged the net to make his throw and tucked the pull rope into his belt. He made a couple of preparatory feints, then, miraculously, the net sailed out and over the water. It didn't open as wide as John's cast, nor go as far. But Daphnis had managed it.

John leaned close as Daphnis readied to pull the center line. The old man spoke to him for a moment, then the boy pulled at the rope, reaching as far as he could and leaning back, wedging the line with his deformed arm, then leaning forward for another tug.

The net came in, and again John reached into the water. Amanis could see fish wriggling in the mesh. She heard John's cackle and saw him clap Daphnis on the shoulder. The old man faced her then and held aloft the dripping net as if it were a trophy of war. They began wading toward shore.

"Mother, I did it! I caught some fish! Look!"

John reached into the net and brought out a silvery mullet almost as long as his forearm. "Get one of the others, boy," he said, setting the net in front of Daphnis. "See if you can catch it by the lower jaw, like this. And watch out for that front fin. It's got spines."

The tip of Daphnis's tongue showed between his lips as he bent over, trying to take up his catch. He straightened, holding up another mullet almost as large as the one John had, its belly swollen with eggs. The grin on his face seemed to Amanis like a long swallow of sweet wine. Suddenly the mullet flapped violently, swatting Daphnis with its forked tail. He yelped and dropped the fish onto the shingle. John laughed as he toed the flouncing fish away from the water.

"Let's get a fire built, Daphnis, before our catch swims away."

They fished for mullet until summer's heat ended the spawning season and sent the fish to deeper water. John showed Daphnis where to look for clams and mussels, how to find the hiding places of the small octopi that lurked among the shallow reefs, where the best places were to take the spiny lobsters and crabs. And in the thick heat of the afternoons, they sat in the entry of a cave upslope from the huts and let the deep earth exhale its cool breath on them. It was here that John found out about Daphnis's agility with letters.

"The boy makes a better scribe with one hand than any two-handed man I ever saw," John said to Amanis one evening as he and Daphnis returned to the huts from a clam digging expedition. "I gave him some papyrus and ink and had Demetrius put him through his paces. He's well taught, that one."

"There was a man in Athens who took an interest in his learning. Go get that mud off yourself," she said to Daphnis. "There's a bowl of berries and some bread to eat when you're cleaned up." Daphnis went toward the hut.

Amanis was working in the beans, pinching off the sprigs of grass and weeds, trying to get a foothold. John set down the basket of clams and squatted beside her. "Would it be all right with you if I gave him some work to do?"

"What kind of work?"

"Writing. My eyes are too old for it and my mind too slow. But there are some things I need to have written out, while it's still in my head how they should go. Demetrius does well enough, but it would be good if the boy could help him sometimes."

Amanis smiled down at her hands as she worked her way along the rows of bean plants. "I think Daphnis won't mind too much if it means he can spend more time with you."

"Well, I guess you could say that works the other way, too. He's a good boy. You've done a fine job with him."

She felt a little bloom of pleasure. "All right, then. But when I need help with the beans or with anything else—"

"He's yours, Amanis of Nubia. No questions asked." She felt his hand on her shoulder. He got to his feet and started to walk away.

"John. Your clams."

"Best to boil them with a little salt. Eat them with olive oil, if you've any extra." He walked away toward his hut.

Daphnis was troubled. Amanis could see it in his face, in the way he held himself, even in the slow way he ate. She watched him finish his supper and shuffle to the doorway to sweep the scraps from his bowl. He stood for a long time, staring outside at the last of the daylight.

He would be a man before too much longer. In certain types of light she had noticed the sparse beginnings of whiskers on his chin. Sometimes his voice broke in the middle of a sentence, and a flush would steal up his neck. He kept to himself more these days; often he would sit in a study, much like this, and when she asked him if anything was the matter, he would give a small, annoyed shake of his head. But tonight's mood was different. This was about something specific, she thought.

"A long time to stare at something as still as those rocks out there," she said finally.

He didn't move. She thought she'd annoyed him somehow until he said, "Who is my father?"

The silence that followed made her think of trying to gather up broken glass in a dark room. "What caused you to wonder about that?"

He sighed and slouched back toward her, plopping down across the cold fire pit from her. "John, today at the cave," he said, picking up a half-burnt twig and idly marking with it on a rim-stone. "He started remembering one of the times when Jesus was talking to some of the people at the Jewish temple in Jerusalem. Jesus called Himself the 'light of the world,' and the temple people accused Him of speaking what couldn't be verified.

"Over and over again in His stories it happens. Jesus talks to the people, and they don't believe Him. They even call Him mad, an infidel. I can't understand it. How could they fail to accept Him? I asked John, and he smiled in that way of his. He said it reminded him of something he heard Jesus' mother say a long time ago: 'Those who have known only darkness can't understand the light. What they can't understand, they must control, or destroy.'

"John said Jesus told the people, 'I am the one who testifies for myself; my other witness is the one who sent me—the Father.' And they wanted to know who His father was. Then Jesus told them if they knew Him, they would also know His father. He knew where He came from and He knew who He was. And because of that, nothing anyone else could say or do had the power to change Him.

"There was a lot more He said after that, but those few words kept going around and around in my head, even while I wrote down what John was saying. 'He knew where He came from, and He knew who He was.'"

Now he looked at her. It pained her to see the anguish written on his face as clearly as a slap. "Mother, how will I ever know who I am?"

She longed to hold his head against her and still the distressing questions with her whispered reassurances.

"I don't know," she said. "And I don't think even John knows that. The answer lies somewhere inside you, I think. You must find out where. You're the only one who can."

"John talks a lot about light and darkness. Some of it I understand, some not. Sometimes it reminds me of one of the books old Dionysius used to have me read, Plato or one of those others. John says light is always stronger than darkness. I understand that part, I guess."

"There is much light within you, I think."

He gave her a tiny smile. "Thank you."

"Start there then. And let God guide you."

He nodded. "I love you, Mother."

She made herself stay still. "And I love you, my son."

Just before winter closed the shipping lanes, a vessel anchored in the harbor. One of those who disembarked was a Christ-follower from Ephesus. He hiked up from the shore to the small community on the hillside. His name was Gaius, and John and the others greeted him with loud cries of joy and many embraces.

Gaius was carrying a letter to John from the Christians in Ephesus. Amanis saw John huddled with his companions as Demetrius read it to them. She heard enough to know that all was not well. The proconsul was suspicious of the church's gatherings, for one thing. Banishing John to the prison island had not satisfied him, it seemed; the followers were continually harassed, sometimes detained for examination by torture. But this didn't seem perplexing to John. He was concerned for them, she gathered, but not surprised by official censure.

More worrisome to him was what the believers told him about some of the teachings among the Christian communities in Asia Province. Amanis didn't understand much of it, but it sounded like a mishmash of the old Greek mystery stories and a tangled version of a few of the Jesus narratives. John shook his head and muttered into his beard.

John kept Demetrius and Daphnis busier than ever at the cave that fall and winter, dictating line upon line. It was as if the news from Ephesus had created in him a fevered rush to get the words in his mind onto a page, where others could look at them.

Amanis fretted about Scaevolus. His healing was painfully slow, and the colder weather was hard on him. He huddled in front of the brazier for days at a time, his cloak pulled closely around him. Amanis took him hot soups and broths, but Tarquinius and Othar told her he ate but little. Still, all he would talk about was taking ship for Ephesus as soon as the days warmed. She doubted that even John would be able to deter him come spring.

Their bean field made an exceptional yield. She really could have used Daphnis's help to get in the crop, but she was reluctant to take him away from his work with John. It took her, Othar, and Tarquinius several days to strip the drying stalks of all the pods, and several more to shell the beans into as many spare pots and baskets as they could scavenge.

"I wonder if we'll run across Damon and the others when we get back to Ephesus," Tarquinius said one evening, reaching for another handful of pods. "I've tried farming, and it doesn't suit me. I'm ready to get back on the road with the troupe and the game."

"You haven't tried farming enough to know," Othar said. "You'd better think again. You're not as young as you used to be. Maybe you're not as lucky, either. Get back!" he said, swatting at the head of the ferret. The lithe animal scuttled sideways, then edged back toward the beans. Othar had found the ferret as an infant, stranded in a rock outcropping at the top of the hill behind the huts. He named it Himdul, after a sentry god of Germania.

Tarquinius sent the German a skeptical look. "What are you

talking about? I'm one of Fortuna's favorites. I survived the shipwreck, didn't I?"

Othar looked as if he were going to reply, but thought better of it. He worked for a while in silence. "You believe in John's God, don't you?" he asked some time later, looking at Amanis.

"Well, yes, I do. I have ever since I knew Damaris."

Himdul picked up one of the bean pods and padded toward the corner where he slept.

Othar chewed on Amanis's answer. Tarquinius was also keeping oddly quiet, she noticed.

"I think I believe in Him, too," Othar said finally. He kept his eyes on his fingers. "I've thought much about my life and you and Damaris and the others in Athens. How they took you and the boy in. How free-handed they were to Daphnis, schooling him and feeding him and us. And about John." He gave her a quick glance, then ducked his head again. "If your God can make people like that, I think I want Him to be my God, too."

Tarquinius sat perfectly still now, his face turned away from both of them.

They took Othar down to the harbor a few days later. John insisted on coming. Daphnis was there, of course, and Demetrius and Gaius. No one brought up the absence of Tarquinius; he had left the hut well before sunrise, and no one had seen him since.

The day was clear and warmer than recent ones. "A good thing," John joked as he, Othar, and Amanis waded out into the water. "If this big lout freezes, we don't have enough people to drag him back uphill."

"I was reared in Germania," Othar said. "Your puny Greek winters are nothing to me." Despite Othar's bravado, Amanis felt her teeth chattering well before the water was up to their waists.

John lifted his face and hands to the sky and said, "O Lord, God of the universe, for the sake of Jesus Christ Your only Son, I ask Your blessing on Your child, Othar. Let him now be washed clean of all sin, and let him receive the Spirit of the Christ, who lives forever. Amen."

As Othar had requested, Amanis placed her hand on his head as he dipped himself below the surface. When he came up, he wrapped his arms around her, squeezing the breath out of her. He released her and swiveled around to catch hold of John, who did his best to return the embrace, though his arms barely reached the back side of Othar's ribs. There was a wide grin on Othar's face.

They waded back toward shore where the others waited holding dry wraps. Othar had to hug each of them, too, in turn: Gaius, then Demetrius, then Daphnis. Othar picked the boy completely off the ground. "You must teach me everything, boy," he said, his graying beard crushed against Daphnis's cheek. "Everything you know."

"I will, Uncle. I will."

Twenty-five

"Why have you come back?" her father said.

It pained Amanis to see him. His eyes were red from weeping. He wore an iron collar with a chain bolted to it. He crouched in his own filth as though he had not moved for days.

She was juggling five balls, the most she'd ever attempted. She had been going for what seemed like hours without a pause, but he only stared at her, asking the same question over and over again: "Why have you come back?"

Patroclus was there. He took the chain from its bracket in the wall and gave it a cruel jerk. Her father's head snapped back and forth as if he were a rag doll.

"Well?" Patroclus said, glaring at her. "Are you ready to join him?" He held out his hand, from which dangled another chain and collar. "I've got everything prepared." She opened her mouth to scream, but the only sound that came out was the thin wail of a starving infant.

She had to listen to the sound of Daphnis's breathing for several moments before she realized she had been dreaming. She closed her eyes and tried to go back to sleep, but the images kept playing through her mind: her father in chains, the fatigue in her arms, the need to keep going, to keep from dropping, the baby's cry coming from her throat. The spite on the face of her former master.

Her former master? In the eyes of the law, Patroclus was still her master. The thought nagged her, had been nagging her for some days now: If she were Patroclus's property, wasn't her escape a form of theft? Everything in her recoiled at the thought of placing herself in his power again, but what should she do? Surely the Christ didn't expect her to return to Patroclus. Did He?

The only person wise enough to give her counsel was John, and he hardly came out of his cave at all these days. He seemed in a trance much of the time, as if he were seeing things no one else could see, hearing words that sounded to everyone else like silence or the stirring of the wind. She was a little afraid of him these days, truth be told. She could easily see why the men in the harbor village kept away from them.

But their second winter on Patmos was rounding toward spring, and she had less and less time left before Scaevolus would insist on leaving. She couldn't bear the thought of not trying, at least, to help him find the girl. But to be in Ephesus again... She wasn't sure she had the courage.

Dawn finally crept across the threshold. She laid aside her coverings and got dressed. She went out into the rose-gray light and climbed the slope behind the huts. She felt her breath coming harder, felt the muscles in her legs protest at such a rude awakening. But she pushed herself until she reached the spine of the hill. She stood in the stillness of the early morning and stared west across the Aegean toward Athens. Far below her the surf thrashed at the shoreline. She held her elbows in her hands and tried to bring some order to the thoughts scrambling around inside her mind.

What would You have me do? Is it Your will that I should go back? Would You have me enslaved again in a household that doesn't know Your name? Was it not for the sake of Daphnis and Damaris that You took me to Athens in the first place? What of that now? How will my child manage if I'm taken? Must he suffer for actions I took, even before he was born?

She waited, but the only thought that formed was that of her father with the collar around his neck. And her own feelings as she beheld him: pity, disgust—and shame, as if in some way she was at fault for his condition. Or maybe it was that she had some responsibility toward him, unknown before, that was still unmet.

She turned then and looked down the slope toward the cluster of huts. No one stirred yet, not even so much as the bluish curl of a cooking fire.

She thought about everything that had been since that day when she rescued the little girl from the slopes of Mount Pion: of creeping through the darkened alleys with Othar and Tarquinius; of the jostle and tumult of her escape in the midst of the troupe; of the days on the road, the strange dream, the unsuspected things she had learned from her traveling companions. She thought of Damon, and of the look on his face that morning on the docks of Smyrna when he had given her the leather balls and said farewell. Of the years in Athens. Of

Damaris and her unflagging kindness. Of Daphnis. How could she ever get her mind around all that Daphnis had been and would be to her?

It came to her that she had fled much more than slavery in Ephesus. But the time for running was almost over.

As the days lengthened and warmed, John posted a watch on the eastern headlands to advise them as soon as a sail was sighted. The word came close to noon on the sixth after the tenth of Thargelion, a day when fleecy clouds were scattered across the sky in ranks as far as the eye could reach.

They readied themselves quickly; very little had survived the wreck, so not much had to be gathered. Amanis shouldered her pack and Daphnis clutched a small satchel containing some styluses, an ink block, and a few sheets of papyrus, all gifts from John. Othar and Tarquinius carried a few loaves of bean bread and some skins of water. Scaevolus carried nothing, but steadied himself by holding onto Othar's shoulder.

John met them at the path leading down to the harbor. "Well, my friends, I'll say good-bye here," he said, smiling. "Your case won't be helped if the procurator's officers see you with me, I'm afraid." He held out his hands, and Scaevolus took them. John peered into the eyes of the other man. "I bid you grace and peace, Scaevolus. May your journey end in joy."

"Thank you, John. I'll do as I said, I promise; I'll speak to the governor. I may still have some little influence."

John laughed. "Better keep your reputation intact. But I thank you, all the same." He gripped Othar's forearm. "God speed you, my German friend. The Spirit of Christ be with you."

"And with you, Brother John. Here." He brought a hand out

of his robe. The ferret was there, squirming and licking Othar's knuckles. "Himdul's pretty good with the bugs and mice. You'd better keep him. I don't know how he'd do on a ship."

John took the ferret from Othar. "I'll do my best to care for him."

John turned toward Tarquinius, but he brushed past without looking at John or saying a word. The old man gave Daphnis a sad little smile and a shrug, then embraced the boy. "My young amanuensis. How will I get my work done without you?"

Daphnis tried to speak, but his throat was blocked by too many feelings. Amanis put her hand on his shoulder. John took her other hand and kissed her on each cheek. "Dear sister. How many more children will you save for this earth, I wonder?"

"That's not why I'm going to Ephesus."

His eyes twinkled at her. "Really? How do you know?"

"Grace and peace to you, Brother John."

"The peace of Christ be with you, Amanis of Nubia."

Gaius came with them; he carried a leather case containing the writings that had consumed John for most of the winter. He was charged with distributing the letters among the churches in Asia Province and beyond.

The six of them reached the harbor's edge just as the prison ship dropped anchor. They watched as men came out on deck, between columns of armed guards, and were herded down a rope ladder into a boat. The boat put out from the ship and came toward them, its oars manned by the prisoners. Four soldiers stood distributed the length of the boat. The morning sun gleamed on the naked gladii in their hands. The boat scudded onto a sandy spit, and the soldiers barked orders. The prisoners, maybe a dozen, slogged ashore.

"Not the same guards as the boat I came in on," Gaius said quietly. "That's good, at least."

"Well, we'd better get the negotiations started, don't you think?" said Scaevolus. The soldiers were preparing to push off when one of them noticed the group moving in their direction. Quickly the guards stood shoulder to shoulder, the points of their gladii leveled at Amanis and her friends.

"What do you want?" one of them said.

"Peace, friends," said Scaevolus. "I'm an old, sick man, and none of us has any weapons. We don't mean any harm."

The soldiers were staring at Othar. He grunted, shook his head, and held out his hands, palms facing the soldiers.

"Tell me, is Marcus Lucius Caprius still centurion of the harbor squadron in Ephesus?" Scaevolus asked.

The commander of the detail gave Scaevolus a doubtful look. "How do you know Marcus Lucius?"

"We're old friends. I sold him Cales."

The guard's eyes widened. "The bodyguard? The big one?"

Scaevolus nodded. "I used to do quite a bit of business in Ephesus. I was on my way back there with my friends and…servants here, and we ran into a bit of unfortunate weather. We're fairly anxious to get off this island." He reached into his belt and took out a small pouch. He jiggled it in his palm so that the dull clank of coins was easy to hear. "We're more than willing to pay for our passage."

"I've won a lot of money betting on Cales," the soldier muttered, his eyes never leaving the purse in Scaevolus's hand. "I've told Marcus Lucius a hundred times he could make some good money putting Cales with a lanista and hiring him out as a gladiator." He looked them over a final time. "All right, then. You can come as far as the ship. But if the captain won't take you, the lot of you'll have to swim back. And I want that German blindfolded with his hands tied."

To Amanis's great relief, the commander of the vessel was a person known to Scaevolus. For the sake of the acquaintance and a few pieces of gold, he brought them on board and weighed anchor for Ephesus. The wind stayed favorable, and they were through the strait of Samos a little after noon. By sunset they were approaching Ephesus.

As the harbor came into view around the Koressos headlands, the captain, standing in the bow, let out a string of curses. "They're dredging out the harbor again," he said. "We'll have to go around to Miletus if we don't want to sit out here all night like a duck on a pond. They ought to just give up on it. Fast as it silts up, Ephesus'll be landlocked pretty soon."

When Amanis told Scaevolus what the captain had said, his face filled with dismay. "Miletus! That's nearly forty miles. Five days walking at a good clip."

"We could always wait until the ship can get back to port."

"No! I've had a belly full of waiting."

He went to the rail and stared at the city across the harbor as the ship swung gradually about. "So close," he said, pounding a fist feebly on the rail. "So close."

They followed the Meander out of Miletus until it turned west, then they picked up the trail through the highlands. Scaevolus walked like a man dragging a millstone. Even with Othar's arm around his shoulders, it was all he could do to move one foot in front of the other. There were times, especially in the hill country, when Othar all but carried him. Finally, after six days, they slogged toward the Magnesian Gate.

"I am Marcus Licinius Scaevolus," the old man wheezed at the guards. "I am a citizen in good standing." The soldier looked at his squad leader, who gave a quick nod.

Gaius left them quickly once they were in the city. "I'm sorry, friends," he said, "but I must get this letter from John to the elders as quickly as I can. They'll want to make copies to send out." He gripped Scaevolus's shoulder. "I pray you find your daughter."

They attracted more than a few stares as they made their way through the streets. Amanis found herself wondering how many of the onlookers might remember her. At any moment she expected to hear Patroclus's voice behind her, ordering her arrest.

They made it to Scaevolus's villa on Marble Street. It sat behind high stone walls, back from the street and a little way up the slope of Pion's western face. From the top story, Amanis could overlook the tiled roof of the Harbor Baths and, farther left, the theater. She stared toward the harbor. Somewhere down there, in the tangle of the waterfront, was the Jewish house of worship—if it still stood. What were the chances that the old man she had entrusted the baby to was still alive? She racked her brain, trying to remember the name of the family that had adopted the baby. Wasn't the man a leatherworker of some kind? She couldn't be sure. It was so long ago.

There was a place she needed to go in Scaevolus's large estate. She went down the stairs to the main atrium. She crossed to the middle of the courtyard, then paused, looking about uncertainly. Such a long time ago. She went along a small colonnade to some large wooden doors at the end. She pushed on them and they swung open. For a moment the smell held her still; her heart began to race. She had forgotten the smell.

There were very few furnishings: just a large, square room with a high ceiling and big windows. She closed her eyes, and the images came rushing back: the red-faced man with the big paunch, peering down at the small boy with huge eyes, occasionally leaning over to prod the boy with a finger or ask him a question in a loud voice; the painted acolyte from the temple of Diana, standing with a finger on her lips as she tried to choose from among the several girl babies being displayed in the arms of Scaevolus's women; the woman with the hawkish face who held the girl—not much older than Amanis at the time—and jerked her this way and that, peering at her from every angle through squinted eyes.

She could see her father's back as they walked into the room. He wouldn't look at her, hadn't looked at her since he told her to get up and come with him. She asked him where they were going, but he wouldn't answer. He just started walking down the street. Amanis had asked herself many times through the years whether he would have known or cared if she had simply run the other way.

Scaevolus was standing at that end of the room, near one of the windows, she remembered. He had nodded gravely at her father as they approached, then his eyes quickly slid over her, gauging price and condition and suitability.

And now Scaevolus lay on his couch in a nearby room, barely clinging to life. The strangeness of it filled her. It pushed the world aside for a moment, made her see her life, Scaevolus's life, the life of every person in Ephesus, as threads in a weaving. They crossed each other in one place, then another, then another, and the design of the joinings and partings was no more apparent to them than the color of stones at the bottom of the sea.

Do you see? Is the pattern of your choosing? Do you know why I'm here, in this place, at this moment?

"He calls for you."

The voice made her jump. She turned around. It was the factor, the man she had fought for the newborn girl.

He was pointing through the doorway. "The master says he is ready to go."

Twenty-six

When Amanis entered Scaevolus's chamber and saw him on his bed, she knew he wasn't going anywhere. His eyes were closed, and his chest labored with each breath as if he had just run a race. The flesh around his mouth was pale; sweat glistened on his forehead. If possible, he looked worse now than when they had arrived here. He opened his eyes.

"Ah, you…found her, Hilarion. Thank you." His head fell back.

Othar was kneeling beside the couch. "He is too weak," he said.

"Must…find," Scaevolus gasped. "Rested…then go."

Amanis turned to the factor. "You have to talk to him. He can't do this. He won't live long enough to walk to the harbor."

Hilarion's eyes went to his master. "Yet, if he doesn't find her soon, that will kill him, too. The years of this pursuit have made of him what you see. The hope of its success is all that keeps him alive."

Daphnis's uneven tread sounded behind them. He entered the room, and Gaius was with him.

"I delivered the letter to the elders," Gaius said. "I came here as soon as I could." He went to Scaevolus's bedside and took the sick man's hand. "I'll help you find your child. I have friends who will do all that can be done."

Scaevolus's lips moved weakly, but no sound came out.

Gaius turned to Amanis. "Tell me whatever you can remember about the night you took the child."

She told him of walking down Mount Pion and slipping into the city through the Koressos Gate. She described the appearance and, as best her memory allowed, the location of the synagogue. When she mentioned the old, one-legged Jewish man, Gaius's face brightened.

"Simeon! I remember him. He used to sit in front of my father at the First Day gatherings."

"Is he still—"

The smile wavered. "He died. Six, maybe seven years ago."

"If only I could remember that name," Amanis said, kneading her forehead.

"What name?" Gaius asked.

"The name of the family that took the girl. I remember the old man told me someone took her, but I can't remember the name. It's been too long. Something about leather, maybe, but…I can't remember."

"Thomas the tanner."

Amanis stared at Othar. "What did you say?"

"That morning, when we were on our way to meet the troupe. You ran across the street to the Jewish place and nearly got caught by the patrol."

"Yes, but—"

"I followed you. I heard what the old man said when you asked him about the baby. 'She is in the home of Thomas the tanner,' he said."

Her mouth hung open. "How did you remember that?"

Othar shrugged.

"Thomas the tanner," Gaius said, chewing his lip. "Doesn't mean anything to me, but I'll ask some people." He paced quickly toward the doorway.

Amanis realized Hilarion was looking at her strangely. When he noticed she'd seen him, he looked away.

The house of Scaevolus had many rooms. Walking in its court-yards and along its colonnades, it was easy for Amanis to imagine the house bustling with slaves, with the comings and goings of commerce and daily affairs. But the rooms were quiet now and mostly empty. Grass sprouted between the flagstones of the courtyards; the paint on the columns and plastered walls was blistered and peeling.

Hilarion parceled them out among the rooms. Amanis and Daphnis shared a chamber nearly twice as large as their tenement room in Athens. It was a far cry, she thought as she lay down that night, from the last place she had slept in Ephesus.

A disturbing dream woke her while it was still dark, but its images faded like smoke on the wind as soon as she realized she was awake. All that was left was a darkness pressing on her, the vague impression of a sorrow too deep for words. It was enough to keep her from returning to sleep. She rose, pulled her robe around her, and padded quietly through the doorway.

She leaned against a column just outside her door and listened to the sounds of the darkness, wondering how close it was to dawn. As she stood there, she saw a figure come out of the room directly across the courtyard and pass along the colonnade. Robed and hooded, its tread made no sound.

Amanis felt her heart quicken its pace. She held her breath as the figure made its way toward the main atrium. She decided to follow.

When she was certain its back was toward her, she ducked into her room and grabbed up her sandals and the sikhimi. She leaned slowly around the edge of her doorway and saw the figure go through the arched entry to the main atrium. She followed as silently as she could.

When she reached the atrium, the figure was nearly to the main door. It put out a hand to the latch, then paused. It began turning back toward her. She tried to back quickly around the corner, but the tip of the sikhimi scraped the wall as she moved. The sound seemed as loud as a scream.

The figure was looking her direction. Now it was walking slowly toward her. Amanis drew the sikhimi and held it in front of her, and the figure halted ten paces away. "The last time you struck me with a rock. This time will you stab me?" A hand reached up and pushed back the hood. It was Hilarion.

Amanis let her breath out slowly as she straightened. She let the blade fall to her side. "Where are you going with such secrecy?" she asked.

"I might ask what you're doing awake at such an hour."

"I couldn't sleep. I saw you walking down the colonnade."

He stood very still for a long time. "Gaius spoke to you of the elders," he said, finally. "Are you a follower of the Christ?"

"Yes. The boy and the German, as well."

"The German? Really?"

She nodded.

"Well then, if you must know, I'm going to the First Day gathering."

"At night?"

He glanced up at the stars. "It'll be sunrise before too much longer. We gather while it's still dark. While most of the proconsul's watchdogs are in bed."

"May I come with you?"

He looked at her a moment, then gave a single nod. "But you won't need that," he said, pointing at the sikhimi. "And you'd better put those on," he added, pointing at her other hand.

Amanis looked down and realized she was still carrying her sandals.

Once again she was sneaking through the darkened streets of Ephesus. Unlike the last time, however, they had no close pursuit. Other than glancing behind and about them occasionally, Hilarion kept a steady pace.

"After our failure to contact you in Smyrna, Scaevolus sent me back here, to continue overseeing the household and trade," he was saying. "He consumed everything in his search for her. Gradually he liquidated all his business enterprises, the land he owned here and in Phrygia, his livestock, even his collection of ancient scrolls and inscriptions. In the last few years, when he commanded me to start selling off the household slaves, I knew things couldn't go on the same way much longer."

"I hope we can find her."

"Gaius is a good man. If it can be done, he'll do it."

"How long have you been a Christ-follower?"

"Nearly two years now. In a way, it was the master's situation that brought me to it."

"How?"

He took a few paces. "I've managed Scaevolus's slave trade for many years. I've seen many slaves and many masters. Some masters use their slaves well, some not. Some slaves serve their masters well, some not. None of it's any of my business, of course. But for a while now, I've been noticing a few masters who seem different somehow. They don't poke and prod the stock in the buying room; they speak kindly to them. When I see their servants in the agora, I don't see bruises on them, don't see them limping or moving stiffly.

"Then I started to realize that some slaves didn't speak poorly of their masters. They didn't loiter in the agora, didn't spend their peculium on whores or the taverns. Even the ones who had hard-handed masters seemed—well, peaceful, somehow. Like I always imagined the old philosophers being. Even some of the people of my own household were starting to act differently. Calmer. Less needful of my constant watching.

"Then Propylus, who'd been here since before I came to serve Scaevolus, fell ill. Suddenly people were coming in to comfort him as he died. People I'd never seen. Slaves, most of them. But some of them were free tradesmen I'd never even seen before. And women, some of them quite well-to-do—matrons of some of the best households in Ephesus. Why were all these people so concerned about the dying of an old man who'd been a slave all his life?

"The day he died, I was there. Five or six of these people were there, too. They were weeping over him and praying, calling on a god I'd never heard of before."

"Jesus Christ."

He nodded. "But I wasn't sure. They also kept saying *anastasis,* over and over. I wasn't sure if the name of the god was Jesus Christ or Resurrection. They said one almost as often as they said the other. And when Propylus took his last breath, they asked if they could take his body and bury it according to their customs. I had no objection, of course. Less expense for me to pay from a quickly dwindling purse.

"But the more I thought about it, the more it bothered me. What god could bring together people of such different stations with so little in common? There was even an old African woman who came sometimes toward the end." He turned toward Amanis. "She reminded me of you, actually. I wondered if she knew you."

"You've thought so much about me all this time?"

"Considering my master's preoccupation, I assure you I've thought of you a great deal. But the woman didn't know you, as it happened.

"Anyway, one day not long after that, I asked one of the few remaining household servants—the Christ-followers were the last to be sold, as you can imagine—some questions about this philosophy of hers. 'Come and see,' she said. So the next time one of their First Days came, I got up in the dark and went with her to a gathering.

"It was at one of the big houses, up on the side of Koressos. When we got there, I realized it was some kind of special gathering of all the Christian communities in Ephesus. There were many people there unknown to Sylvia—the one who brought me. She said they were all gathering to say good-bye to someone. A leader of theirs who had been banished."

"John."

"Yes, that's right. You know of him?"

She told him about the shipwreck. "But you were saying—"

"Well, this John was an interesting fellow. Everyone there was weeping and falling on his neck. He alone seemed undisturbed. 'Little children,' he kept calling them, and telling them not to worry. After a while, John asked someone to bring the letter. They all seemed to know which one he meant. He read it to them. And I began to understand a little about why these Christ people were so different. It was a letter written quite a few years ago by someone named Paul."

"I've heard others talk about him," she said.

"He told them things you might expect of any philosopher: wishes for them to have wisdom and revelation, admonitions to patience, truthfulness, sobriety, temperance. Even the advice to slaves sounded familiar: Don't just do well when someone's watching you, but serve your masters from your hearts.

"But then this Paul tells masters, 'Don't threaten your slaves. Treat them well, since you know you, too, have a master in heaven.' That was something I'd not run across before. Masters who don't abuse their slaves are more respected, of course, but to actually call them to account?

"I started going with Sylvia after that, almost every First Day. I watched the way they spoke to one another. I saw landowners kneeling in front of slaves to ask forgiveness for some fault, and watched as the slave prayed over his master, then embraced him, sometimes with tears. I'd never imagined anything like it. And before long, I knew I wanted to be a part of it."

They walked a while in silence, and something in Hilarion's narrative began to nag at her. The troubling notion of her responsibility toward Patroclus came again to the front of her thoughts. *What would You have me do?* she prayed, thinking even as she prayed it that she already suspected the answer—and it brought her no comfort.

They came to the meeting place: a small house just around the corner from the Harbor Baths. A few people were already there. Two men smiled at Hilarion as they walked toward him. They exchanged the kiss of greeting, then turned toward Amanis.

"This is Amanis. She's a believer," Hilarion told them. "She's just arrived from Athens. She knows Gaius—and John."

Their eyes widened at this, and they both gave her the greeting. "Come and sit with us, sister," one of them said to her.

"Tell us about John," said another. "How is it you know him? Did you see him on Patmos? Is he well?"

As briefly as she could, she explained about the journey from Athens, and how they had been cast up on Patmos by the storm. She told about Gaius and the mission that had brought her back to Ephesus.

"Thomas the tanner," one of them mused when she finished. "No, I don't recognize the name. But we'll do everything we can. We have to be careful, you know. The procurator is no friend of the Way. But—"

The other man leaned across and laid a hand on the arm of his friend. Someone was standing in front of the assembly. He raised his hands and angled his face toward the sky and began to sing. As he sang each line, the gathering chanted the words in response.

There is one Physician, both fleshly and spiritual,
begotten and unbegotten, God who came in the flesh.
True life in death, both of Mary and of God,
first passible then impassible,
Jesus Christ, our Lord. Amen.

"Just as the Christ suffered, brothers and sisters," the man said, "we, too, will suffer. Some of us have been imprisoned. Some have been tortured. Our beloved brother John languishes in exile, a man who has wronged no one, but did good to all and never stopped reminding us to pray for the Emperor and all those in authority."

He finished by telling them that the only real deliverance and healing was that given by the Christ. "He is the true physician who comes from God," he said. "One day, He will heal not only us, but all the world. Until that day, brothers and sisters, watch and pray."

They all stood for the benediction. Afterward a few people went to the man who had presided and gave him money or loaves or flasks of oil. The rest stood about in small groups talking. The two men who had greeted them were asking Hilarion about the search for his master's daughter.

"Is it even known whether she is still alive?"

Hilarion shook his head. "This is the woman who took her up on the day she was born." He gave Amanis a crooked smile. "Best not to cross her, as I learned that day."

"You took her to Simeon?" one of the men asked.

"Yes. I never knew his name, but that was what Gaius called him."

The man wore a studied look. "Thomas the tanner. I know some of the Jewish families in Ephesus, but I never heard of a tanner named Thomas."

They drifted toward the doorway. Amanis felt Hilarion's hand on her arm. "There she is," he was saying. "Come, Amanis. You should meet this woman. I think she's maybe a countryman of yours, at least."

He guided her toward an old African woman. Even at her age, though, it was easy to see she was still strong. She was tall, like Amanis, though slightly bent at the shoulders. She carried herself with an ease and fluidity that belied her age.

"Neria. Here's someone I want you to meet."

The old woman turned to face them. Amanis stared at her briefly before catching herself. The old woman reminded her strongly of her father. Hilarion was right; she had to be Nubian.

"Well met, good mother," Amanis said, one of the few phrases she remembered in the language of her people. The old woman's eyes widened. "And to you, daughter," she said, completing the formula. "Who are you?"

"What do you mean?" Amanis asked.

"Who are your people, child?"

"My father—" The dream reared up before her. *Her father in chains…Patroclus shaking the empty collar and glaring at her…*— "my father was called Lucius. He was a metal worker, a smith."

"You say, 'was'? Do you think him dead?"

"I haven't seen him in many years." *The collar…squatting in his own filth…*"Why have you come back?"

Amanis felt the woman's hand taking hers. Her grip was strong. "Come, then. It's time you saw him again."

"How do you know him?"

"He is my brother."

Twenty-seven

awn was rising over Ephesus as the old woman led Amanis along the streets. Amanis stared at the woman as they walked, barely able to hear anything above the pounding of her own heart. Could it be true? Could this woman really be her aunt? She tried to remember the scraps of mention from her childhood: two sisters, taken as slaves at the same time as her father. Once they reached the slave market at Alexandria, he never saw them again. He thought he heard the Greek who bought them say he was taking them somewhere in northern Greece—Macedonia, maybe. She had never even heard him say their names. Neria? Was that what Hilarion had called her?

She realized the woman was saying something to her in Nubian. She shook her head. "I don't understand. I don't remember too many words in Nubian."

"I was telling you I've been praying to Jesus Christ to bring you back here. Your father needs to see you. He needs to believe."

"Believe…?"

Neria pushed on a door and pulled her into the courtyard of a small house. It was the same dusty yard, with thin chickens scratching in the dust. The same small shop behind the house. She almost expected to see herself as a child, running from the house to see the visitors at the gate. Almost expected to hear the sound of her mother's singing.

She heard the clang of a hammer on an anvil, and a rush of memories closed her throat. Her fingers dug into Neria's shoulder. "No," she said in a low, panicked voice. "I can't."

"Come on, little one," Neria said. "It will be well. You'll see. You'll see."

They walked toward the shop. There were no walls, only wooden columns to support the mud and wattle roof, just as Amanis remembered. She saw a man, his back to her, bent over an anvil. He raised a hammer and brought it down with a clatter. Then they were in the doorway.

"Napti. Look here. Now will you believe?"

Napti. That was her father's name, his real name. Everyone else in Ephesus knew him as Lucius the metalsmith.

He put down the hammer. With his tongs he picked up the metal, still glowing a dull red, and inspected it, turning it this way and that. Still he had not turned to face them. He dipped the metal in a nearby tub; steam leaped up to the roof. He laid the tongs on the anvil and turned.

Somehow, in her mind, she had not allowed for the years since she had last looked on him. But this man was much older, much harder used.

He still held himself straight. In that, she now saw, he was like his sister. And though the flesh of his upper arms hung a bit looser than she remembered, the muscles and tendons were still firm.

But it was in his face that she chiefly noticed the changes. In the droop of his mouth, the sag beneath his eyes. His hair and beard were almost completely white.

"Who is this?" he asked, but his eyes told her he already knew. She had to fight to keep herself there in his presence.

"I am Amanis, Father. The daughter you sold into slavery. Remember?" She heard the quaver in her voice, but couldn't do anything about it.

"I told you, Napti. I told you I was asking Jesus Christ every day to bring this daughter back to you."

"I have not come back to him," Amanis said. "I came here because you brought me. And I don't care to be called his daughter. I was no more to him than some coins from Scaevolus's purse."

Neria grabbed her, pulled her around to face her. "Both of you have the same disease. It tastes like hate to you, and it tastes like hopelessness to him, but it's the same sickness." She brought her face even closer to Amanis. "I served a woman who watched her daughter walk away and stay gone until the daughter was a grandmother herself. They said she came back at the end, when it was almost too late. So many times I wanted to say something, but I was only a slave. Well, now I am not a slave anymore. I will fight against this sickness. My brother passed it to you, maybe. But it ends here. Today. Now. In the name of Jesus Christ I say to you, it ends now!"

Napti sank slowly to his knees, leaned forward and picked up handfuls of dust. He put the dust on his head; some of it filtered down onto his face. Wet from his sweat and tears, it ran down his face in muddy rivulets, tan against the ebony of his skin. He sobbed, louder and louder.

Amanis watched him, fascinated and ashamed. The long grief poured and poured and poured from him. "Merume," he said. "Merume, I'm sorry. I'm sorry, Merume, I'm sorry."

Hearing her mother's name shifted something in Amanis. Merume had loved them both once. Was that enough? *What would You have me do?* she prayed. And realized she already knew the answer.

Slowly, as if walking past a sleeping lion, she crossed to him. She knelt beside him, in the dust of the workshop, and put her hands on him. She felt the beginnings of her own tears.

She stayed in her father's house all that day, and the two old people sat across from her and listened as she told about the baby and how it all began. She told them about her escape and her wandering. She told them about the other babies in Athens, then about Daphnis.

Amanis realized she was talking more to her aunt than to her father. It was still hard between them. It probably would be for a long time—maybe always. But at least she was here. At least he was listening, for now. There was a chance.

The emptiness of her stomach made her realize it was well into the afternoon. "I have to get back. Daphnis will be worrying about me, likely, and I need to find out how Scaevolus is faring."

At the slaver's name, her father looked away.

"He has lost a child, too," she said in what she hoped was a gentle tone. "Maybe I can help him."

"You must bring the boy to us," Neria said. "Daphnis. I want to see him."

"I'll try, but I have to be careful. If Patroclus finds out I'm here—"

Her father scrambled to his feet as if something were burning him. "Wait. Don't go," he said and went quickly to an iron-banded wooden box in the corner of the room. He came back with a folded piece of parchment. "Here. Open this."

She turned the packet over in her lap. It was yellowed with age, and it had been sealed so long ago that the wax was dry and crumbled. What was left of it, though, looked like the seal of Patroclus. She looked at him questioningly.

"Just open it," he said. He wouldn't look at her.

The rest of the seal flaked off as she ran her thumb beneath the flap. The parchment was written in Greek characters. "I can't," she said. "I don't know how to read."

"Tell her," said Neria, looking at her brother. "Tell her, Napti. She has to know."

"Tell me what?"

Still he wouldn't look at her. "Not long after you . . . you left, word got out that Patroclus was in trouble with his creditors. He had to sell almost everything. He opened his veins rather than face the public shame. But before he did, I . . . I went to him and bought this." He pointed at the parchment. "He sold you back to me. He told me that's what the paper says."

"All this time...I've been—"

"You don't belong to Patroclus anymore, even if he were still alive. I give you the writing. It's yours. You're free."

"I'm—"

"You see, Amanis? He never forgot, not really," Neria was saying. "There was something in him that hoped, even after all the hurt. Even though he tried not to let himself believe it. And the proof of it is in your hands."

Walking back to Scaevolus's house, she had to continually remind herself not to break into a run. Maybe her father had it wrong. Or perhaps Patroclus, in some fit of vindictiveness, had lied to her father about what was written in the paper. Even when Neria got out her own paper, the one her former mistress in Philippi had given her, and showed Amanis how many of the Greek letters looked the same in both documents, still Amanis could not let herself trust it. Hilarion would tell her. She had to get to him. With promises to come back soon, she rushed away from her father and his sister.

The sun was nearing the top of Pion when she came through Scaevolus's gate. "Hilarion!" she shouted. "Where are you? I need you!"

"Mother, where have you—"

"Not now, Daphnis," she said, rushing past him. "Where is Hilarion? I have to see him, right now."

"In with Scaevolus," the boy said in a hurt voice.

"Hilarion!"

He came running from Scaevolus's chamber. "What? Have they found her?"

Amanis thrust the paper at him. "Read this. Tell me what it says."

His eyes scanned the writing; his lips moved silently. He looked up at her. "It says Patroclus sells you to some freedman named Lucius for—" he glanced at the paper—"three thousand sesterces." His eyebrows arched. "Three thousand. Not a bad price, if you're the seller. Who is this Lucius?"

There was a roaring inside her head. She reached out to find the wall.

"What's wrong?"

She shook her head, tried to hold her mind still enough to form words. "Nothing. I...Lucius was—is my father. He bought my freedom from Patroclus, my former master."

"Patroclus...yes, I remember him. Got into some trouble with the bankers. Killed himself, didn't he?"

"So...this paper means I no longer belong to Patroclus or anyone in his family?"

He looked at it again. "It's properly witnessed, and it looks like your father registered it at the temple of Serapis." He handed the parchment back to her. "Perfectly legal and binding."

Three thousand sesterces. Amanis tried to imagine what her father had thought about, the day he decided to gather the money and climb the twisting street up the flank of Mount Koressos to the home of his beleaguered patron. She wondered if he dickered with Patroclus for her life, or if he simply paid whatever price her former master had asked. She wanted to believe the latter. But maybe that didn't make any difference. He had done it; that was the inescapable thing. Her father had climbed outside the isolation of his despair long enough to act upon a wild, unlikely hope.

"Of course, technically you belong to your father," Hilarion was saying.

"Yes. I know that. But...it's all right."

Several days went by, and still no word came. No one knew a Jew named Thomas who was a tanner. Gaius told them inquiries had been made among the tanner's guild and among as many of the synagogues as had friendly relations with anyone among the Way.

Scaevolus was still clinging to life. He faded in and out of consciousness. When he was awake, Hilarion or Othar would do their best to give him some thin broth or a few sips of water. Now and then he had strength enough to talk to them a little.

None of them gave him the bald truth about the discouraging progress of the search.

Tarquinius mostly kept to himself. Amanis sometimes saw him wandering in one of the courtyards or along a colonnade. If she tried to engage him in conversation, he would answer in as few syllables as possible and find the earliest excuse to take himself somewhere else. He made it a point to be elsewhere when Gaius or anyone else from the Way came calling. Sometimes he gathered with the rest of them for meals, sometimes not.

"What's wrong with Uncle Tarquinius?" Daphnis asked one day as he was copying out a document for one of his clients.

"I'm not sure," Amanis said. "But he hasn't been the same since Othar's baptism."

"I know. He wouldn't even say good-bye to Father John when we left Patmos."

She looked at Daphnis as he bent carefully over his parchment. "What do you think he needs to hear?" she asked him.

He sat up and carefully wiped his stylus. "I think someone should ask him why he's so afraid of hope."

She shook her head as she looked at him. "Sometimes I think you are really a philosopher, only pretending to be a boy."

"Such things you say, Mother." He took up his stylus, spat on his ink block, and again leaned over his work.

Later that day, Tarquinius slipped through the main gate. Amanis walked to the entry and watched as he hobbled down the path leading to Marble Street. He turned south toward the theater. On a sudden impulse she ran to her room, grabbed her head covering, and trotted after him.

She kept a good distance between them, though his stature made him difficult to locate at times. He continued past the gymnasium and the theater. Finally he turned aside at the fountain on the east side of the agora.

It was a market day, and the colonnades and porticos surrounding the square were crowded. Tarquinius found a seat on one of the stone benches fronting the fountain. He watched the crowds. After a while she walked over to him.

"May I sit, or are you meeting someone?"

"Following me, are you?"

She shrugged.

"Well, I can't keep you from sitting, if you want to."

She sat and watched the marketgoers for a while. Pity she hadn't brought her juggling bag; she could probably make some money today.

"It's getting on toward summer. I wonder if the troupe will be through Ephesus anytime soon."

"I hope so. When they do, I'll leave with them," Tarquinius said.

"What makes you think they'd have you back?"

She could see the red working its way up the back of his neck.

"I'm joking, Tarquinius."

"You can say what you please, like anyone else."

She looked over her shoulder at the shaded alcove where the fountain spilled into its stone basin. The spout was carved in the shape of a lion's head. A little boy cupped his hand under the water and brought it to his mouth, then dashed away after his father. "This is where we first ran into each other, isn't it? This fountain. I never expected to be sitting here with you again, especially in broad daylight on a market day."

"Well, things have changed, haven't they? You can do as you please now."

"I know. That's why I'm here."

"What's that supposed to mean?"

She waited a moment before answering. "This morning, I asked Daphnis what he thought you needed to hear. Do you want to know what he said?"

No response.

"He said, 'Someone should ask him why he's so afraid of hope.'"

Tarquinius fidgeted and mumbled something unintelligible.

"What did you say?"

He jerked around to face her. "I said, 'Easy for him to say.'"

He jumped from the bench and vanished into the crowd.

Twenty-eight

"What should I call him, Mother?" Daphnis wanted to know.

"His name is Napti. But most people in Ephesus know him as Lucius."

"But he's your father. Shouldn't I call him 'Grandfather'?"

"You can if you want to." She looked at the gate, hesitant to enter. If it weren't for the steadying presence—and the insistence—of Neria, she wasn't sure she'd have brought Daphnis for this visit. She took a deep breath, then pushed on the gate; it swung inward. She heard the rattle of iron in the workshop. Amanis called Neria's name as they went to the door of the house.

Neria was seated by the fire pit, stirring something in a large iron pot. She looked up when they came in, and Amanis saw the widening of her eyes when she saw Daphnis.

"Oh! You are the boy, then. Come closer." She waved him over.

Amanis stood by the door as Daphnis shuffled toward her

aunt. Neria reached out and took his withered arm in her hand. She looked at Amanis. "I don't know why, but when you told me about him, my mind saw an African boy." She chuckled, shaking her head. "I'm a silly old woman." She looked at Daphnis's face, held his chin with her fingertips. "Sit down, boy. I want to talk to you."

"Should I tell Father we're here?"

"Not yet. Come over here, Amanis. Sit with us for a while. Now tell me, Daphnis. Tell me what you remember about the day you were born."

He looked helplessly at Amanis. "But…I was only a baby—"

"Yes." Neria nodded slowly. "A baby, and at the very beginning. Beginnings are so important, boy. They tell so much, show so much." She cocked her head, watching him. She let the silence lengthen.

"Well, I…don't really remember anything about…about the woman who bore me. I only remember Amanis." He looked at Amanis when he said it. "I remember her hands, her voice. I remember that she took care of me always."

A gentle smile started on Neria's face and grew until her face shone with its warmth.

"I remember this, too," Daphnis said. His voice sounded surprised, wondering. "I remember the first time I knew my skin was different than Mother's. I wanted to rub pitch into it, or something else dark, so it would be like hers." He laughed.

Neria laughed with him, shaking her head. "No, no boy. Not like that. There are other ways of being like her. Inside ways."

"There is something I worry about sometimes," Daphnis said, his face becoming more serious. "I've even talked to Mother about it once."

"What is it, boy?"

"Will I ever really know who I am?"

Neria took on a faraway look. She stirred the pot for a long time without saying anything. "Go back to the place you were born," she said finally.

Amanis felt a thrill of apprehension. "Back to Athens?"

"No. Not the city. The place. The inside place. There is a place inside everyone at birth. Sometimes we lose that place. We forget what made us, how we are made. We have to find the place again. Then we can remember who we are." She looked at Daphnis. "You can find the place." Then she stopped stirring and pointed at Amanis. "And you can show him the way."

She stirred a bit more, then leaned over and looked into the pot. "This is ready. Now you can go and tell my brother to come in."

As Amanis rose to go get her father, she realized she knew the place Neria was talking about. And she knew how to help Daphnis find it.

The western slope of Mount Pion rose away from them, orange in the late afternoon light. The summer heat still blared from the stony ground; Amanis felt it soaking through her sandals. She led Daphnis up the twisting path toward the summit, pacing herself to accommodate him. She stopped climbing and signaled him for quiet. They stood still for a while, listening for the cries. Nothing.

"Maybe there aren't any here today," she said, leaning forward into the climb. "That's what you always hope for, of course. But some days…"

"What if we find more than one? What if we find more than we can manage?"

"'What if' is the beginning of a prayer to fate. Trust God, Daphnis. He won't give you more to do than you can manage. Or so I have found it to be up until now." The breeze tossed his hair as she looked at him. She felt big with love for this boy who was now on the verge of becoming a man. *You can only toss and catch one ball at a time.*

They had been going out nearly every evening for two market intervals now. The day Amanis scooped a baby off the ground and settled it in the crook of Daphnis's arm, it was as if he were hearing his own name for the first time. He said nothing the entire way down the mountain and through the streets to the house where they took the foundlings. He stared into the face of the infant he held, reading something there she guessed was intended only for the child.

They took the babies to the home of Thallia, the widow of Tyrannus, a longtime teacher and lecturer. The house was built onto the back of the spacious hall where her husband had lectured for so many years. It was close to the synagogue where Amanis had gone that very first night, where she had knocked on the door of kindly old Simeon and his shrewish daughter. Simeon was one of the first to receive Paul's teachings about Jesus Christ in those early days, Amanis had heard. No one mentioned the daughter.

Things were much easier with the babies now. Upon her husband's death, Thallia had converted the lecture hall into a kind of inn for the families of those who were dispossessed. During the times when the procurators' suspicions toward the Way ran high, there might be as many as twenty or thirty persons there, not including children. Most of the offerings from the First Day gatherings went to Thallia.

Word of the rescue efforts by the African woman and her

adopted son spread quickly from Thallia's household throughout the Christian communities of Ephesus. Rarely was a baby at
Thallia's more than one or two nights before some family came
forward to offer it a home. A few even began to join in the daily
search among the crags and copses of Mount Pion.

Evening deepened as Amanis and Daphnis returned to the house
on Marble Street. It was near midsummer and though the sun
was well below the horizon, the heat of the day still hovered in
the air like a weighted net. She tugged on the gate, then paused.
An unfamiliar racket of voices came from one of the inner atri-
ums. She and Daphnis went through the archway from the entry
yard and saw a crowd in the atrium, lamps and sconced torches
scattered throughout the open space. People were talking and
laughing; it looked like a feast was well underway. Amanis's first
thought was bafflement. Her second was indignation—
Scaevolus was on his deathbed; this was no place to hold a revel.

Tarquinius scuttled over to her. "Well, look who's finally
back! Come on, come on. Damon's been asking about you."

"Damon?"

"Yes. Has the heat made you blind? The troupe's here."

She peered around the atrium. Yes, there was Harim, leaning over with a dagger to spear a morsel from a bowl, laughing
at something Turash had just said. They looked amazingly
unchanged, almost as if the years she had spent in Athens had
not been. Maybe it was the lamplight. Or maybe she was seeing
more with her memory than with her tired eyes. And there was
Artemisia, one of the fortune tellers. Did she look a little heavier
than Amanis remembered? But there were Horatius's bird cages,
and the old man squatting between them. Wait…no. The bird

keeper turned to reach for a wine bowl, and Amanis realized it was a far younger man than Horatius. Tarisia, the dancer, was not present. There was her partner, Tyche, but now Tyche wore the habit of one of the fortune tellers. She looked closer and failed to find Thyrsis among the grandmothers. So time had not overlooked the troupe, after all.

"Who told these people to come here?" she said, rounding on the dwarf. "This is the house of a dying man, and we're guests here, not hosts. And besides that, who paid for all this food?"

Tarquinius stared at her. "What happened to all those notions of charity you learned from your Christ-follower friends? Isn't it better for them to sleep here than in some ravine outside the city walls?"

"It's one thing, Tarquinius, to share what you have with another. It's something else to make free with what belongs to someone else."

He stomped away in a huff.

"I'd better go check on Scaevolus," she told Daphnis.

"I'll come with you."

She was glad that shutting the door of the sick man's suite also shut out most of the noise from the courtyard. Hilarion was attending his master, and Othar slumped with his eyes closed against a wall near the bed.

"How is he?" she asked Hilarion in a low voice. Scaevolus appeared to be asleep.

"About the same. He wakes, takes a little broth or water, and drifts away again. His breathing is still clear and regular. He hasn't spoken all day, though. Still no word?"

She shook her head, looking down at the dying man. *Please grant him the mercy of finding her before he dies,* she prayed. *A man should see his children, even if he got them in the wrong way.*

"I'm sorry about all those people in the atrium. I don't know what Tarquinius was thinking."

"They came about midafternoon," Othar said without opening his eyes. "Tarquinius ran across Damon in the agora. They brought food and offered to share it with us in exchange for a night's shelter. We've been eating boiled beans for a long time. Hilarion and I told them yes."

"Have you eaten then?" she asked.

Hilarion nodded his head and smiled. "One of the women brought us each a bowl of meat and cheese not long after they got here. Your friends live pretty well for wandering performers. And right now my belly is glad for it."

"Damon especially wants to see you," Othar said. "He's asked about you several times."

She went out, promising to return with something for Daphnis to eat. Among the food piled in the atrium, she found some new crop figs, almonds, walnuts, and apricots. There were several skins of soft cheese, and even a little bread remained. She gathered some of each into a bowl to take back to her son. As she was turning to go, she heard someone calling her name. She turned around and saw Damon, stepping carefully among the groups of people seated cross-legged on the flagstones as he made his way toward her.

He reached the place where she waited and stood for a moment, maybe an arm's length away, smiling at her. "Hello, Amanis. I hear you've learned something about juggling."

"Maybe. And one or two other things besides, who knows?"

They watched each other for a few more moments. "I need to take this food to my son," she said finally. "Then maybe we can see."

"Son?"

She tilted her head, inviting him to follow.

He pulled open the door for her, and they stepped into the hush of Scaevolus's quarters. Daphnis was on the floor beside Othar, talking quietly with the German.

"This is Daphnis," she said, handing the bowl of food to the boy. "Daphnis, this is an old friend of mine. He taught me to juggle, though he didn't know it. His name is Damon."

"A skilled teacher indeed who can instruct without realizing it," Hilarion said.

Damon smiled. "Let's see how well you learned before we decide how well I taught."

"My things are in another room," she said.

"By your son's look, I'd say you never saw his father," Damon said when they were outside.

"I found him in Athens. He was exposed. I retrieved him from under a laurel bush and named him Daphnis. He has a good mind. I think it almost makes up for his crippled arm and foot."

"Still the rescuer then?"

"When you've been rescued yourself, how can you do anything else?" She looked at him. "I worship the Christ now, Damon. It's because of Him I saved Daphnis. But as it turns out, Daphnis has saved me, too."

"I hear much about this Christ. In every place we stop, more and more people are talking about Him."

"Here's my room." She went in and picked up her satchel. She reached in and took three wooden balls and, after a moment's thought, brought out two more.

When Damon saw the five balls in her hands, his eyebrows arched. "Five?"

"I had a good teacher."

They went back to the atrium. Suddenly she felt nervous and a little foolish. She hadn't worked more than once or twice since they'd been back in Ephesus.

She started with three. Damon held the other two, watching her with critical eyes. At least he didn't laugh at her or turn away in disgust. Gradually the patterns began to sort themselves out; the balls crossed in front of her, and she could see the whole without having to think about the individual arcs. The popping of the balls into her palm settled into the familiar rhythm.

She nodded, and Damon tossed her one of the balls. She nodded again, and he tossed her the other. The five balls rose and fell in the firelight; people were watching, drifting over to form a circle around her and Damon.

He reached into his pack, taking out five balls. He juggled for a while and then tossed a ball to her just as she tossed one of hers to him. Soon the balls were flying back and forth in the air between them, flying in and out of their patterns and weaving the two into a single, interlocked whole.

The circle of watchers was quiet. The only sound was the brush of skin against the wooden balls, the quiet breathing of the jugglers. Amanis felt her mind reach outward to take in Damon, his quick hands and intent eyes. Then her mind reached to the audience, standing around them as still and respectful as stars. Her mind opened further and held Daphnis, Othar, and Hilarion, sitting silently in the room with Scaevolus. She enfolded Scaevolus then and reached even further, to the whole of the darkened city with its crisscrossed streets and its myriad of people. Somewhere in the city, she sensed, a particular girl sat beside a lamp or hung emptied food baskets on pegs in the ceiling beams or readied her pallet for a night's sleep.

She was there, Amanis knew—held fast in the fingertips of God.

Twenty-nine

It was then that he first started to believe, Damon told her years later. Poor Tarquinius. He thought he was leaving Ephesus in the company of the same, familiar people he had left on the dock at Smyrna. But they weren't the same at all. Everyone had changed, either for better or for worse. She prayed for Tarquinius for years, even after the troubles forced her out of Ephesus. That dwarf was as stubborn as he was short, though. Some of them had told her that close to the end, maybe… Ah, well. God was merciful; best to leave it with Him.

Amanis shifted on the stool. She realized her mind had wandered during Berenice's reading, weaving in and out of the words of her letter like a thread across the face of a loom.

"The elder, to the chosen lady and her children," Berenice had read, "whom I love in the truth—and not I only, but also all who know the truth…" Amanis smiled. Hearing John's words brought his image to her mind. She would never forget the day Demetrius handed her the packet containing this letter. "He said he wrote it either for you or for the churches in Ephesus,"

Demetrius had said. "I tried to get him to say which, but he just shrugged and said it was better to let you keep it and share it as you thought best."

Her letter. The church's letter. It worked out to much the same thing. Lots of people came through Thallia's house in those days: travelers from Christian communities in some other part of Asia Province who needed a place to stay, Ephesians whose homes had been destroyed by fire or earthquake, refugees from a procurator's oppression. And of course, there were always the children.

On her deathbed, Thallia told Amanis of her wish to bequeath the house and hall to someone who would continue the work with the abandoned babies. "And who better than the one who got the whole thing started?" she'd said.

After a while, she acquired the epithet, "Mother of Ephesus." It always embarrassed Amanis when someone said it. It sounded too much like something originating from the old temple of Diana, but it also made her sound better and more gracious than she knew herself to be. Yes, she had helped some people through the years. Yes, the number of young Ephesians among the Way who called her Mother—then, after a while, Grandmother—had grown immensely over time. But she knew that inside the kindly old woman everyone saw still lived the spirit of the restless wanderer, the one who fretted at every constraint. She looked at Berenice, at the other young women who stayed with her and treated her so kindly. What would they have made of the rebellious slave who crept out of Ephesus to escape the wrath of her master?

Ah, but if she hadn't… If she hadn't bridled at the abandonment of that tiny girl, so many years ago, many things would have ended differently.

There had been rains during the night, she remembered. The low growl of the thunder had kept her awake long enough to think gratefully of the coolness that the shower, so unusual in the summer, would lend to the morning air. The patter of water draining from the roof onto the flagstones had soon lulled her back to sleep.

She woke Daphnis the next morning and told him they were going to look for babies that morning, rather than waiting for the late afternoon. It would be hotter then, and if any infants were left out in the rain, they needed to get to them all the more quickly.

As they were going up the path, they met a woman and her daughter coming down. The daughter cradled a baby and tried to feed it goat's milk from a small leather flask. Were they of the Way? Amanis hadn't seen them before, but there were gatherings in many places throughout Ephesus, and she didn't usually come here in the mornings.

"Where was she?" she asked them, gazing down at the tiny girl. She cupped her palm around the crown of the tiny head.

"Behind some rocks, up there," the mother said, pointing to the three large rocks that guarded the outcropping where Amanis had found the first baby so long ago. She looked at the baby, then at the girl holding her and trying to feed her. A pretty girl with fine features. She looked to be maybe a little older than Daphnis.

"That's where I found my first one, many years ago," Amanis said.

The woman looked at her closely. "Are you the Nubian woman? Amanis? The one who came here from Brother John?"

Amanis nodded. The mother was looking at her now with a wide-eyed, almost fearful expression. Her jaw was trembling.

"What's wrong?" Amanis asked.

The woman fell to her knees and grabbed the front of Amanis's clothing. "You! I've thought of you for so long but never dared to seek you out. And now that God has put me in front of you, it's as I feared: I have no words to thank you." She buried her face in Amanis's robe.

Amanis stared at her, then at the girl. "Who are you?" she asked, hardly daring to hope for the answer.

"My name is Rachel," the girl said in a quiet voice. "That is the name given me by my father when I came to live at his house."

"Came to live…?"

"I came there from the house of Simeon, an old rabbi—"

"—with one leg," Amanis finished. There was a pounding in her ears.

"Yes."

Amanis felt the ground tilting. She put out a hand and grabbed Daphnis's shoulder to steady herself. "Then your father—the man who took you from Simeon's house—was a tanner named Thomas?"

"My husband," the mother said. "Thomas died a year after Rachel came to us."

"We've been looking for—"

"I know." The woman raised herself slowly to her feet. "In all the churches, people have been asking the whereabouts of Thomas the tanner. I'm surprised no one remembered I was his widow, but that was quite a few years ago, and Thomas never…never really approved of the Way."

"But why didn't you say something?"

"I was afraid! Don't you see? Rachel is the only one I have left. All we were hearing was that a Greek man who claimed to be her father wanted to see her. What if he decided to take her? What if I never saw her again?" She turned her face toward the ground, unable to meet Amanis's eyes.

Amanis looked at the girl. "Did you have no wish at all to see the man who sired you?"

The girl drew herself to her full height. "My mother is the only parent I've ever known. I would never do anything that might hurt her."

Amanis turned back toward the mother. "Listen to me—what is your name?"

"Olympia."

"Listen, Olympia. You must bring Rachel to Scaevolus. That's his name, Scaevolus, and he's dying. He's clinging to life with his last strength, and do you know why? Because the only thing he wants in all the world is to see this girl."

"Then why did he abandon her?"

"He didn't. He… Never mind that now. I ask you, I beg you, you must let him see her. He won't keep her, Olympia. He can't. He's almost too weak to breathe, much less take away your daughter."

Olympia was looking at her now, but her face was filled with doubt.

"Olympia, listen. I understand something about being afraid. For nearly thirteen years I ran from this man because I thought he either wanted to send me back to my master or kill me. And all he wanted was to ask me where his daughter was."

"Rachel, I want to tell you something." It was Daphnis. He stepped close to the girl. "Amanis found me on a hillside, just the way she found you. Only she didn't take me to someone else. She cared for me as her own child." He smiled at her. "She's the only parent I've ever known, and I would never do anything to hurt her. Rachel, you can trust this woman. You can believe what she says. I've been with Scaevolus, too, and I know she's telling the truth."

Amanis saw the tinge of pink in his cheeks as he finished, but he held the girl's eyes until she looked at her mother.

"I believe him, Mother. I'll go."

"All right, then. But I'm coming, too."

Amanis would never forget the look on Hilarion's face when they came into Scaevolus's room. He looked first at her, then at Rachel, and he knew. He leaned over and spoke softly to Scaevolus. The old man's eyes fluttered and opened. Hilarion put an arm behind his frail shoulders and lifted him while Othar rearranged the pillows behind his head.

"Scaevolus, I've found her," Amanis said, leading Rachel forward. *Thank You, oh, thank You.* "Her name is Rachel. She's come to see you."

Scaevolus's eyes glittered with a fearful intensity. His lips moved, and Hilarion leaned down to put his ear near his master's lips.

"He wants you to come closer," Hilarion said, beckoning Rachel. "He wants to tell you something."

Amanis thought she had never seen anything braver or more beautiful than the few steps Rachel took toward the bed of the dying Scaevolus. She leaned down, and the cloth covering her hair slipped away. Strands of dark, curly hair spilled over Scaevolus's face and chest. She gave a little embarrassed cry and made as if to rearrange her covering.

"No," said Scaevolus. It was the loudest word Amanis had heard him say since their return to Ephesus. Rachel looked at him doubtfully, then leaned over him again. Her hair brushed his face, and Scaevolus closed his eyes. Amanis felt tears stinging the corners of her eyes.

Scaevolus whispered into Rachel's ear for some time. His limp fingers flinched, then stroked her wrist once and again. She straightened, looked at him, and stepped back from the couch. She went back where Olympia stood. They all looked at her and waited.

"He told me he had spent his life loving me, even though he never saw me," Rachel said. "He told me that you—" she looked at Amanis "—were someone I could always call on in time of trouble. He said he had little left to give me, but that it would give him great pleasure if I would live in this house after his death with anyone I cared to have around me."

Olympia's eyes widened.

"He said, 'In the end, love is all that's left.'"

There was a long silence.

"Is there anything you want to tell him?" Amanis asked.

"It's too late," said Hilarion. "He's dead."

"'And now, dear lady,'" Berenice read, "'I am not writing you a new command but one we have had from the beginning. I ask that we love one another. And this is love: that we walk in obedience to His commands. As you have heard from the beginning, His command is that you walk in love.'"

Walk in love. There had been many, many good days, Amanis thought. When Daphnis and Rachel presented her with her first grandchild, this fine, strong girl they named Berenice—that was a good day. She would always treasure the look on Daphnis's face as he gazed at his daughter, cradled in his wife's arms.

And the day John came back from Patmos, finally freed by the death of Domitian and the reshuffling of the consular ranks—that had been a good day. The love of the Ephesian Christians for this old man—more stooped than Amanis remembered—was so strong it was almost palpable.

And what else but love could have eased the hard places between Amanis and her father? Because of Neria's gentle persistence, Amanis and her father gradually found a way toward each other through the wasteland of mistrust and despair that had kept them apart for so long. Amanis would never stop being grateful to her aunt for loving them both enough to help them retrieve something they would never have found without her.

She looked at the box in which she kept her treasures. It was the only thing she wanted from her father's house when he died.

Even the day she had left Ephesus for the relative safety of Pisidia was a day she remembered with love. The church had sent a delegation to beg her to leave the city, but she had given them every protest she could fashion: there was too much work still to be done among the foundlings and orphans; any day now, the proconsul would turn his attention to other things; she had no wish to be so far from her granddaughter; the inland winters were too cold; the inland summers were too hot. But in the end they had persuaded her that she was of more value to the churches of Asia Province alive and in Antioch than imprisoned or dead in Ephesus. A crowd accompanied her to the Magnesian Gate on the morning she left. Some of them were women and men she or her helpers had found as abandoned babies, and who now had children of their own. Some of them were people nearly as old as she who had been followers of Christ since the days of Paul. Othar was there. With tears moistening his long, white beard, he gave her the kiss of fellowship.

"Take care of my son and his family," she told him. "And don't take in any more cats. You must surely be feeding half the cats in Ephesus as it is."

He grinned through his tears. "They keep down the vermin."

It had grieved her almost beyond bearing to receive word of Othar's death this past summer. He went peacefully, Daphnis had written her. In his sleep.

"'I have much to write to you, but I do not want to use paper and ink,'" Berenice read.

Amanis was so grateful for this time with her grandchild. Daphnis and Rachel had sent her with a group of believers who were on their way to Galatia. The young women of the churches in Antioch had loved Berenice immediately, and it was easy to see why. She had her father's quick mind and sensitive heart, and her mother's loveliness and good grace. She had been of inestimable comfort to Amanis.

"'Instead, I hope to visit you and talk with you face to face, so that our joy may be complete.'"

Not long now, Brother John, she thought, *not long. Soon I will be where you are, and our joy will know no bounds.*

"'The children of your chosen sister send their greetings.'" Berenice folded the parchment and put it carefully back in the leather pouch. "That's all, Grandmother."

"Thank you, child. Just put it back in the box with the other things, will you? It goes down at the bottom."

Berenice replaced the letter and closed the lid. It fell into place with the click of a well-fitted joining. Even after all this time.

"I'm tired now. I think I'd like to sleep." Amanis got up with a grunt and shuffled to the woven straw pallet beside the box. Some of them hounded her to put a couch in her room, but she had slept on a floor pallet all her life and didn't mean to change this late in the day.

Berenice ushered the other young women from the room and closed the door softly behind them. She came over to where Amanis lay and arranged the blankets over her. "Are you warm enough, Grandmother? Shall I move the brazier closer?"

"No, dear. I'm fine." Such a thoughtful girl. Amanis felt a pleasant drowsiness settling over her. "I'll rest for a bit, and then it'll be time to start thinking about supper."

"Yes, Grandmother. I'll sit with you, if you like."

"That would be nice, Berenice." Amanis reached out a hand and stroked the side of the box. It made her feel better knowing everything was within reach.

Berenice hummed a tune under her breath. Amanis began to fall asleep to the soft, comforting sound.

The publisher and author would love to hear your comments about this book. *Please contact us at:*
www.multnomah.net/motheroffaith

–Experience–
The Daughters of Faith Series

Daughter of Jerusalem

Journey back to the time of Jesus and be on hand as Mary Magdalene—one who was lost, then found—reaches in compassion toward other wandering sheep of the house of Israel. Through Mary's eyes, you will experience the birth of the infant church and the excitement of the days just following Pentecost.

THOM LEMMONS

ISBN 1-57673-477-3

Woman of Means

Whatever happened to Paul's first European convert? What was the trouble between Euodia and Syntyche mentioned in Philippians? Discover potential answers in this imaginative, extraordinary novel.

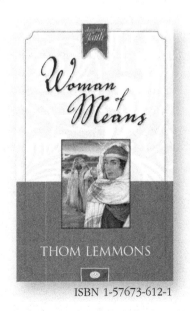

THOM LEMMONS

ISBN 1-57673-612-1

Let's Talk Fiction is a free, four-color mini-magazine, created to give readers a "behind the scenes" look at Multnomah Publishers' favorite fiction authors. *Let's Talk Fiction* allows our authors to share a bit about themselves, and gives readers an inside peek into their latest releases. *Let's Talk Fiction* is free, and is distributed in the fall, spring, and summer seasons. It features our fiction titles released during these seasons, and is filled with interactive contests, author contact information, and fun! Take a moment to review *Let's Talk Fiction* on-line at www.christian-fiction.com and tell us what you think. Or let us know if you would like a hard copy in the mail. We'd love to hear from you!

www.christian-fiction.com

Printed in the United States
by Baker & Taylor Publisher Services